GUNS OF FREEDOM

A Western Duo

GUNS OF FREEDOM

A Western Duo

RAY HOGAN

Five Star
Unity, Maine

Copyright © 1999 by Gwynn Hogan Henline

An earlier version of "Fire River" appeared under the title "Return to Rio Fuego" by Clay Ringold, first published in a paperback double novel by Ace Books. Copyright © 1968 by Ace Books, Inc. Copyright © renewed 1996 by Ray Hogan.

Five Star Western
Published in conjunction with Golden West Literary Agency.

June 1999

First Edition, Second Printing

Five Star Standard Print Western Series.

The text of this edition is unabridged.

Set in 11 pt. Plantin by Minnie B. Raven.

Printed in the United States on permanent paper.

Library of Congress Cataloging in Publication Data

Hogan, Ray, 1908–
        Guns of freedom : a western duo / by Ray Hogan. — 1st ed.
        p.   cm.
        ISBN 0-7862-1573-9 (hc : alk. paper)
        1. Frontier and pioneer life — West (U.S.) — Fiction.
2. Western stories.   I. Title.
PS3558.O3473G825   1999
813'.54—dc21   99-19834

Editor's Note

When Ray Hogan originally wrote the story he titled "Guns of Freedom," it found no acceptance among book publishers because it was set in Cuba in 1851. Yet, as was also the case with Ray Hogan's SOLDIER IN BUCKSKIN which sold very well, indeed, as a Five Star Western, the parameters of what editors of even ten years ago considered a Western story simply did not reflect the purview and interest of readers. Those elements of character, situation, and dramatic tension always found so abundantly in a Ray Hogan story are certainly present in "Guns of Freedom"—and something more, that heroic, revolutionary spirit that has always been so close to Americans since their own revolution against oppression. Yet, because this text was somewhat shorter than customary for a Five Star Western, "Guns of Freedom" has been combined with the short novel, "Fire River," set in the rangeland of New Mexico, for so many years Ray Hogan's adopted state. This story, which opens this book, is actually the original version of a short novel that Ray Hogan wrote under the pseudonym Clay Ringold for an Ace double paperback book published in 1968, combined there with a much longer novel by another author, John Callahan (pseudonym for the late Hal Lewis). In its present form, "Fire River" is being published here for the first time. Ray Hogan's Western fiction is notable for its pacing, its exploration of ethical questions, and its celebration of human honor and integrity. Given the overall quality of his Western stories it is not surprising that he came to have such a wide and loyal readership.

TABLE OF CONTENTS

FIRE RIVER

I

Joel Kane looked down from the ridge and studied the small scatter of structures that made up the Circle K. He had realized something was wrong at his father's ranch when he received the letter—and now, having his view of the place, the assumption became a visible fact. Everything was in an advanced state of disrepair: roofs sagged, doors hung from broken hinges, corral poles were down, several missing entirely. Dry leaves, trash, and brush littered the yard. The cottonwood trees that once had spread their thick, protective shade over it all were dead or dying.

Joel considered the scene soberly. It had been ten years since he'd turned his back on the Circle K, vowing never to return, but even in that length of time he knew Amos Kane would not change enough to permit that sort of neglect. Such, actually, had been the seat of their trouble. Amos was a strict, unbending man who demanded perfection in all things. He brooked no excuses, countenanced no variations, insisting that his way alone was the right way. Joel had lived in his despotic shadow until he was fifteen years of age, and then moved on. It was no grievous loss for either. He and Amos had never been close, even after the death of his mother, which ordinarily would have welded the relationship between a father and a son into a firm bond. To the contrary, the chasm between them had widened, just as the bitterness had grown, and thus it was inevitable that the day should come when the boy could stand it no longer.

Consequently, the letter Joel received had come as a

shock. It had trailed him four months before finally over-taking him in the Three Forks country of Montana where he was working for Webb Preston. Typical, the note had been brief and to the point.

Need you. Come home, Son.
Amos Kane

Joel's first thought had been: *The old man's hard nose and smart mouth have finally bought him something he can't handle.* Joel had had an impulse to throw the letter away, forget it, but somehow the word Son stuck in his mind. He couldn't recall when Amos had ever employed that term of paternal affection to him. And that his father would actually ask for help had also been astonishing. Amos Kane's creed had been to obligate himself to no one, regardless of need. If a situation arose in which he alone could not handle it, the consequences, however painful, were accepted. It was a narrow, Spartan way of life in which he made no friends and discouraged all overtures, but it was how he wanted it, and all those with whom he came in contact thereafter avoided him and went their own course.

Joel had mulled the matter over for a day and a night be-fore coming to a final decision: he would return to the Circle K to see what it was all about. He owed Amos nothing, but still, he was a Kane—and there was something to the old saw that blood ran thicker than water.

Accordingly, he had loaded his saddlebags with his few belongings, had cut south across a corner of Wyoming, had ridden the depth of Colorado where snow still banked the higher peaks, and had come eventually into the beautiful Fire River country of New Mexico. He had camped one night on the banks of the stream, which took its name from the glow imparted by sunlight striking water flowing over red sandstone, and the following day had skirted the rimrocks to the west of the Circle K, reaching the ridge south of the ranch around mid-morning.

Everything looked the same, Joel thought, except the ranch, and that—he drew himself to sudden attention. Two men emerged from the barn and were strolling lazily toward the main house. One, a squat, huskily built man with a black beard and thick mustache, was twirling a pistol in his right hand. The other, slim, narrow-faced, and dark, wore a bright red bandanna around his neck. They were not working cowhands—that was easy to see. Kane watched them move by the corral where four saddled horses dozed in the warming sunlight, cross the yard, and seat themselves on a log bench near the back door of the ranch house. They were discussing something, and several times the squat one laughed. His partner, however, apparently saw no humor in what was being said; not once did the sober, cold lines of his features relax.

What would men of this sort—obviously gunmen—be doing on the Circle K? Joel ran that question through his mind slowly. Amos Kane had no use for their kind, and more than once Joel had watched his father, shotgun cradled in his long arms, order them off the property when they paused, supposedly looking for work. Suspicion began to build slowly within Kane. Men such as those two would not be there unless something—or someone—had forced Amos to permit it. That fact, coupled with the general run-down appearance of the ranch, could only mean. . . . Again Joel's thoughts came to a stop. The screen door leading off the kitchen at the rear of the house opened, and an old man, water bucket in hand, shuffled out into the yard. He was tall, angular, and bent with years; his hair was iron-gray and shoulder-length. The clothing he wore was faded and torn and hung slackly from his frame.

Head down, the oldster walked haltingly toward the well. The thick-set gunman said something to him. He paused, half turned, and looked to the south. Shock traveled through Joel. There was no mistaking that sharp, hawk-like face. The old man was his father, Amos Kane.

The outlaw with the pistol raised it and leveled it at Amos. The dry clack of the hammer being cocked carried clearly across the hush. Abruptly the gunman laughed, as he lowered his weapon. Amos Kane stared at him briefly and then, shrugging wearily, plodded on toward the well. Joel watched in disbelief. This was not the Amos Kane he knew and remembered; this was an old, broken man, devoid of spirit, and utterly without hope.

The windlass creaked loudly. Amos wound up a dipper keg of water, poured it into his bucket. Grasping the bail, he swung slowly about and started back for the house. When he drew abreast of the toughs, the thin one thrust out a foot, Amos tripped and went to his knees, spilling the water and sending his tormentors into uproarious laughter.

Anger now a steady flame within him, Joel watched his father pull himself stiffly to his feet, retrieve the bucket, and return to the well. Again the windlass squealed its protest, and once more Amos Kane filled his bucket. Cautiously, now, he wheeled and headed for the door, but this time he swung wide to avoid the men on the bench, who continued to laugh and taunt him until he had finally disappeared into the house.

Joel remained motionless, anger and wonder filling him with a harsh grimness. There was no doubt now that his father was in some sort of desperate trouble, and he no longer questioned the old man's change of heart and his appeal for help. Forgotten were all the differences of the past, all the bitterness. Joel Kane saw only that his father needed him —and, judging from his frail appearance and evident weakness, needed him quickly.

He considered his best move. It would be foolhardy simply to ride down, announce himself, and attempt to drive the outlaws off the ranch. There were more inside the house—at least two, if he could calculate from the number of horses waiting near the corral. There could be more in the barn or elsewhere on the Circle K. He'd play it smart—go down and ask for a job. There would be nothing unusual in that. Cowboys were always on the move, and hardly a day passed when a rancher did not have two or three dropping by, looking for work. In that way he could get a closer look at them, size up the situation, and figure out his next move. Before he could make any plans at all he must know just what he was up against. There was one drawback in following that course: if Amos recognized him, he would be in immediate trouble unless he could somehow warn the older man in time. He gave that several minutes' thought and then shrugged. It was a risk he'd have to run, he concluded. Heeling his sorrel horse lightly, he started down the long slope.

II

Kane reached the edge of the yard, broke through the fringe of encroaching rabbitbrush and snakeweed, and pulled up beside the four horses standing near the corral. He swung from the saddle with studied, deliberate movements, hearing rather than seeing the two men by the house rise and drift quietly toward him. Taking his time, he looped the sorrel's reins around a pole and turned. The outlaw wearing the red bandanna blocked him on the right; the husky one had taken up a position to the left.

"Now, where do you think you're going, mister?"

The squat rider stood, legs apart, thumbs hooked in his belt.

Joel forced a grin. "Looking to see the head man."

The outlaw threw a sardonic glance to his partner. "You hear that, Clete? He's wanting to see the head man. What do you reckon for?"

The thin-faced gunman's expression did not change. "Maybe he'll tell us," he drawled.

Joel could feel the steady press of their eyes upon him, sizing him up, making their assessment. "Need a job. Figured to try here."

Clete folded his arms across his chest, spat, and nodded to the husky man. "Haven't heard of any jobs around here, have you, Bill?"

Kane, too, had been judging quietly. Bill would be a brawler. Clete was the more dangerous of the two—a man who lived by his gun. It was written there in the flat, emotionless depths of his eyes, in the stillness that lay upon him.

"Sure haven't," Bill said. "So you might as well mount up, cowboy, and ride on."

The frozen grin did not leave Joel's lips. "Reckon I'll let your boss tell me that."

"Far as you're concerned," the squat outlaw snapped, "I'm the boss of this outfit . . . and I'm telling you!"

Kane clung to his temper. After seeing their treatment of his father, he would like nothing better than taking on the two men and teaching them a lesson, but he couldn't afford to at that moment. It wasn't in him, however, to back down.

"You look like the hired help to me," he said, starting for the house.

"The hell . . . I'll show you!" Bill yelled, and lunged.

Joel took a quick half step to the side. He reached out, caught the husky rider by one shoulder, and spun him off balance. Placing both hands against Bill's shoulders, Kane shoved him hard into Clete. Both men swore as they came together. Kane, drawing his pistol, glanced to the barn where two more figures, attracted by the shouts, rushed into the open, then halted.

"Damn you . . . I'll pull you apart!" Bill gritted, regaining his balance and wheeling fast.

Kane nodded and looked beyond him to Clete. The outlaw's hand rested lightly on the butt of his pistol. He made no further move, aware of the weapon already in Joel's grasp. In that same instant Bill charged. Once more Kane pulled away. As the husky rider rushed in, Joel raised his arm and clubbed the man sharply on the side of the head. Bill groaned and went to his knees.

Eyes still on Clete and conscious of the two men now approaching from the barn, Joel turned half around, keeping them all within his field of vision. He bobbed his head coldly at Clete.

"Either draw that thing, or forget it."

The gunman did not move.

Kane's eyes hardened. "Maybe you'd better get rid of it," he said. "Use your left hand."

Clete considered for a long moment, then, reaching across, drew his pistol and tossed it into the brush.

Joel brought his attention back to Bill. The bearded outlaw was on his knees, shaking his head to clear away the cobwebs. Over to his left the pair from the barn had halted and were watching narrowly. Neither was armed. Hostlers,

Joel guessed, hired to look after the horses and gear. He dismissed them from his mind.

Sliding his weapon back into its holster, he reached down, grasped Bill by the arm, and dragged him upright. "You done?"

Bill jerked free. "Hell no, I ain't done!" he shouted, and struck out savagely.

The unexpected blow caught Kane in the ribs, sending a stab of pain through his body. He grinned at his own carelessness and danced away to avoid the man's lumbering rush.

"Get him, Bill," Clete said in a taut, hopeful voice. "Back him up against the corral."

Kane halted abruptly, struck out with a straight left, followed by a swinging right. The left stalled the outlaw in his tracks; the right rocked him to his heels. Clete said something else, but the words were lost to Kane. The hostlers had eased in nearer, and he realized he was pressing his luck—if they all moved in at once. He smashed another right into Bill's middle, drove a second blow straight into the outlaw's jaw. Bill began to wilt. Relentless now, Kane moved in close, chopped the husky rider with a vicious right, cocked his left for a finishing follow-up, then hesitated. Bill was sinking slowly. Stepping back quickly, Joel dropped his hand to his pistol. The hostlers checked themselves. Clete, absolutely motionless, watched in silence.

Joel met Clete's gaze, and then shifted his hot glance to the hostlers. Both looked down. At that moment a voice from the house cut through the sudden quiet.

"What's going on out there?"

Kane turned. A tall, powerfully built man with flaming red hair had come into the open. Behind him, a Mexican in *vaquero* trappings lounged in the doorway of the house.

"You're getting what you wanted," Clete said.

Joel continued to stare at the redhead. "Who's he?"

"Berryman . . . Cass Berryman."

The name struck no familiar chord in Kane's mind. "He the foreman?"

"He's the whole damned works," Clete said dryly. "You were looking for. . . ."

"Clete!" Berryman shouted again. "What's the trouble down there?"

The thin-faced gunman wheeled lazily. "Jasper here rode in looking for you. Wants a job. Bill got some other ideas."

Berryman considered that. "Ideas about what?"

"About hiring, I reckon."

"Bill's getting a mite too big for his britches," the red-haired man said angrily. "Bring him on up here."

He turned, started for the door, paused, and waved at the two hostlers. "One of you throw a bucket of water on Taney, get him to his feet," he said, and pushed by the *vaquero* into the house.

Both men hurried toward the water trough. Clete eyed Kane and jerked his head.

"You heard him. Get moving."

Joel Kane nodded, took a forward step, and then pulled to a halt as Clete veered aside to retrieve his pistol. The outlaw caught Kane's steady attention on him and shrugged. "No sweat," he murmured, and dropped the weapon into its holster.

Joel shrugged. "Just for luck, I'll walk behind."

The gunman made no answer, but simply strode on, his booted feet sending up small geysers of dust each time they touched the ground. It must have been a dry winter, Kane thought absently. Back near the corral there was a sudden splash of water followed by a mumbled curse. The hostlers had brought the black-bearded Bill Taney to consciousness.

Reaching the house, Clete leaned forward and pulled open the dust-clogged screen door. Joel paused and shook his head. The outlaw's eyes flickered, but he moved on, and Kane trailed him into the room. Halting, the younger man glanced around, at once remembering old and familiar objects from the days gone. He was in the kitchen. The big nickel-trimmed Pacific cook stove still stood in the corner; the heavy, oblong table his father had built, along with the two benches that served as chairs, were still in use. On the wall was the framed lithograph depicting a platter heaped with apples and peaches, still in its exact place—nothing had changed.

"What kind of work're you looking for?"

Cass Berryman's voice had a deep harshness to it. Joel brought his wandering attention to a halt. The red-haired man stood near the door that led into the rest of the house. At his elbow was the sly-faced Mexican. Across the room a turkey-necked, balding oldster with a stringy mustache worked over a narrow bench built against the wall. He was peeling potatoes and slicing them into an iron spider. Amos Kane was not in evidence. Joel breathed a bit deeper as he realized that.

"Cows," he said. "Been working cattle all my life."

"Not all you've been doing," Berryman said, glancing through the doorway to the corral. "Somebody tell you I was taking on hands?"

Joel shook his head. "Saw your place. Looked pretty big, so I figured it'd be a good bet to stop."

Berryman considered that. He glanced at the *vaquero,* then at Clete. "Where'd you come from?" he asked, bringing his eyes back to Kane.

"North . . . several places."

The Circle K was no longer a working ranch, that much Joel had already decided. Just what did go on under the guise of cattle raising he had yet to learn—just as he needed to know where Cass Berryman and his hardcases fit.

"You come through town?"

"Town?" Joel repeated, making a question of it. The less they thought he knew of the country, the better.

"Cedar River. Twenty miles east or so of us."

Kane shook his head. "Wasn't anything but open country, the way I rode in." He looked up as the doorway filled and Bill Taney stepped into the room. The bearded man's face was beginning to swell, and there was a dark welt under one eye. Berryman gave him critical appraisal.

"Never learn, do you?"

Taney's features reddened, and he took a step forward. "I'm not done with that god-damn' saddle bum yet! I aim to. . . ."

Berryman waved him back. "Like I said, you never learn."

"Took me when I wasn't looking," Bill grumbled, glancing at Clete. The gunman only stared.

Berryman came back to Joel. "Nothing much doing around here as far as cattle goes. Handle a few head now and then. More interested in a man who can use his fists . . . and his gun."

"Done my share of that kind of work, too. Not backing off, but just what'll I be doing?"

"Special sort of jobs . . . for me."

"Jobs like robbing a bank, maybe?"

Berryman laughed, a hollow, mirthless sort of sound. "Could be. We keep plenty busy around here," he said, and pulled aside slightly.

Amos Kane, moving unsteadily, came through the

doorway. At close range he appeared even worse off than he had from the ridge. There was a starved look to his sunken, lined face, and his eyes had receded into deep, shadowy pockets. One corner of his mouth sagged noticeably, and the firm set of his jaw that Joel always remembered was gone.

"Hurry it up, old man," Cass Berryman snapped impatiently.

Amos stumbled slightly in his haste, caught himself against the table. He looked up at Joel. A frown pulled at his brow, and his lips tightened briefly.

"You hear me?" Berryman snarled and, reaching out, gave the oldster a hard shove.

Anger whipped through Joel. He drew up stiffly, thrust out an arm to steady Amos. The old man nodded, pulled free, and crossed over to where the cook still worked at his counter.

"Well, what about it?"

Berryman's voice cut into Joel Kane's suppressed fury. Lowering his head to hide the tautness of his features, he shrugged. "Not sure I want that kind of work."

"Why not? Be no chore to you . . . especially when word gets out how you cleaned Bill's plow."

"It's not getting around," Taney broke in hotly, " 'cause I figure to change things first."

"You haven't done much good so far," Berryman taunted.

"We'll see about that," Bill yelled, and lunged at Joel.

Amos Kane, in the process of crossing to the stove, moved into the outlaw's path. The two men collided. Taney swore, struck out wildly. The blow drove Amos to his knees. Taney kicked him savagely in the ribs. The old man groaned, fell forward.

Blinding fury rocked Joel. Forgetting his precautions, he stepped in fast, smashed a hard blow to Bill Taney's belly. As the outlaw buckled, he straightened him up with a stiff uppercut. Taney staggered back, hands clutching his middle, mouth blared wide as he gasped for wind. Joel, thoroughly aroused, closed in swiftly. He heard Berryman yell something, and then caught a fleeting glimpse of the *vaquero* coming at him from the left. He jerked away, came up solidly against Clete. Spinning, he rapped the gunman with a short left, started a right.

"Joel . . . look out!"

His father's frantic warning caused him to duck, wheel again. He had a quick vision of the Mexican swinging his pistol at his head, pulled back. The blow missed, and the Mexican, off balance, reeled by. Joel gave the man a hard shove, sending him crashing into the wall, and wheeled once again to face Clete.

"Hold it!"

Cass Berryman's harsh voice overrode the confusion. Joel, barely hearing, swung wild at Clete, missed. Momentum carried him into the outlaw, and for a moment they were locked together. A gunshot blasted inside the room with deafening effect. Joel felt Clete's arms loosen as Berryman's voice again sounded.

"You hear me? Stand away, all of you! I'll shoot the next man who tries anything!"

Joel, arms at his sides, turned slowly. Clete had pulled him back against the wall and was breathing heavily. Bill Taney still held his belly, and the Mexican, a knife in his hand, was crouched in a corner.

Berryman, holstering his revolver, gave Joel a quick glance, and then stepped to where Amos was struggling to regain his feet. Leaning down, he grasped the older man by the arm and pulled him upright.

"Did I hear you right?" he demanded, shaking Amos roughly. "You called him Joel?"

The elder Kane said nothing.

Light flared in Cass Berryman's eyes. Raising his hand, he slapped Amos across the face sharply. "Answer me . . . damn you!"

The old man's head wobbled grotesquely. Joel surged forward, fresh anger overcoming him. Abruptly he halted, feeling the hard, round pressure of Clete's pistol against his spine.

"Leave him alone," he said, facing Berryman. "Sure, he called me Joel . . . it's my name."

III

A slow smile parted Cass Berryman's lips, and a slyness came into his eyes. He leaned back against the table.

"Well, what do you know," he said in a quiet, satisfied way. "The old he-bear's cub has come home."

The *vaquero* looked up, frowned. "This is the son?"

"This is the son," Berryman said. "The old man used to talk about him a few years back. Haven't heard much about him lately, and I reckon he just sort of slipped my mind."

From across the room Bill Taney, finally recovered, said: "That change things any?"

Berryman shook his head and stared at Joel. "What brought you back? The old man send for you?"

"Just riding by," the younger Kane said.

Berryman wagged his head slowly, the frozen grin still breaking his lips. "That's a god-damn' lie. You wouldn't have come in here asking for a job, if that was it."

"Suit yourself," Joel answered disinterestedly. He glanced at Amos, and temper stirred him again, but he held himself in check. He'd stand no chance bucking the four of them. It'd be best to bide his time, try to figure a way out without a showdown.

"I'm asking you . . . what do you want?" Cass Berryman's voice had dropped to a lower pitch.

"I have to want something?" Joel countered. "Can't a man drop by to see his folks?"

The red-haired outlaw chief shook his head again. "Amos told me you'd up and run off. You wouldn't be coming back now unless you had a reason."

Berryman was prying, digging, trying to learn what he knew, Joel realized. So far that totaled up to nothing except that his father apparently was a helpless prisoner on his own ranch.

"You heard my reason. Just dropped by."

"Hogwash!" Berryman snapped, and then leaned forward. "Who'd you talk to in Cedar River?"

"Never came that way. Do I have to say everything twice for you?"

Bill Taney muttered a curse and shifted restlessly on his feet. Berryman motioned to Clete.

"Take his iron," he ordered, and then to Joel added: "I figure you're lying."

The gunman pressed up close to Joel, lifted the Forty-Five from its holster, thrust it under his own belt. Immediately Cass Berryman lashed out and struck the younger Kane across the mouth.

"I want some straight talk . . . you hear?"

Fighting anger, Joel brushed at the blood oozing from his crushed lips. "You heard it right. I've talked to nobody."

Berryman stared at the younger man intently for a long minute. Finally he shrugged. "Maybe it is the truth," he said with a sigh.

Bill Taney pushed forward instantly. "Let me have him, Cass," he begged. "I'll sure as hell get it out of him."

"Doubt that. You haven't looked so good mixing in with him so far. Anyway, he's not the talking kind."

"I got ways," the husky outlaw promised.

Berryman only smiled, turned lazily to Amos. "How about you, old man? You want to do some talking?"

Amos Kane, head bowed, stood motionless. Cass, suddenly angered, grasped him by the shirt front, jerked him up sharply. "You send for your pup? You tell him how things are around here?"

Amos turned away. Berryman yanked again, almost pulling the older man off his feet. Instantly Joel pushed in between the two and knocked the outlaw's arm aside.

"Let him be," he said coldly, ignoring the gun Clete held to his back. "You don't and I'll kill you."

Berryman's eyes flared with surprise, and then his grin returned. "Expect you would at that . . . leastwise you'd try."

"Let me take care of him, Cass," Bill Taney pleaded in that same anxious way.

Berryman shook his head. "And have him lying around for somebody to find and start asking questions? Not much. I've got a better idea."

"Ain't no idea better'n getting rid of him before he stirs up trouble," Taney muttered.

"Not saying there is. I'm talking about the how of it."

"The how?"

"Sure. This is something that's got to be done right. Can't have anybody questioning my inheritance."

A grin spread slowly across Bill Taney's bearded face. The *vaquero* laughed. Amos Kane turned his head and looked at Joel helplessly.

"The way I see it the time's come to collect, especially since we've got the pup here, too. Now I can handle things first-rate, without any loose strings hanging down . . . no heirs to worry about."

Joel could make no sense of Cass Berryman's words. He was wishing now that Berryman didn't know he hadn't been in Cedar River. It seemed to have an important bearing on the situation.

Taney scratched at his beard, cocked his head to one side. "But how are you going to collect this inheritance thing without . . . ?"

"Without a fuss? Easy." Berryman glanced around the room. "We'll just pay a little visit to Mud Lake."

Mud Lake, Joel remembered, was a swale ten miles or so across the valley that had been a deathtrap for many an unwary steer and horse. Fed by underground springs, the sink was filled with a thin, slimy clay that quickly engulfed any luckless creature blundering onto its surface, much as did the quicksands of the Río Grande.

"Sure . . . that's just the ticket!" Taney yelled. "The old man and the pup'll just drop out of sight . . . and you'll take over."

"All according to law," Berryman finished.

Except for the promise of death outlined for him and his father, it was no more than a jumble of words to Joel Kane, but he wasted no time endeavoring to puzzle them out. He knew only that he must act quickly, that, if he delayed longer, he would be in no position to do anything. Whirling, he drove his elbow into Clete's belly, knocked away the pistol the outlaw was jamming against his body. As the gun exploded harmlessly, he leaped for Cass Berryman.

He caught the man by the neck, struggled to spin him around, to use him as a shield while he clawed for the pistol in the other's holster. Berryman yelled, hung onto the edge of the table. The *vaquero* rushed in, knife glittering in his hand. He went down abruptly, tripped by Amos Kane.

Berryman yelled again, began to thrash wildly about. Joel felt his grip slipping, felt other hands pulling at him. He shook loose, tried to leap onto the table and get behind Cass Berryman, but he was being held down. His fingers slipped, and he realized Berryman's throat was in his grasp. He shut down tight, felt the outlaw shudder.

"Call them off!" he shouted. "Or you're dead!"

A wave of pain slashed at him as Clete, or one of the others, struck him across the back of the head with a gun barrel. He fought off the clouds of darkness that were swirling about him, tightened his grip. Berryman began to wilt. Another blow smashed into his head. As if from a great distance he could hear someone yelling. He could feel himself sinking, falling away. And then it was completely dark.

IV

Joel Kane opened his eyes. It was half dark, hot and stuffy, and it was several minutes before he realized he was lying on the floor in a small, windowless room. He remained motionless, conscious of dull, throbbing pain, while he endeavored to get his bearings. A slight sound caught his attention. Turning only his eyes, he saw the bent silhouette of his father hunkered beside him. Unsteady, he pulled himself to one elbow. Instantly the older man leaned forward.

"You all right, Son?"

Amos Kane's voice was anxious. Joel nodded slowly and, then remembering, said: "How long have we been in here?"

"Half hour or so."

"Where are we?"

"Storeroom. Off the end of the house."

Joel couldn't recall the room, guessed his father must have built it after he had gone.

"Was afraid Jordan had done you in."

"Jordan?"

"Clete. The one holding a gun on you. Hit you with it a couple of times when you jumped on Berryman."

Joel's senses were finally clearing despite the unrelenting pain. Touching the back of his head gingerly, he drew himself upright and made a slow tour of the room. There was only the one door around which light filtered to provide meager illumination.

"Joel," the elder Kane said hesitantly, "it's good to see you again. But I'm wishing now I hadn't sent that letter. Didn't aim to get you in a fix like this."

Joel returned to his father's side and sat down. He could feel the stiffness between them, a sort of barrier. "It's all right, Pa," he said, trying to brush it away. "Not the first tight I've been in . . . probably not the last. They hurt you?"

"Nope. Reckon I'm used to it."

Silence hung between them after that for a long minute, and then Joel said: "Who's this Cass Berryman?"

Amos stirred wearily. "Biggest mistake I ever made . . . and I've made some humdingers, like letting you leave."

"We both had a hand in that. Don't blame it all on yourself."

"My fault . . . just the same. I did a lot of regretting later."

Again there was quiet. "Berryman," Joel pressed gently. "What about him?"

"Was my foreman. Been working for me seven, eight years. One of the best . . . or was in the beginning."

"What made him change?"

The old man wagged his head. "Don't rightly know. Things were running along pretty well. The stock was doing fine, market stayed high, and we were having a stretch of good winters and summers. I sort of started taking it easy. I was getting a mite tired, so I just let Cass handle everything, run things to suit himself."

"And he finally took over everything."

"That's what he did. I woke up one day to find all my boys gone, and Cass had new help on the place . . . his boys, only they weren't regular cowhands . . . they were tough hardcases who didn't know anything about cattle raising."

"They the only kind around now . . . gunfighters?"

"No. Berryman's got half a dozen to take care of the stock he brings in."

"Brings in?"

Amos Kane lowered his head. "Rustled stuff. They drive it in, small jags mostly. Then they use running irons, change the brands to Circle K, and sell it off as my stock."

"And nobody ever catches on?" Joel asked in an amazed voice.

"Reckon nobody even thinks about it. Like I said, Cass and his crowd pick stock up in small bunches, and when there's a sale made . . . usually to the Army or one of the Indian agents . . . the steers all carry the Circle K brand."

Joel nodded. "People just naturally don't figure you'd be mixed up in anything like rustling."

"That's it. Nobody'd bother to check, anyway."

Joel could understand that. Amos had closed his gates to

any who would be friendly. As a result he was left strictly alone by other ranchers and townspeople.

"Can't you do something about it when a sale is made? There're papers to be signed . . . ?"

"Part of that mistake I was telling you about. Cass handles everything, does all the business for me. I gave him that authority." The older Kane paused, then said: "You know, I haven't been off the place in five years."

"Five years," Joel echoed. "He's keeping you prisoner?"

"Just what he's doing. It's been more'n a year since I was farther'n yelling distance of this house."

"And now he figures to get rid of you . . . of both of us . . . for good in Mud Lake." Joel frowned, remembering something else Cass Berryman had mentioned. "What's this inheritance thing he was talking about?"

Amos Kane sighed deeply, rubbed at his jaw. "It was the biggest fool thing of all that I did."

Joel stared at his parent through the gloom. "He's actually going to inherit the Circle K, when you're dead?"

"That's the way I fixed it. It came up about a year ago. Cass made me a proposition. Mentioned I was getting old. Said if I'd make out a will giving him the ranch when I was gone, he'd take care of me the rest of my days. Deal was, I'd have a roof over my head, grub, spending money, and somebody to look after me when I couldn't get around on my own. Sounded like a fair offer at the time, and I took him up on it. The will was made out, giving him everything, all legal and such. He even brought Henry Testman out from the bank to do the witnessing."

Impatience stirred through Joel. Amos Kane should have known better, and words to that effect sprang to his lips, but he let them go unsaid. Amos was old, and he was tired. Berryman's offer would have sounded good. He was sud-

31

denly aware of his father's intent stare.

"You see," the older man said, "the way things were, I never expected to lay eyes on you again."

"I understand, Pa," Joel answered quietly. "What made you send me that letter?"

"I finally woke up to what was happening. Things went along fairly well for a few months, then I could see Cass was changing. He and his bunch started pushing me around, making my life mighty miserable. Didn't take much thinking to realize what was up . . . the sooner I was dead, the sooner Cass could take over. That's when I slipped a drifter a gold eagle to mail a letter to you. It was all I could figure left to do."

"Surprised you knew where to find me."

"There was a pack peddler through here about a year before that. Said he'd run into you up Wyoming way."

Joel remembered the man. They'd met accidentally in a saloon, got to talking. When the peddler mentioned he was going down into the Fire River country, Joel had told him that was his home, that his father had a ranch near the town of Cedar River.

"Took that letter four months to catch up," Joel said. "I'd moved on twice."

"I was wrong to send it. All it did was bring you back so's you could get yourself killed."

"Not dead yet," Joel murmured. "There anybody we can go to for help?"

"Can't think of anyone. The way Cass does things, it all seems to be on the up and up. Be a mite hard to get anybody to believe what I've told you."

Such was the truth, Joel realized. Berryman was smart—smart enough to keep his dealings strictly legal—and anything that was to be done he would have to do it. The will seemed to be the key to the situation. As it now stood, the paper was nothing less than a death warrant. If he could get his hands on it, destroy it. . . . "Who's the bunch Berryman keeps with him?"

"They handle the rough stuff. Bill Taney and Clete Jordan and the Mexican, Dobe Rivera. Those three are always with Cass."

"How about the cook?"

"Name's Ben Stoyers. Never known him to lean one way or the other. Sort of gets along with everybody."

"He stand by you or with Berryman?"

Amos considered that. "Ain't sure. Been with me about ten years, little less. Only old hand left on the place."

Joel rose to his feet and crossed to the door. Placing his ear to the widest crack, he listened. He could hear nothing. Apparently Berryman and his outlaw hired hands were not inside the house—but there was no way to be sure. There was also the possibility of a guard posted somewhere nearby. He turned back to Amos.

"Got to figure a way out of here. Can't risk breaking down that door. Any ideas?"

Amos started to move his head negatively, and then sat up straighter. "Just happened to remember that I ran out of nails when I was putting down this floor. There's a couple of boards over there in that corner that I didn't fasten."

Joel hurried to the opposite side of the small room, began to pull away several sacks and other odds and ends piled there.

"Always intended to finish the job," Amos said, moving to his side. "Just kept forgetting, I guess."

"Good thing that you did," Joel replied, dropping to his knees. Thrusting a finger into a knothole, he tried one of the planks. It came up easily. The one next to it was also loose. The third, however, had been anchored securely. It didn't matter.

"Wide enough to crawl through," Joel said. "What's it like under the floor?"

Amos thought back. "Joists're about a foot off the ground."

"Any openings in the foundation?"

"No foundation. I just piled rocks at each corner and set the timbers on them. Be easy getting out. And there're tall weeds all around. Nobody's apt to spot you until you get into the open."

"Us," Joel corrected. "You're coming with me."

"No. I'd just be in the way. I got into this mess. It's only right I don't hurt your chance of getting out."

"We'll get out of it together," Joel said firmly.

Amos stared at the younger man for a long moment, and then nodded humbly. "All right, Son. Whatever you say. Only thing . . . what do we do once we're free?"

"First thing'll be to get you to a safe hiding place. Then I aim to get back that will you signed. It's Berryman's trump card. Once I've done that, then we'll be holding the aces."

The elder Kane grinned into the darkness. "For a fact! Tearing that paper up'll put an end to his game powerfully quick. Getting it, howsoever, is going to be a sizable chore."

"I know that, but I'll ford that creek when I come to it. Main thing is to get out of here before somebody shows up. You ready?"

"Ready," Amos said.

Joel lowered himself through the narrow opening in the floor and stretched out full length on the cool earth beneath. There was scarcely room to move, but by keeping himself prone he wormed his way to one side. While he waited for Amos, he glanced around.

Sunlight trickled through the thick brush and weeds growing along the edge of the structure, and he easily determined the location of the corners where Amos had stacked flat rocks to support the timbers. It would be wise to emerge from a side not facing the yard, he decided, and turned his head to see how Amos was faring.

The older man was clear of the opening and now behind him. Joel immediately began to work his way toward the far side. He was anxious to get away from the house as soon as possible. Likely Berryman planned to wait until nightfall before taking them to Mud Lake, so every minute gained would put them that much further ahead of the outlaws.

He reached the edge of the building and halted. Amos was a few feet away, pulling himself painfully along. It was a hard task for the older man, and his strained features reflected the effort. When he caught up, Joel touched him on the shoulder.

"I'll go first and have a look around. If it's clear, I'll call."

Amos signified his understanding, and Joel, reaching forward, brushed aside a narrow tunnel in the rank growth and crawled into the open. He lay there a full minute, listening carefully. From the muted sounds coming from the kitchen, he guessed the cook was busy preparing the midday meal. Convinced there was no one close by, Joel finally raised himself to his knees and, turning, threw his glance into the yard. It was deserted—even to the horses that had been standing near the corral.

That was a disappointment. He had planned to make use of them, taking his own sorrel and one of the outlaws' mounts for his father. Now he would have to risk entering the barn. There was one good thing: the absence of the horses meant Berryman and the others were off somewhere and not hanging around the house. He wouldn't need to worry about encountering any of them.

Turning, he leaned down into the opening in the weeds and whispered: "All clear." He braced himself to give whatever assistance he could to his father. A few moments later they were crouched in the tall, musty-smelling rabbitbrush at the edge of the yard.

"Need horses . . . and a gun," Joel said, looking toward the barn. "Are there likely to be more than those two hostlers I saw working when I rode in?"

"Never is," Amos replied. "We can get horses, sure enough. Got my doubts about a gun."

"Rifle on my saddle," Joel said. "If they put my sorrel in the barn. . . ."

"That's where he'll be." Amos pointed to the end of the sprawling building. "Side door over there. Be easier getting in that way instead of the front."

Joel nodded, took a quick survey of the surrounding area to assure himself no one was near, and started along the rear of the corrals for the larger structure. They reached the side entrance without incident. There was no concealing brush at that point, and they were in the open, but Joel spent a full minute listening, trying to locate the two men he expected to be inside. He could hear nothing, however, except the occasional movement of a horse. Bending low, he drew back the door carefully. With Amos close on his heels, he moved into the gloomy interior of the structure.

Cautioning the older man, Joel continued down the corridor-like area in front of several empty stalls until he reached the intersecting runway. There he halted abruptly. The two hostlers were just inside the front doors. One sat propped against the wall, dozing. The other was indifferently mending harness.

In the stalls directly across from them Joel could see the heads of several horses. He located his sorrel in the second compartment. Turning back, he rejoined Amos.

Getting the horses was going to be difficult. There was no approach except up the runway, and he had no weapon of any sort. While the hostlers—as he had noted earlier—were unarmed, they could yell, set up an alarm, and bring someone who did possess a weapon.

Joel related this to Amos, who nodded his understanding of the problem. When the younger man had finished, he thought for a moment, and then pointed to a corner on the opposite side of the runway.

"Tools stacked over there. Maybe you just might find something we could use."

Immediately Joel returned to the intersection, looked again to the hostlers. Both now dozed. Signaling to Amos, he waited for the older man, and together they crossed over and moved to the tool bin. The most powerful weapon appeared to be a pick handle. Joel chose one, turned away, and then paused when he saw Amos also take up one of the lengths of hickory. The oldster grinned.

"Figure I might get a chance to help."

Joel smiled back, and together they returned to the runway. The hostlers had not stirred. Moving quietly, Joel worked his way along from stall to stall toward them. Amos was no more than a step behind.

They gained the partition occupied by a barrel-bodied little buckskin just below the two men. Joel could see his horse by looking over the intervening cross boards, felt relief when he saw the sorrel was still saddled and bridled, that his rifle was yet in its scabbard. They would need time only to throw gear on a mount for Amos.

He brought his attention back to the hostlers. He would

move in silently, knock out the nearest man with a blow on the head, turn quickly, and fell the second man before he could cry out, if possible. If he. . . .

Joel drew back abruptly as a sudden rush of hoofs sounded in the yard. The hostlers came alive and bounded to their feet. Joel swore under his breath. Berryman and the others had returned.

He watched the four outlaws wheel up to the corral and swing down. One of the hostlers sauntered into the open, looking expectantly at Berryman. The outlaw leader turned away and, with the others trailing, walked to the house and entered. The stableman shrugged, then returned to where his partner waited.

"Reckon they aim to ride out again."

The older man of the pair grunted. "Bill said something about being busy tonight . . . reason they didn't want the sorrel put in the back. You about done with that harness?"

"Just about."

"Soon's you are, we'll. . . ." The hostler stopped, stared across the runway. "Say, who . . . ?"

Joel gathered his muscles, pressed hard against the side of the stall. The man had spotted him.

"What's wrong?"

"Thought I saw somebody . . . in there with the buckskin."

The younger man laughed. "What's eating you, Ike? You going loco? Nobody but us has come in here since morning."

"Just the same, I think I saw something," Ike insisted and moved toward the stall.

Kane waited, muscles tense. The hostler reached the corner of the partition and stepped in closer. Silent as a shadow, Joel brought the pick handle down in a short, swift arc. Ike grunted, dropped to the straw-littered floor.

"Find anything?" the younger man called.

"Only me," Joel said, leaping from the depths of the stall and swinging the pick handle in a single motion.

The hostler slammed back against the wall, doubled forward, and sprawled in the runway. Joel tossed the length of hickory aside and, taking the man by the shoulders, dragged him out of sight. Amos, wasting no time, was already busy throwing gear on a long-legged gray in the adjoining stall.

Chore completed, Joel backed the sorrel into the runway. While he waited for Amos, he checked the rifle. It was still fully loaded. He glanced then to the house. Cass Berryman and his friends were still inside. Joel grinned tightly. So far he and Amos had not been missed.

"All set," the older man announced finally.

Joel turned immediately and, leading the sorrel, retraced his steps down the runway to the side door through which they had entered earlier. Halting, he made a careful check to be certain there was no one around, and then stepped into the open. The door was barely large enough to permit passage of the horses, but they managed, and shortly the two Kanes were mounted.

"Which way are we heading?" Amos asked.

"Need a good place to hide. It's too far to town. Got any ideas?"

The older man thought for a moment, nodded. "That old trapper's shack, back up in the rimrocks. Nobody ever goes up there any more."

"Just what we want," Joel said. "Let's go."

V

An hour later they were high in the rock-studded country west of the valley. Joel had forgotten about the cabin until his father had brought it to mind, and, visualizing it and its location now, he was certain it would be an ideal place for Amos to hide until he could bring matters with Cass Berryman to a head. Just how he would manage to get the outlaws off the Circle K was still unclear in his mind. However, at the moment, his thoughts centered only on the will his father had made and its recovery. With it destroyed, he reasoned, the threat to Amos Kane's life would be removed—or at least diminished.

The next move would then be Berryman's, and ideally the outlaw and his crew would simply pull stakes and drift on to greener grazing, forgetting the Circle K. But Joel had few illusions on that score. Cass Berryman had a good thing going for him on the Kane ranch, and he wouldn't toss it away without a bitter fight.

"Shack's on the other side of that shoulder," Amos called.

Joel looked ahead. The narrow trail veered sharply to his left, cut its way through a narrow slash in a huge bulge of granite. If it came down to a war with the outlaws, here would be a good place to make a stand, he thought. A man with a rifle, well hidden in the rocks, could hold off a small army.

Rounding the corner, they broke into a small clearing covered with matted clumps of yellow mountain daisies. Set back on the far side, the stone and log cabin appeared half buried in the dark soil. Buckbrush, sage, scrub oak, and other shrubs crowded in from all points, giving the place a desolate, abandoned appearance.

Crossing over, they dismounted, and, while Amos went

inside to have his look, Joel led the gray around to the rear and picketed him in the dense undergrowth where grass was plentiful. Returning, he found his father standing in the doorway.

"Nobody's been here for years."

"Just the place we need," Joel said, "but don't take any chances. Stay inside and don't build a fire. Berryman will be hunting for us."

"If I hear somebody coming, I'll take to the brush."

"Do what you figure best. The main thing is not to be seen. Expect I'll be back about the middle of the afternoon."

"Going to return to the ranch?"

Joel nodded. "Aim to get that will. Any idea where Berryman keeps it?"

The older man clawed at his chin. "Pretty sure he isn't carrying it on him. Most likely it's in that old desk of mine in the parlor. He took it over for his office. How're you going to get inside so's you can search with them there?"

"I figure they'll pull out and start looking for us as soon as they find we're gone. Shouldn't be anybody left but the cook, and I can get by him."

"Stoyers won't give you any trouble."

"Maybe not, but I don't intend to give him the choice." Joel turned to the sorrel, swung aboard. "I'll bring back some grub and a couple of blankets."

The older man's brows lifted. "We going to stay here a spell?"

"Hard to say. Depends on Berryman. *Adiós*."

"So long, Son," Amos answered as Joel cut back to the trail. "Take care."

Joel halted, when he reached the foot of the rocky slope. It seemed unwise to move directly toward the ranch.

Berryman could be aware of their escape by that hour and have men searching. He decided to keep well in the deep brush until he knew exactly how matters stood.

Accordingly, he swung right and began a circuitous approach. It was almost noon, and ordinarily the outlaws could be expected to be sitting down to their midday meal—but that wouldn't necessarily hold true, if someone had opened the storeroom door. If that had occurred, the hunt would already be under way.

Evidently it was. Kane realized it a short time later when he halted on a hill south of the buildings and looked into the yard. The horses were gone. Considering the hour, they should still be there unless. . . .

"There he is!"

The voice came suddenly from the trees to his left. Instantly a pistol cracked, and Joel heard the clip of leaves as a bullet sped through the foliage beyond him. He threw a quick glance to the side as he spurred around. The shot had come from Bill Taney. A short distance behind the husky outlaw, Berryman, and Dobe Rivera were wheeling their horses about in response to Bill's shout. He saw nothing of the fourth outlaw, Clete Jordan.

He wasted no time locating the man. He'd be somewhere nearby, little doubt of that. Heading the sorrel into the dense brush, he sent him plunging forward, away from the trail that led toward the cabin where Amos hid. More gunshots crackled through the hot stillness, but he didn't hear the snap of bullets, so he guessed the outlaws were shooting blindly.

Abruptly he broke out of the thick undergrowth into a long, twisting wash. He would be an open target there and immediately veered the sorrel to the right, topped out the rim of the slash, and raced on, driving hard for a grove of trees a hundred yards distant. It was going to be close. Reaching down, he pulled the rifle from its boot. Clamping the stock of the weapon under his arm, he levered a shell into the chamber and looked back. Taney and the missing Jordan were just appearing above the edge of the wash. Taking quick aim, he pressed off a shot.

Sand spurted a few paces in front of the men, and both swerved hastily. Joel grinned, levered another cartridge into the rifle. He'd spoiled their opportunity.

He heard Cass Berryman's voice just as he entered the grove, glanced back. All four outlaws were streaming across the flat. Berryman was waving his arms, shouting for them to split up, box him in. Kane snapped another bullet into the general direction of the oncoming men, saw the *vaquero* jerk to the right as the slug droned by him. They hadn't figured on his having a weapon, and this fact was laying a caution upon them.

He lost sight of them a moment later, when the trees closed in behind him, and immediately began to slow the sorrel's rush while he tried to figure his best move. He had led them away from the trail into the rimrocks, and he felt now that Amos would be in no danger. To keep going straight on, to the opposite side of the ranch, seemed the logical course.

Spurring the sorrel again, he drove on, winding in and out of the pines, hoping the outlaws had not lost sight of him entirely. Reaching the upper end of the grove, he slowed and looked back. Almost immediately a gunshot flatted across the hush, and again he heard the sharp clipping of a bullet tearing through the brush. He had cut it a little too thin.

He felt his nerves tighten as he sent the sorrel hurrying on. Half turning in the saddle, he fired another shot at the blurred shapes coming through the shadows. A flurry of pistol shots was his answer, but only one bullet sounded near.

Suddenly he was again in the open, racing across a narrow, almost level field. On the far side was another stand of pines that ran all the way to the cliffs on one side, to the valley on the other. He would never have a better chance to shake the outlaws.

Leaning forward on the straining red, he deliberately veered toward the lower end of the trees, as if heading downslope into the valley. A fresh burst of shots broke out at that moment, but he paid no heed. They had seen him and that was what he wanted.

He gained the trees, continued on downgrade until he was well within the grove and entirely hidden. He swerved sharply then, altering his course completely, and began to double back toward the cliffs. He followed that procedure for a short distance, allowing the heaving sorrel to move at a fast walk, finally cutting back at right angles through the grove until he reached its fringe.

Dismounting, he worked his way through the brush until he could see the open field. Far below, the outlaws were just entering the trees. They had angled across the flat, hoping to cut down his lead by taking a more direct line. When they didn't find him, they would assume him to still be ahead, trying to reach the valley. Kane heaved a sigh. Each step was taking them farther from the ranch. He could now return and carry out his search for Amos Kane's will without fear of interruption.

VI

He rode into the ranch from the east side and hid the sorrel in a strip of tamarisk Amos had planted years ago for a windbreak. No sounds were coming from the house, and Joel wondered briefly if Stoyers, the cook, had gone—perhaps to town for supplies. If so, he would be in luck, but he had his doubts about it.

Working his way to the corner of the house, where he had a grand view of the yard and the barn standing at its far end, he halted. There was no sign of the hostlers either, and that didn't seem normal. He didn't believe he had struck either man hard enough to cause serious injury, and both should be about. Could they be inside the main house?

It was a possibility, and a risk he'd have to accept. He couldn't afford to delay a search of the house for long. Eventually Cass Berryman and his men would return. Dropping back, Joel made his way along the east wall of the house to one of the bedrooms. The window was open, but a square of wire had been tacked on the outer frame to ward off insects. He spent another ten minutes quietly prying out the tacks and removing the screen. That finally done, he listened to be certain he had aroused no one. Finally satisfied his efforts had gone unnoticed, he hoisted himself through the opening and into the room.

Again he paused to listen. The place was in dead silence, and the conviction grew within him that Ben Stoyers was absent. Crossing to a door that led into a hallway, he entered and followed the corridor to where it opened into the parlor. Amos had said the will would most likely be found in the old rolltop desk now used by Berryman. He spotted it, standing against the back wall and, moving to it, immediately began a search of its drawers and hinged compartments.

The distant pound of a hammer brought him up short. He stepped back to the hallway and listened, while he tried to locate the sound. Coming from the barn, he decided, likely one of the hostlers. There was no threat there as long as the man continued his labors.

Returning to the desk, he resumed his inspection, carefully checking every paper, even going through the pages of several account books in hopes Berryman had secreted the will in that manner. He found nothing other than an indication of the outlaw's business ability—and that he was salting money away in the Cedar River bank.

At a loss as to where to look next, Joel returned to the hall. The bedroom—the one used by Cass Berryman. He crossed to the nearest, began to go through the dresser drawers, the clothing hanging in the closet—nothing.

Unsure as to which were Berryman's quarters, he followed a similar procedure in the adjoining room. There he found his pistol, taken from him earlier by Clete Jordan, but no more than that. Holstering his weapon, he stood in the center of the dimly lit room to think. He had searched all the logical places and turned up nothing. He began to wonder if it wasn't likely Cass Berryman carried the paper on his person. It didn't seem possible, yet—Kane shook his head. The will was hidden somewhere in the house—it had to be. Wheeling, he went back to the first bedroom, since the clothing there appeared to be that of the red-haired outlaw leader. He'd have to move fast, however. Time was running out, and his luck wouldn't hold indefinitely.

Again he ransacked the drawers, examined each item of clothing, even to checking the insides of three pairs of boots he discovered on a shelf. To no avail. He turned to the bed, pulled it apart, paying particular attention to the mattress. Again a blank. From there he went to the carpet tacked to the floor and felt along its edge for a bulge while he listened for the crackle of paper. That, too, proved fruitless, and he next removed the framed pictures hanging on the wall and checked them carefully. When this also failed to turn up the missing paper, he abandoned the bedroom and went once more to the parlor.

He hadn't given the furniture a going over, he realized, and at once began a thorough investigation of the chair bottoms, the springs in the dust-covered couch, the underside of the heavy lion-footed table. A braided rug was spread on the floor, and, heaving the furniture to one side, he kicked it into a heap. There was nothing hidden beneath it, either.

He paused and studied the desk, wishing now he had asked his father about secret drawers or compartments in the massive old piece. Most desks like this contained some, he knew, each elaborately concealed in an unlikely spot. With that in mind he began to go over the desk, removing drawers, checking for false bottoms, thrusting his hand deeply into vacated slots for a second container. Eventually he found it—a smaller drawer that fell into place when the front member was entirely removed. It was filled with folded papers and a few gold coins. Hurriedly he dumped it all on the desk and then, one by one, began to unfold and read the yellowing sheets. Deeds, bills of sale, letters—but no will.

Disappointed, he returned the papers and money to their container, reset it, and continued the search. There could be a second secret compartment, but he knew it was a slim possibility. He didn't like the thought of admitting it, but the fact that the will was not in the house was becoming clearly evident. Either Cass Berryman was carrying it or—Joel Kane's thoughts came to a full stop. A faint, scraping sound had registered on his consciousness. He felt a slight prickling along his spine. He'd pushed his luck too far. Arms hanging at his sides, he slowly turned to face the doorway.

Ben Stoyers, a shotgun cocked and ready in his hands, stared at him. Stoyers said: "What the hell do you think you're doing?"

The old man's eyes were deep-set, hard. He took a short step into the room, glanced about at the disorder and confusion. Joel moved slightly. Stoyers was instantly alert.

"Get your hands up . . . away from that pistol!" he barked, waggling the shotgun threateningly.

Kane raised his arms slowly. "I'm Joel . . . Amos's son."

"I know that. What's it got to do with your being here, tearing the place to pieces?"

"You're Pa's friend . . . been with him a long time, he said."

Ben Stoyers only watched in his sharp, bird-like way.

"I'm trying to help him."

"Against Berryman?"

Joel nodded. "You know the deal and what they're trying to do to him. I'm going to stop it."

The old cook was silent for a time. Then: "Where's he now?"

"Hid out where they can't find him. Soon as I get what I want, I'm moving in on Berryman and his bunch and driving them off the place."

Stoyers grunted. "Bit yourself off a big chaw."

"I'll get help, if I have to."

"From who? The old man hasn't got any friends."

"I'm doing it, not him," Joel replied, vaguely angered. He stirred impatiently. Time was slipping by and with it his margin of safety—Berryman and the others would be returning.

Stoyers jerked his head at the room in general. "You looking for something?"

"That will Pa's signed, giving everything to Cass Berryman when he's dead."

"It's not here. He keeps it safe in the bank," Stoyers broke in, and then bit off his words as if he had spoken more than he intended.

"The bank," Kane murmured. He hadn't given that possibility any thought, but it stood to reason. Berryman had gone to great lengths in every other way to make things appear legal and above board.

"Amos change his mind?"

The question was clearly unnecessary, but Joel said: "He has. Way it stands now Berryman's in a hurry to see him dead so's he can take over. Once I get that will back and destroy it, he won't have a reason."

"Won't make any difference to Cass. He's got the place, and he'll hang onto it. Your pa's signing that paper just made it easy for him . . . kept it all legal-like."

"He can *try* hanging onto it," Joel corrected quietly. "And he'll be doing it without any real claim." He studied the old man for a moment, then said: "Where do you stand, Ben?"

"What's that mean?"

"Pa said he figured you for a friend, only you were stringing along with Berryman and his bunch because you didn't have much choice."

"About the size of it," the cook said with a shrug. "Man looks out for himself. Reckon I was working for Amos a long time before Cass and his boys came along."

"That means you're still siding him?"

Stoyers lowered the shotgun. "Reckon it does."

Joel Kane sighed and lowered his arms. Undoubtedly the

outlaws were close by at that moment, but he could leave now. He knew where to find what he sought.

"You want to help?" he asked, stepping to the doorway where he could better listen for approaching horses.

"Sure."

"Better understand what it'll mean. Like you said, Berryman won't give up easy. Going to be some people hurt before it's over with."

"I'm old enough to know that. What do you want me to do?"

"Best you get out of here. Berryman learns you've thrown in with Pa and me, your life won't be worth much."

"Where'll I go?"

"To where Pa's hid out. Take along some grub and a couple of blankets . . . and that scatter-gun. How about the two men in the barn?"

"Berryman brought them here."

"Leaves them out. Can you get away without them knowing about it?"

Stoyers bobbed his head. "Expect I can manage. Where's Amos at?"

"Old trapper's cabin . . . south end of the rimrocks. Take the trail below. . . ."

"I know where it is. I've done some hunting up there, off and on. Where'll you be?"

"Paying the bank a call. Once I get my hands on that will, we'll give Berryman a chance to pull out. If he doesn't, we'll drive him off."

"Take more'n you and Amos . . . and me."

"Could be."

"You thinking about bringing in the law?"

"If I have to."

Stoyers shook his head. "That's not such a smart idea.

Way things have been run around here, I doubt if Amos'll want the law poking into how he gets his beef and what he does with it."

"That's Berryman's doings, not Pa's."

"Proving it won't be easy. Amos's name is on the bills of sale."

Joel swore softly. Berryman was a careful man, too. He had taken pains to cover all possible problems. It would be hard to convince people Amos did not participate in the rustling that went on—more difficult yet to make them believe he was powerless to stop it. Loner that he was, he was certain to be misjudged. But all that would come later; there were immediate things now to be handled.

Kane moved into the hallway. "Got to get out of here before Berryman and the others show up. Best you do the same," he said, walking hurriedly toward the bedroom where he had entered.

Stoyers trailed him down the hall. "Where'll we meet you?"

"Stay put at the cabin. I'll come there as soon as I've finished my business with the bank."

The cook nodded.

Joel thrust a leg through the window, then hesitated. "Be careful leaving here. Don't let anybody follow you."

Stoyers grinned. "Don't go worrying about me," he said.

VIII

Very little of Cedar River was familiar to Joel Kane. He had been in the town only a few times, and during his early childhood at that. As he turned into the single main street, he glanced about curiously: several saloons, a café or two, barber, harness and gun store, and all the other shops and offices found in similar settlements scattered across the West. *They all look alike,* he thought, singling out the bank and angling toward the hitch rack fronting it.

Halting, he dismounted and wrapped the sorrel's reins around the crossbar and then swung his eyes back over the way he had come. Across the dusty, rutted strip and down a few doors the town's marshal had moved out onto the walk and was regarding him with quiet interest. Joel returned the lawman's gaze, nodded slightly, turned, and entered the bank.

Except for an elderly man wearing steel-rimmed spectacles and a green eye shade in the teller's cage and a well-dressed individual seated at a desk, the place was deserted. It would be Henry Testman at the desk, Joel guessed, and made his way to that point.

The banker, sallow-faced and clad in a soft gray suit, glanced up as Kane halted in front of the desk. "Something I can do for you?"

Joel said: "You Henry Testman?"

The man nodded cautiously.

Kane offered his hand. "I'm Joel Kane . . . Amos's son. Been away for a spell."

Testman frowned, shook hands limply. "Son?" he repeated, and then added: "Yes, I remember now. How long ago was it?"

"Ten years, more or less."

Testman motioned at a chair. Kane drew it up next to the desk and sat down. The banker cocked his head to one side. "What brought you back?"

There was something about the banker's attitude that rubbed Joel wrong. He would have to overlook it, he realized. He couldn't afford to antagonize Testman. He shrugged. "Man comes home . . . eventually."

Testman said: "Yes, I suppose so. What can I do for you?"

Bankers, he'd learned, liked the indirect approach. "Looking for information mostly . . . sort of getting acquainted again," he said. "Pa and I were talking this morning. Said he'd made out a will."

Henry Testman nodded.

"I'd like to have a look at it."

The banker settled back, bridged his fingers, and frowned. "Why?"

"Pa's getting old. Not too sure what he put in it."

"He signed it."

"I know that, but like I said he's getting pretty old and doesn't think too good." Joel paused. He was treading on thin ice. The banker could get angry, flatly refuse his request, but he had to risk it. "There some reason why you don't want me to see it?" he demanded suspiciously.

Testman leaned forward quickly and shook his head. "Of course not, only . . . well, it's not customary. A will is a private paper."

"He's my pa," Joel said. "He sent me. If you don't believe that, saddle up, and we'll ride out and ask him."

"No need," the banker said wearily. Reaching out, he pulled open a drawer, removed a leather folder, and began to sort through a thick sheaf of papers. Selecting one, he handed it to Kane. "Afraid you're going to be disappointed," he said. "Won't find your name in there."

"That's what Pa told me," Joel replied, and unfolded the sheet.

It was as Amos had said: everything had been signed over to Cass Berryman. Kane studied the document briefly, then refolded it, and thrust it into his shirt pocket.

"Better take this along. Pa's aiming to make some changes."

Henry Testman came forward angrily. "You can't do that!"

"Why can't I? Belongs to my pa. He wants it."

"But he didn't leave it with me. It's somebody else's property!"

"Cass Berryman's?"

"Matter of fact, yes. He entrusted it to me . . . to the bank . . . for safekeeping. I can't turn it over to you unless he says so."

"Not his property," Kane said evenly.

"It is!" Testman snapped. "If you walk out of here with it, it will be robbery . . . the same thing as a bank hold-up."

The banker's voice had lifted sharply. The teller moved out from behind his screened cubicle and glanced toward the door. Joel drew his pistol and rose to his feet.

"Forget it," he warned the clerk, then brought his attention back to Testman. "No reason to get riled up about this. Man has a right to change his own will. If you're worried about Berryman, make out some sort of receipt, and I'll sign it."

"I don't want a receipt . . . I want that document back!"

"We'll leave it up to Pa. If he wants you to have it, I'll bring it back . . . after he's through making his changes."

"No!"

Joel looked keenly at the banker. "Maybe you don't want him changing it. Maybe you want it left just like it is. You got a deal going with Cass Berryman?"

Testman's face darkened. "That's neither here nor there. You've got no right to take that paper."

"Got every right," Joel drawled. "And if you're smart,

you'll just sit tight and forget it."

"Trouble here, Henry?"

Joel whirled at the question. The town's lawman was standing inside the doorway. A tall, lean man with iron-gray hair, he had entered so quietly Kane had heard nothing.

The lawman saw the pistol in Joel's hand. His jaw settled into a firm line and his eyes narrowed. "This is a hold-up?" he asked coolly.

Kane shook his head. "Just picking up a paper for my pa, Marshal."

"Why the gun?"

"It's a hold-up, Tom." Testman broke in before Joel could answer. "Says he's Amos Kane's boy. Maybe he is, maybe he's not. Forced me to hand over the old man's will."

"Forced?"

Testman, on his feet, pointed to the weapon in Joel's hand. "Why do you think he's holding that?"

The marshal placed his flat gaze on Kane. "Can't see as it matters what you're after. Using a gun to get it makes it a hold-up. Now, put that weapon away and give Testman back that paper."

"It's important that I don't," Joel said. "You want to hear my side of it?" He had considered laying the whole story of Berryman's duplicity before the law and asking for help, if it became necessary. This could be the opportune moment.

"Not interested," the marshal said. "Only thing I want is to see you put that iron in its holster, and fork over that paper."

"Then what?"

"Then we're taking a walk over to my jail. I'm putting you under arrest, while I get to the bottom of this."

"Arrest! On what charge?"

"You've heard it . . . hold-up."

Impatience ripped through Kane. "Not a hold-up, Marshal, and you know it. If you want to do something, get on your horse and go back to the Circle K with me. That's where some law's needed."

"What's wrong out there?"

"He's all heated up because his pa's leaving the ranch to Cass Berryman," Testman offered. "He ran off ten years ago . . . left the old man flat. Berryman stepped in and has been looking after things all this time. Now he's come back, wanting his share."

The lawman nodded thoughtfully. "That the way of it? You pull out like Henry says and just now come back?"

"He's right. . . ."

"That will leave everything to Berryman?"

"It does, but that's not the reason I'm here. Pa sent for me. He's in trouble."

"Why would Amos Kane send for him?" Testman persisted. "He disowned him after he left. Be the last man he'd go to for help . . . if he *was* in trouble, seems to me he'd go to you."

"Makes sense," the lawman agreed.

"How do you know?" Joel demanded. "You ever drop by the Circle K, see how things were going?"

"Well, can't say as I have. Just never had no reason to, and your pa . . . he ain't the friendliest man I ever met."

"Then you don't know . . . ?"

"I know just one thing, Kane," the lawman said, his voice going brittle, "you'd better do like I tell you, or you're in real trouble, because I'm not letting you walk out of here."

"I'm walking out, all right," Joel said, abruptly out of patience. He brought up his pistol, leveled it at the old lawman. "Get over here with Testman. You, too," he added, motioning to the teller.

The two men moved slowly up beside the banker's desk. Beyond them the door to a closet stood partly open.

"In there," Kane said crisply.

Testman and the clerk began to back slowly toward the small room; the lawman did not stir. Temper finally got the best of Kane. He stepped in close, lifted the older man's pistol from its holster, flung it into a corner.

"Move . . . damn you!" he snarled. "I don't want trouble with you!"

The lawman stared at Joel for a several moments and then began to retreat with the others. "You've already got trouble, mister," he said. "Plenty."

There was no key for the closet door. Kane dragged up a chair, wedged it under the knob, blocking it securely. Turning then, he left the bank and mounted the sorrel. Swinging off into the street, he shook his head. *Now I've got the law and the outlaws both gunning for my hide,* he thought.

VIII

The sun was well on its westward swing, when Joel Kane reached the trail leading to the rimrocks. He was feeling much better. The will was in his possession, thus removing the immediate threat to Amos Kane's life, and now it would be only a matter of time until Berryman and his outlaw following could be driven from the Circle K. He regretted the measures he had been compelled to take where the marshal of Cedar River was concerned. He had never been at odds with the law, and he didn't like the idea—but he had been given no choice. Henry Testman had made an issue of surrendering the will, either because of some arrangement he had with Cass

Berryman, or possibly due to a sense of loyalty to what he considered his duty as a banker. Joel was uncertain which. Regardless, when it was all cleared up, he'd go to the old lawman and explain why he had been forced to act as he did. With his father's backing and a presentation of the facts concerning Berryman, he should be able to make the marshal understand.

The sorrel, tired from the long day, picked his way slowly up the rock-studded path. Joel did not push him. It would be too late, when he reached the cabin, to do anything but rest anyway, and there was no point in punishing the big red. He touched his pocket, reassuring himself that the will was there. He'd let Amos tear it up, burn it. It would give Amos pleasure and perhaps act as a sort of stimulant for the job that lay ahead. Joel still had no definite plan of action in mind. He guessed it would be a good idea to talk things over with Amos and Ben Stoyers, get their ideas, and then start things rolling in the morning. He hoped the old cook had remembered to bring along some grub. He hadn't eaten since morning and was feeling the need for food.

At the first granite ledge the sorrel halted, unsure of the rain-washed surface. Joel swung down, intending to lead the red across its narrow width. At that moment he heard a faint halloo coming from below, and halted. Frowning, he moved to the edge of the ledge and studied the rolling, brushy contours of the distant valley.

Motion to the south caught his eyes—several slow-moving dots winding in and out of the gray-green undergrowth. Berryman and his men, he decided, continuing the search. More dots appeared, working now toward a central point. Methodically he counted them. Ten riders in all.

A hard grin pulled at his lips. These men weren't outlaws; this was a posse from Cedar River. The marshal had lost no time organizing a pursuit. It looked as if the old lawman was following no specific trail, however, but was hunting blind—he was now swinging his men north, away from the rimrock country.

He had nothing to fear, Joel concluded. The posse would search until darkness fell and then give it up. They might possibly return at daylight, depending on how great the injury to the marshal's pride had been and how strong were his powers of persuasion. Thinking about it, Kane hoped they would come again; perhaps he could devise a plan whereby he would lead Berryman and his followers into the hands of the posse. Amos could then lay the facts before the marshal and press whatever charges he desired.

Charges? Joel considered that thought. *What charges?* That Berryman had been unnecessarily hard on him? That he planned to murder him in order to take over the Circle K? They would be difficult to prove, and any verification from Joel would be discounted, just as it had been in the bank—the son, returning home and resenting the fact that an outsider was to inherit his father's property. He would have to handle Berryman himself, Joel realized. It would be best to keep the law out of it, at least until he'd made the first move and had the outlaws on the defensive.

The posse had all but disappeared, cutting to the east now. The ranch lay in that direction and, twenty miles beyond it, the town itself. Chances were better than good that the lawman and his men would encounter Berryman somewhere along the way. He wondered what the outlaw would tell the marshal when he learned they both sought the same fugitive. It would be a good story; Berryman was a smooth one to deal with.

Tugging at the leathers, he led the sorrel on across the ledge, remounted, and continued up the steep trail. A short time later he broke out onto another bench and saw the shoulder of rock beyond which the cabin stood. *Almost there*, he thought with relief. In a few more minutes he'd be out of the saddle and easing his tired muscles while he satisfied the hunger now gnawing at him. He hoped Ben Stoyers had coffee ready.

Amos and the old cook had heeded his warning. The shack appeared as deserted as ever. Joel rode in slowly, anxious to arrive, yet restrained as always by an inner instinct that, throughout his life, had unremittingly refused to accept any situation at face value. As he had done many times in the past, he tried to brush aside the caution, telling himself that the evident absence of life, the lack of greeting, was to be expected, that it was something of his own doing, since he had told both men to remain hidden, taking no chances. But the uneasiness persisted. He reached the edge of the clearing, the sorrel moving in slow, weary steps, and halted, eyes on the closed door. He sat for a moment, studying the weather-beaten panel, and then, ignoring his misgivings, he swung down. Ground reining the sorrel, he hitched at his gun belt and started for the door.

"Joel, trap!"

The muffled warning brought him up short. He heard something fall inside the cabin and clawed for his pistol just as another sound came from his left. He spun fast to see Bill Taney and the *vaquero* break suddenly from a screen of brush.

Kane lunged to one side as Taney fired. The bullet thudded into the front of the cabin, sending up a puff of dust. Joel, snapping a quick reply at the outlaw, whirled again. Directly ahead was Berryman and not far from him, Clete Jordan. They were trying to box him in, push him back against the shack.

Escape on the sorrel was out of the question. He leaped

aside and ducked behind a clump of sage, going full length and rolling fast until he was in the deep shadow of a scrub cedar.

"Get him . . . god-damn it!" Berryman yelled. "He's in that brush!"

Guns crackled, drowning the outlaw's strident command. Bullets smashed into the sage, churning the feathery leaves. Crawling, Joel gained the shelter of a rocky ledge, drew himself to a crouch. He couldn't see the outlaws, but guessed they were closing in on the clump of sage, expecting him to be there.

He darted off, running low and quiet, circling in behind the cabin. There was no way he could return to the sorrel, but Amos's horse was picketed in the undergrowth back of the shack. If he could reach—he caught sight of the gray. The horse was thirty feet away, head lifted, ears pricked forward as he looked curiously at Kane's crouched shape. Keeping low, Joel hurried on.

"He ain't here!"

Bill Taney's voice was shot with surprise. There was a muffled curse and then Berryman's impatient shout: "Got to be there! I saw him jump in behind that bush . . . and with all that shooting! Look again!"

"Must've missed him. He sure ain't here!"

"Doubt that." Cass Berryman's tone was less insistent. "Bound to have winged him, so keep hunting. He can't have gone far."

Joel reached the gray, jerked the reins loose. He started to swing onto the saddle, but thought better of it. Mounted, he would be above the brush and easily seen.

Leading the horse, he dropped back another ten yards and then, believing himself well screened, stepped into the saddle. Instantly a gunshot blasted through the quiet, and he felt the shock of a bullet searing across his shoulders.

"Over here! Over here!" Clete Jordan's voice shouted.

Throwing himself forward in the saddle, Joel dug spurs into the gray's flanks and pointed him for the higher ledges of the rimrocks. The gray began to labor on the rough up-grade almost at once. Kane swore in frustration; the horse had no bottom—he'd go down in another hundred yards at that pace. He swore again, wishing he had the sorrel; tired as he was, the big red at his worst was twice as good as the gray.

He looked back. Berryman and the others were some-where below. They couldn't be far, but the rocky outcrop-pings and dense undergrowth hid them from view. He could hear them shouting, and now and then came the rattle of displaced gravel and the dry slap of brush.

The trail veered to the right, breaking its steep ascent, and leveled off on a sparsely grassed shelf. Immediately the gray caught his wind, picked up speed, and for a brief time gained rapidly on the pursuing outlaws. And then again the path turned upward, now following a narrow gash in the granite face of the mountain. Joel began to feel the sting of the wound across his shoulders. With one hand he reached around to explore it gingerly. The skin was barely broken, although there was considerable blood. Jordan's bullet had just skimmed his body, slicing a shallow furrow in its flight. If the slug had been a half inch lower, he'd be back at the cabin helpless, possibly dead.

Near the top of the crevice the gray stumbled, churned his hoofs to regain balance, and sent a quantity of loose rock cascading onto the ledge below. Yells went up, and a solitary shot echoed through the gathering darkness. Kane heard no thud of a bullet and guessed that whoever'd fired had simply aimed in the general direction of the racket. He stared ahead. The gray was beginning to wilt and would need rest at once. Kane could see no break in the trail. It continued to climb seemingly straight up as it pointed for the upper crests and ridges.

Berryman and his men were still hidden from view, and the sounds of their coming seemed more distant. He had almost lost them at the gash when he turned off, he realized, and they had lost time doubling back. If the gray hadn't stumbled and set off a disturbance, he might have gotten into the clear. But that didn't help now. The gray had to be given a few minutes' rest—and, besides, he must somehow get back to the cabin. Amos and Ben Stoyers were probably prisoners, likely hurt. Something had happened inside the shack when Amos had yelled his warning. If Joel could turn off the trail, hide and allow the outlaws to bypass him, he could cut back down the mountain. Under cover of darkness it wouldn't be too difficult. Anxiously, he again peered ahead. The trail ran on, hemmed in on both sides by sheer rock.

He wondered how Berryman had found Amos. The last he'd seen of the outlaws they were far off in another direction. It had been by sheer accident, he supposed—or possibly Berryman had known of the cabin and had led his men there on an outside chance he'd find the Kanes. If so, the hunch had certainly paid off for him.

A darker area loomed up to his left. Hope rose within him, and he strained his eyes to determine the nature of the break in the otherwise solid wall of rock. A narrow cañon, filled with thick-growing piñon trees which apparently extended the complete depth of the slash. The trees were not large but were so crowded they formed an almost impenetrable screen.

Using spurs, he goaded the winded gray to a faster pace.

No turnoff was apparent, and, if he could make the swing without being seen by the outlaws, they would simply assume that he had continued on toward the summit. Reaching the draw, he cut the gray around and broke into the first of the piñons. Brush crowded the ground beneath the trees, and for the first dozen strides the horse had little easier going than on the steep trail, but shortly the clumps of scrub oak and sage thinned out and progress became much simpler.

He rode the gray well back into the pocket of the cañon and halted. Staying in the saddle, he turned to watch. The piñons were like a solid green wall, shutting off all except what was immediately before him. Dissatisfied, he slipped from the saddle, anchored the gray, and made his way forward until he could look upon the trail.

The outlaws were only minutes behind him. He heard first the sharp click of a metal shoe against stone and then the dry squeak of leather. Kane tried to locate them in the darkness, but the moon was not yet strong, and the men were evidently beyond the mouth of the cañon.

Cass Berryman's voice broke the hush. "Ought to be pulling up on him. That gray's wind-broken. Hasn't got it in him to do much hard climbing."

"That why we aren't hearing him?" Taney asked. "Reckon he could've turned off, given us the slip?"

"Turned off where?" Berryman's voice was ragged, impatient.

One of the others said something in a low voice—the *vaquero,* Joel thought—but he couldn't make out the words. That left Jordan to account for. The sound of their passage was clear now, and a moment later he saw the upper portion of their bodies silhouetted against the faint, rising glow. Three riders only. Where was Clete Jordan?

"Be a damn' good place for him to be hiding," Bill Taney said, pulling to a stop abreast the cañon. "Hard to find anything in there."

The others halted.

Berryman said: "It's worth a look." Then: "Where the hell's Clete?"

"He tried a swing to the west . . . figured Kane could've dodged that way."

"Ought to be showing up. Nothing but cliffs through there. Man can't get to the top unless he sticks to the trail."

"He knows that. He'll be catching up. Want me to take a sashay through the trees while we're waiting?"

Joel threw a hasty glance around. Taney was certain to spot the gray. He'd best move farther back into the grove, try to find taller growth. He turned, felt his foot strike against a stone. A thought passed through his mind, and, leaning over, he picked up the rock. It might work. Moving forward to where he had room, he threw the stone uptrail as hard as he could. It fell with a hollow thud, creating a small gravel slide.

Berryman swore. "He's not in there. Still ahead of us."

"Not far either," Bill Taney replied. "We go on or wait for Clete?"

"Keep going. Sounded like we're pretty close. Jordan'll find us."

Immediately Joel heard the sound of their horses as they resumed the trail. He grinned into the pale night. The outlaws had fallen for a trick as old as Indian fighting itself. He'd give them a couple of minutes and head back for the cabin. Jordan? He'd have to go carefully. The thin-faced gunman was below him somewhere, probably on the trail now. While Joel didn't remember much about the mountain, he knew Berryman had been correct in saying it was impossible to reach the summit except by the path. Sheer rock walls blocked every other access. Jordan would have been forced to cut down off the slope, get on the trail.

Kane returned to the gray and mounted. He sat out a long five minutes, wishing Jordan would appear and ride on by. It would make matters much simpler. He gave it another three minutes and concluded he could delay no longer. He'd need plenty of time, once he reached the cabin, to get Amos and Ben Stoyers out of the shack and onto horses—and well down the trail. And if either of the men was injured. . . .

He touched the gray lightly and started down the cañon. It would be smart to stay off the path as much as possible, do his traveling on the shoulder, even if it was slower. In that way he stood a chance of seeing the outlaw before being seen.

A sound to his right brought Kane to a sudden halt. He pivoted and saw Clete Jordan. The outlaw's features registered surprise, and Joel realized the man was as startled as he.

Jordan reacted instantly. His hand swept down for the pistol on his hip. Kane was equally fast, but, wanting no gunshot echoing across the mountain to summon Berryman and the others, launched himself from the saddle. He hit the outlaw with solid force and threw his arms around Jordan's body. Together they went to the ground, thrashing wildly. Joel, on top, fought to keep his grip around Jordan, knowing he must prevent the man from drawing his weapon. But Clete was no newcomer to the rough-and-tumble way of combat. He began to twist, to use his legs, his head. Kane felt his grasp slipping.

Gasping for breath, Joel managed to get his knees under him. He drew himself up slightly and lifted Jordan.

Gathering strength, he lunged forward, smashing Jordan to the ground beneath him. Jordan's wind exploded in a gusty blast, and for a brief instant his efforts suspended. Joel instantly released his grip and drove a balled fist into the outlaw's jaw. Clete groaned, struggled to pull away. Merciless, Kane hammered at his head, his neck and face. Jordan managed to get to his hands and knees. Joel drew himself upright and, standing over the outlaw, drove him flat with a down-sledging blow. Jordan went limp.

Breathing hard, Kane stared at the unconscious man for several moments and then, turning, staggered to where the gray waited. Pulling himself into the saddle, he headed downgrade for the cabin.

IX

Joel swept into the flat at a gallop. Time was too short to worry about noise. He doubted if Cass Berryman and the two men with him, far up on the side of the mountain, could hear the gray anyway. As for Clete Jordan, it didn't matter.

The cabin stood silently in the now bright moonlight, and Joel felt his fears rise again. Amos could be dead. The outlaws could have injured him fatally and thus completed the job they had planned for Mud Lake. Anxious, he swerved the gray in beside the sorrel, leaped to the ground.

"Pa!" he shouted hoarsely, and rushed for the door.

He booted the panel open, then paused. A shaft of silver light reached into the small room and fell across the form of Amos Kane, crumpled in a back corner. A rag was across the lower half of his face, and his hands were bound behind him. Blood crusted his forehead in a ragged streak, but his eyes were open and greeted Joel with a bright feverishness.

"Pa," Joel said again, relief flowing through him. Recalling the situation, he added hurriedly: "We've got to get out of here quick."

He stepped into the cabin—and felt the hard, round muzzle of a rifle jab into his back. Caught off guard, Joel froze while his mind raced to find an understanding.

"Step right in, Mister Kane. Make yourself to home."

Ben Stoyers.

Joel, arms raised, wheeled slowly. He had the answer now as to how Berryman had found Amos. Stoyers was a double-crosser: he'd been one of the outlaw's crowd all along.

"You sneaking bastard!" Joel snarled. "This is the way you pay back a man who's been your friend, given you a job. . . ."

"Friend?" Stoyers echoed scornfully. "He ain't my friend! He's nobody's friend!"

"Fed you, furnished you with a place to stay, and paid you good money for what you did."

"If he'd paid me a thousand dollars a day, it wouldn't have been enough! Working for him's like being a slave."

"You could have quit . . . walked off."

The old cook swallowed hard, but he did not look away. "Maybe, only I. . . ."

"Only you knew you wouldn't get another job as good as the one you had. Nobody'd hire you."

"Nothing good about it," Stoyers muttered. "Up, working daylight till dark. Taking his cussedness, letting him wipe his boots on me . . . but I knew my day was coming."

"And to get it you sold him out to Berryman. When did you decide to do that, Ben? When you saw me at the house?"

Stoyers laughed. "A long time before that, mister. Made my mind up with Cass a couple of years ago. How do you figure he was able to keep tabs on old Amos so good? Was me, watching close, letting Cass know what was going on all the time."

Amos Kane stirred weakly, moaned.

Joel glanced at him, then back to the cook. "Take that gag off him. No need for it now."

Ben Stoyers wagged his head. "Nope, just leave him be. I'm kind of enjoying myself, watching him squirm around."

"He's hurt. At least, let me look at his wound."

"Doesn't amount to anything. Just a little rap on the head. Cass and the boys'll be coming along in a minute anyway."

That same thought had entered Joel's mind. He studied Stoyers quietly, calculating his chances of overcoming the man. If anything was to be done, it would have to be done quickly.

Stoyers, little more than an arm's length away, returned his stare with a crooked grin. He shifted his rifle. "Thinking about jumping me . . . that it?"

Kane shrugged. "Be a fool to try . . . with you standing there pointing that gun at me."

"For a fact. I'd blow a hole in your guts big enough to walk through."

Amos groaned again. Joel, sweat beading his brow, swore harshly. "You have to let me take that gag off. He's having trouble breathing."

Stoyers glanced at the elder Kane uncertainly.

"No risk for you as long as you're holding that rifle," Joel pressed.

Abruptly the cook nodded. "All right . . . but first you turn yourself around. And keep your hands high."

Joel wheeled slowly. He heard a slight sound as Stoyers stepped forward, then felt a lessening of weight on his hip as his pistol was removed from its holster.

"Go ahead," the older man said then. "But you move slow and easy. I'm a mite nervous."

Kane crossed to his father's side and hurriedly pulled the gag loose. Amos stared up at him through dazed eyes.

"Joel?"

"It's me all right, Pa. You're going to be fine now."

"Was afraid they'd caught you, too."

Ben Stoyers cackled. "They have, old man. We've got you both."

Amos frowned. "Who's that?" he asked, trying to focus his gaze.

"Stoyers," Joel answered. In the pale glow of the moonlight that sifted into the cabin, Amos appeared very old—and very tired. The blow on his head had weakened him and left him slightly addled.

"Ben?" he said as if finding it hard to believe.

"He's sided with Berryman, Pa. He's no friend."

Amos stirred wearily. "Never figured Ben'd turn against me. Always sort've trusted him . . . where're Cass and them others?"

"Up on the mountain."

"Looking for you?"

"That's right, Pa. I came back to get you and Ben. He fooled me, too."

Suddenly angry, Stoyers said: "You've done enough yammering. Get back over here where I can keep an eye on you."

Joel rose slowly and turned. The old cook had changed his position. He now stood near the partly open door so he had the light to his back and could see the interior of the cabin better. Kane gave the situation a swift survey. If he could get within reaching distance of that door. . . . Moving with deliberation, he crossed to the wall and leaned against it. Ignoring the stinging pain the pressure evoked in his shoulders, he folded his arms and stared at Stoyers.

"Can't figure you, Ben . . . siding with Berryman. What'll you get out of it?"

"My share," the old man said promptly. "And I'll be my own boss. Won't be anybody walking in on me and chewing me out all the time."

"Maybe. I can't see Cass taking you in, giving you any part of a split."

"He will . . . told me he would."

"And you're fool enough to believe him? Hell, you're not as smart as I figured."

"You don't know a thing about it!" Stoyers yelled, thoroughly aroused. "I'll be getting. . . ."

Joel kicked out like a striking rattlesnake. His booted foot caught the forward panel of the door, which swung hard and slammed into Ben Stoyers. The rifle in Ben's hands exploded, sending the bullet into the floor. The weapon itself went flying into a corner of the room.

"Damn you . . . !" Stoyers yelled, and stumbled backward through the doorway.

Joel was across the room in a single bound, arms reaching for the rifle. Gathering it up, he levered a fresh cartridge into the chamber, whirling to peer through the layers of hanging smoke.

The half bent figure of the cook, Joel's pistol in his hand, was crouched just outside. Stoyers caught a glimpse of Kane and fired hurriedly—missed.

"Drop that gun!" Joel yelled, keeping the wall between him and the man. "You haven't got a chance!"

"The hell I ain't!" Stoyers shouted back and, triggering the pistol again, lunged through the doorway.

Joel Kane fired once. The slug buried itself in Stoyers's chest, halted his forward motion, and slammed him half around. He dropped his weapon and grabbed frantically for the door frame. For several seconds he clung to it, and then abruptly collapsed.

Kane bent hurriedly, scooped up his pistol, and wheeled to Amos. "Got to pull out fast," he said, tugging at the cord that bound the old man's wrists. "Cass and the others are sure to have heard that shooting. Think you can ride?"

"Manage . . . somehow," Amos answered haltingly. "Ben dead?"

Joel nodded. "Tried to talk him out of it. He wouldn't listen."

"He was a fool," the old man said, struggling to his feet with Joel's aid. He leaned weakly against the wall. "Things are sort of fuzzy. Reckon it's that rap on the head Ben give me."

"Soon as you're outside breathing some fresh air, you'll be all right."

Throwing one arm around his father's slight body, Kane started for the door. They reached the opening, stepped over Ben Stoyers's lifeless shape, and moved into the cool, silvered night.

"Horses . . . they're right ahead, Pa," Joel said. "Keep resting on me. We'll make it."

In that next moment Kane realized he and Amos were going nowhere—at least alone. Waiting at the edge of the shadows fronting the cabin was Cass Berryman. Strung out to either side, in a half circle, were Bill Taney, Clete Jordan, and the *vaquero*, Dobe Rivera.

Berryman said: "Go ahead, friend. Load the old man on his horse."

Joel hung motionless in the center of the clearing, Amos leaning heavily against him. A sullen anger was moving through him—not so much at the outlaws but at himself and his own carelessness. He should have used more care. He should have realized Berryman and his men would be near and prepared for them.

"Reckon you better get rid of that pistol first," Bill Taney said.

Kane remained frozen, his mind reaching out, striving to find a means for meeting and overcoming this new emergency. Taney cocked his revolver, the distinct clicks loud in the stillness.

"Now!" he commanded harshly, leveling the weapon.

Joel drew the pistol with his free hand and allowed it to drop.

Berryman laughed. "Put your pa on his horse, like I told you."

Kane, supporting his father, walked to the side of the gray. Cradling the older man as he would a child, Joel lifted him onto the saddle. Amos groaned softly, sagged forward.

"Tie him," Berryman said. "Long ride ahead of us."

Silent, tense with anger, Joel Kane lashed Amos to the saddle with a rope the outlaw tossed to him. That finished, he wheeled slowly. His pistol lay six feet away. The rifle was twice that distance, near the doorway of the cabin where he had dropped it. His chances for reaching either were less than none at all. He raised his eyes to the red-haired outlaw.

"Now what?"

Cass Berryman kneed his horse in closer. Extending his hand, he said: "I'll take that paper you got at the bank."

The will! Bitterness rolled through Joel. It was still in his pocket. He had planned to give it to Amos, let him have the satisfaction of destroying it. Now it was too late. He should have done it himself. "What paper?" he asked coolly.

"Don't try bluffing me!" Berryman snapped. "Raise your hands and keep them up."

Kane lifted his arms. The outlaw leaned forward, probed Joel's pockets, and produced the document briefly, then nodded in satisfaction.

"Old Ben was right," he said, and thrust the paper inside his shirt front. "That god-damn' Testman's going to hear from me about this." His glance paused on the body of the cook, half in and half out of the cabin's entrance. "Get Stoyers's horse," he said to Taney. "Wouldn't be smart to leave him here."

The bearded outlaw spurred off into the brush.

Clete Jordan hawked, spat. "You still figure on taking them to Mud Lake?"

"That's my plan. Best and safest way to handle it."

Joel forced a laugh. "You'll have trouble explaining this."

"Not me," Cass Berryman said, folding his hands on the horn of his saddle. "Your pa'll never be missed, and tramps like you come and go."

"Little different with me. I was seen in town and folks know who I am. The marshal was one of them."

"Eli Pryor? Expect I can handle him. I'll just give him and his missus a side of good beef and that'll end it."

"Said there were others."

"Testman? You mean him and his teller? No problem there, either. Henry knows what's good for him . . . same as the teller. You're barking up the wrong tree, Kane. Made a big mistake trying to buck me."

Bill Taney appeared at the edge of the clearing, a small buckskin in tow. He halted near the shack and dropped the leathers.

Berryman motioned to Joel. "Hand Stoyers across the

saddle. Better lash him down, too. Pick up the guns while you're there," he added to Taney.

The husky outlaw came off his mount as Joel walked slowly to where Stoyers lay. Kane knew he had no choice but to do as he was told—for the time being, anyway. Later his chance might come.

Bill grinned at him as he scooped up the pistol and turned to retrieve the rifle. "You ain't doing so good, mister."

Joel said nothing. He knelt beside the crumpled body of the cook, lifting him easily, and draped him over the buckskin's saddle. Pulling the coil of rope free of the skirt, he tied the body securely into place. Stepping back, he collided with Taney, who was returning to his horse.

"Damn it . . . watch what you're doing!" the outlaw yelled and struck out angrily.

The backhand slap landed on the side of Joel's head. It did no damage, but he recognized his opportunity, and seized it. "Sure!" he answered, and drove his fist into the husky man's middle.

The blow was too high. Taney merely grunted, cursed again, and swung hard. Joel dodged and sent two more quick jabs into the man's face. Berryman shouted something, but Joel was too intent on drawing in Taney to hear. If he could maneuver the outlaw into the right position, he would not only have a shield but could gain possession of a weapon as well.

He pulled back, leading Taney on. The squat outlaw, face red, mouth working with a wild fury, rushed in. Joel, shoulders now to the wall of the cabin, set himself for a blow that would stun the man, stop him cold. Taney lunged within reach. Kane started an uppercut from his heels, cleared the way for it with a sharp left jab to the outlaw's eyes. His knuckles cracked as his fist connected with Bill Taney's jaw. The husky rider halted as if he had walked into a stone wall. His arms fell to his sides, and he began to sway. Instantly Joel leaped forward, caught him around the waist with his left arm, and snatched the pistol from its holster with his right hand.

"Kane!"

Berryman's voice brought him up short. Revolver cocked, he looked across the clearing. His hopes died.

The outlaw chief had spurred in close to Amos. The *vaquero* had swung in also, was now on the opposite side of the old man. Both had their weapons out and were holding them against Amos Kane's bowed head.

"You want to see him die quick, try using that iron," Cass Berryman said.

Joel straightened slowly. Sucking deep for lost breath, he released Taney, who staggered forward, still groggy.

"The gun," Berryman pressed.

Joel tossed the weapon aside, felt a heaviness settle over him. It had almost worked—almost. Now . . . ?

He was aware suddenly of Bill Taney wheeling, swinging a wild blow at his head. He heard the outlaw's enraged voice lashing him, cursing, threatening, as he tried to avoid the man's oncoming fist. Too late. He took a solid jolt to the ear. Lights popped before his eyes, his senses reeled, and he felt himself going down. Berryman was again yelling. His words seemed to come from a great distance.

He was on the ground, only half unconscious from the hard blow. He stirred. The sharp toe of a boot smashed cruelly into his ribs. Hands pulled at him, dragged him upright. He tried to stand, but there was no strength in his legs, and once more he started to sink.

"Hold him, damn it!" someone nearby shouted impatiently. "I'll get his horse."

Through the fog that blurred his vision, Joel made out the face of Clete Jordan. Taney was turning toward the sorrel, and, on beyond, Cass Berryman and the *vaquero* sat their saddles and watched in silence.

The sorrel was in front of him, crowding him. He felt himself being boosted, then dumped onto the saddle. Bill Taney's voice registered dully on his mind.

"We have to tie him, too?"

"Let him set a minute," Berryman answered. "He'll come out of it."

"A wild one," the ordinarily silent *vaquero* commented. "In my country one we would say *muy macho*."

"He ain't so much," Taney grumbled. "Grabbed me when I was looking the other way."

"Doesn't seem to make much difference whether you're looking or not," Berryman said dryly. "Now, keep away from him, hear? I don't want him making another try."

"I'm not done with him . . . not by a damn' sight!" the husky outlaw declared. "Got me a few licks coming and I aim to get them."

"You want us to hold him for you . . . maybe tie his hands behind him?"

Joel, fully conscious, sat motionless with his head down while he listened. It wasn't over yet—not as long as he was still alive.

"Won't need any help!" Bill Taney roared. "Turn me loose with him . . . I'll show you."

"Maybe. Anyway, you're not the only one wanting a piece of him. Clete figures he's got himself a claim, too."

Jordan shrugged, turned to his horse. "I'll collect . . . but it'll be my way. I'm not fool enough to try using my fists . . . not with him."

"Well, I'm not scared of him!" Taney said. "I don't need any hog-leg!"

"You need something," Berryman said laconically. "Shake him a mite, wake him up."

The bearded outlaw whirled, grasped Joel by the arm, and jerked violently. Kane, hoping to maintain the deception further, mumbled thickly, sagged to one side.

"He can ride," Berryman said. "Mount up. I want to reach Mud Lake and get this job over with before daylight."

X

They moved off downtrail. Dobe Rivera was in the lead. Behind him was Berryman, followed by Amos Kane, then Joel, Clete Jordan, Taney, and, last of all, the horse bearing the body of Stoyers. At the start Joel watched his father anxiously, not certain he was in condition to ride, but Amos, securely lashed to the saddle, appeared to be in fair shape although still somewhat dazed.

They descended slowly. Despite the brightness of the moon, shadows lay across the path, spooking the horses and causing them to proceed with caution. For this Joel Kane was grateful. It would take several hours to reach Mud Lake, and he needed every possible moment to find a way out for Amos and himself.

The posse? He thought of Eli Pryor and the men he had seen from the rimrocks, scouring the flats. Had they returned to Cedar River—or had the gunshots at the cabin drawn their attention? It was possible. Sound carried to great distances in the cold, clear air, and the old lawman and his party could, at that very moment, be working up the slope. But it could be no ace in the hole for him. Cass Berryman had spoken as if the marshal was something of a friend and would side with him after taking a bribe to look the other way. And from what he knew of Berryman, Joel had little reason to doubt his claim of influence.

He sighed heavily. There was little hope of help coming from anyone. Everything was stacked against him; it seemed foolish to buck such odds. But Joel Kane was not one to quit; as long as he had breath, he'd fight. Better to die from a bullet, anyway, than in the suffocating layers of slimy gumbo in Mud Lake. He glanced up. Amos, head sagged forward, rode the gray lifelessly, his frail body moving and shifting with the movements of his horse. Beyond him Berryman was a blocky outline in the night. Rivera, the silver trappings on his broad-brimmed Mexican hat glittering brightly, was a length farther away.

Joel ventured a look over his shoulder. Clete Jordan, both hands resting on the horn, face tipped down, rode wearily. He was not sleeping, Kane realized, but was in that nether world of tired half wakefulness. He brought his attention back around. Sheer wall lifted on his right, but to the left a slope fell away, steeply in some places, more gradual in others, and all thickly brushed. A man could break at the proper moment, send his horse plunging into the undergrowth, and possibly make good an escape. It wasn't for him. Cass Berryman knew he would not make such an effort, was so certain of it, in fact, that he had foregone binding Joel's wrists. The outlaw had Amos, and, as long as he did, he knew he held the upper hand.

Joel had to think of something else—something that would provide escape for both Amos and himself. He shook his head wearily. It was a big order, one that would be difficult to fill. The trail began to level off, and Joel realized they were moving onto the flats that stretched out from the base of the mountains. He glanced around once more, growing more desperate for some means of escape. Jordan stirred into life, and Taney, taking note for the first time, gave him a hard-cornered grin.

"Something bothering you, saddlebum?"

Instantly Cass Berryman turned on his saddle. "Shut up back there," he hissed. "I don't want any racket."

The meaning of that drove home to Kane. The outlaw leader had also seen the posse and was hoping to avoid it. Apparently Cass wasn't as sure of Eli Pryor as he had claimed. Or perhaps it was the men riding with the marshal. They would be local citizens of Cedar River, and probably not ones to be intimidated by the red-headed outlaw. Hope began to stir again within Joel.

Abruptly the horse ahead of him stopped. Joel looked up quickly. Berryman, hand raised, was in the center of the trail. Rivera had pulled off to the side and was staring into the brush.

"What's the trouble?" Taney's question was a hoarse whisper.

"That posse we saw, probably," Clete Jordan murmured.

At that moment the *vaquero* wheeled, doubled back to where Berryman waited. He spoke a few quick words to the outlaw. Berryman immediately raised himself in his stirrups and made a quick survey. Obviously he was seeking a place in which to hide.

Again Cass Berryman lifted his arm, this time waving the party off the trail and pointing to a thick stand of juniper and other growth. Rivera spurred off the path, catching the reins of Amos's gray as he crossed. Berryman swung in behind them, and at the same instant Clete crowded by Joel, forcing the sorrel to turn, head into the trees.

"Try something and I'll split your head open," Bill Taney warned, brandishing his pistol as he cut in beside Joel. "Hear?"

Joel nodded. It was not yet time to make a move, if one was to be made. Best wait until the marshal and his men were near and there was no doubt of their passing by. It could be they were only in the area, and Cass Berryman was just playing it safe.

Silent, he lined up with the others in the deep shadows, aware that Clete Jordan had taken up a position slightly to his rear, Taney farther over. The moments dragged. Far off in the distance an owl hooted. A hoof clicked sharply against a rock. Again there was quiet—and then a horse and rider appeared at a bend in the trail. A second moved into view, then a third. Joel strained to make out the first man's identity. Moonlight glinted against metal on his vest. Relief sped through Kane: Eli Pryor, the marshal. It was the posse. Joel tensed, but allowed the seconds to tick by, waited until the lawman was directly opposite.

"Marshal!" he called in a clear voice, and started to spur into the open.

Pryor halted, and instantly Jordan jammed his pistol into Kane's back, murmured: "Sit tight. Take a look at the Mex."

Joel froze and swung his eyes to the *vaquero*. Rivera had his knife out, was pressing the point against the elder Kane's throat.

"Who's there?" Pryor asked, staring into. the black depths of the junipers.

Cass Berryman moved onto the shoulder of the trail. " 'Evening, Marshal," he said easily.

The lawman glared at him. "What the hell do you mean, scaring a man like that?"

Berryman laughed. "Sorry, Eli. Didn't mean to."

The old lawman settled back, still frowning. "You hiding from somebody?"

"Reckon you could say that. Heard you coming . . . weren't sure who it'd be. Pulled off into the brush until we had a look. Lot of owlhoots running loose around here these days."

"So I been told," Pryor said dryly. "Little late to be riding the hills, ain't it?"

The marshal didn't appear to be much of a friend to Berryman, Joel thought, and wondered if he dared trust the man. Regardless, he couldn't be much worse off.

The outlaw leader said: "Heard shooting up in the rimrocks. Some of the boys and I rode up to see what it was all about."

Pryor shifted wearily. "Find out?"

"Sure did. Guess it's a job for you, Marshal. Somebody killed my cook."

The lawman came to attention. "Stoyers? Thought he worked for old man Kane."

"Same thing," Berryman said with a wave of his hand, "seeing as how I'm running the place for Kane."

Pryor digested that, said: "Who did it?"

"Don't know. Whoever it was had lit out. We picked up some tracks heading west. Lost them in the dark."

Surprise stirred Joel. He had half expected the outlaw to name him as the killer—it would have been a simple way for Berryman to rid himself of a problem. But the redhead evidently believed it safer to handle the matter in a different manner. Joel leaned forward. If he could draw Pryor's attention, get recognized. . . . Jordan's gun barrel dug deeper into his spine. "You forgetting the Mex?" the gunman muttered.

Joel relaxed. Pryor drew a pipe from his pocket, tamped it full of tobacco. Striking a match, he puffed for several moments, then returned his attention to Cass.

"You leave Stoyers's body up there?"

"Having the boys bring it down. Aim to give the old man a decent burial. Sure hope you can catch that killer, Eli. Ben never harmed anybody."

"I'll get him," the lawman said, looking up the trail. "Whereabouts did it happen?"

"That old cabin, south end of the rimrocks."

Pryor twisted around and nodded to the men gathered into a group behind him. "Let's get up there, boys. We'll camp till daylight, then start doing some tracking."

"Smart idea, Marshal," Berryman said, shaking his head admiringly. "Killer's probably holed up for the night, and you being there at daylight'll give you a good start. Need any help?"

"Reckon I got enough," the lawman said. "Obliged just the same."

"Just offering to do my part," the outlaw said smoothly. "My place and my men . . . they're available to you any time you say the word."

"Obliged," Eli Pryor said again and, motioning to the riders behind him, started up the trail.

Cass Berryman wheeled around and rode up to Joel. His eyes were narrow and his face was set in grim lines. "Thought you'd pull a smart one, eh!" he snarled, and struck Joel hard across the mouth.

Joel recoiled, tasting the warm salt of blood from his lips. He stared at the outlaw, his own anger a steady, simmering hate. Another chance for escape had failed—and now he was grasping at straws. Berryman was riled plenty. If he could incense him further, cause him to make a false move, create an opening—shrugging, Kane forced a grin. "Remembered you talking about the marshal. Just trying to see if you were the big man you claimed."

"Don't worry about him. He'll do what I tell him."

"Not worrying about anything. I figure that posse'll be back. They didn't swallow that yarn you handed them."

The red-haired outlaw glanced at Clete Jordan, betraying for the first time a thread of uncertainty. It was only a fleeting expression, however. He laughed. "That's what you're hoping."

"Easy to see," Joel said. "Pryor knows me, heard what I told the banker about you . . . and what you're doing to my pa. Trying to pass Stoyers off as one of your bunch was a bad mistake."

Berryman considered that in silence. Joel watched the man closely, searching for signs of his weakening. He had no actual belief in the words he had spoken—doubted if Eli Pryor had even registered the slip about who Stoyers had worked for, but he had to push every possible opportunity, work any and all angles.

Bill Taney spurred up to Berryman's side. "Aw, he's just talking, Cass," he said. "They didn't figure anything was wrong."

"Believing that," Joel said, pressing hard, "will be another mistake. Face it, Berryman. Your string's run out. Better turn Pa and me loose and make a run for it while you've still got a chance."

Berryman raised his head and brushed back his hat. "Not much, I won't," he said, coming to a decision. "The marshal couldn't prove anything, no matter what he might think. And with you and the old man gone . . . lying under twenty feet of mud. . . ."

"Ought to be moving out of here," Jordan broke in,

looking uptrail, "just in case that posse does take a notion to come back."

Berryman nodded. "Expect you're right. The sooner we get them out of the way, the easier it'll be to handle things." He swung to Taney. "Bill, take Stoyers's body and head for the ranch. I want you to stay there and wait."

"Now wait a minute," the bearded outlaw began. "I'm not. . . ."

"Stay there," Berryman repeated in a flat voice. "If Pryor does show up, I want him thinking things are just the way I said."

"He'll be looking for you. Where'll I say you are?"

"In town. Went there to make arrangements for burying Stoyers. I don't think you'll have any problems. There's a chance we'll be back before they show up . . . if they do."

Taney swore. "Why can't Jordan do it . . . or Dobe? Why's it have to be me?"

"Because I'm telling you to," Berryman snapped, and pulled away. "All right, let's move out."

"You heard him," Jordan said, and prodded Joel roughly with his pistol.

Joel, disappointment and frustration again weighting him heavily, put the sorrel into motion, swung in behind Amos. The older man appeared to have recovered somewhat and now seemed aware of what was taking place. He glanced at Joel, smiled wryly, apologetically. Joel nodded faintly, wishing he could convey some reassurance to him.

As before, Rivera led the party. He rode a short distance ahead, continually on the alert as if afraid of encountering others. That seemed unlikely to Joel. At that hour of the night he could scarcely expect anyone to be abroad, especially since they were on Circle K land. One thing he had learned. Berryman was not the all-powerful man he sought to make others believe, and again Joel began to search his mind for a way to tear at the outlaw's self-assurance, create doubts, and provide an opening. One thing was good—with Bill Taney gone he had only three to contend with.

They rode steadily on through the night, crossing the ranch at a long diagonal that would take them from the extreme southwest corner to a point just beyond the northeast boundary. But Joel Kane had no time for interest in his surroundings or the beauty of the warm, silver-lighted darkness. With each passing mile they were drawing closer to Mud Lake—and the end for Amos and himself.

He wondered if Eli Pryor had been suspicious, as he had tried to make Berryman believe. If so, the old lawman had played it cool, making it appear he was going along with what the outlaw had told him. But if that were true, why hadn't he and his posse reappeared? Could it be he was trailing Berryman's party at a safe distance, waiting to see what the outlaw intended to do? Did Cass Berryman also have such thoughts?—he was keeping Dobe Rivera ranging wide, maintaining a sharp lookout.

He couldn't rely on such a frail possibility, Joel knew. There was a chance it was true—but only a chance. Deep within him another conviction relative to the old lawman had begun to form, and grow in strength: Eli Pryor, like so many small-town marshals, was nothing more than a badge—a hollow representative of the law, useful only in serving legal papers and jailing Saturday night drunks.

Joel glanced over his shoulder. Jordan was immediately behind him, watching him with a quiet, deadly intensity. He wished Berryman had sent Clete back with the cook's body and left Bill Taney to guard him. Taney was the sort who could be tricked, and the possibility of escape would have been much greater. Likely Cass Berryman realized that and had chosen Jordan intentionally, thus ridding himself of Taney and potential trouble.

Joel looked again to his father. The old man rode head bowed and slumped in the saddle, but he was no longer limp. Undoubtedly he felt much better—but he would still be of little use in a showdown of any sort. Amos's legs were lashed together, holding him firmly to his horse. But even if he rode free, he could be of small help. Anything that was to be done, Joel guessed, he'd have to do alone.

A long ridge, dark against the star-littered sky, began to take shape ahead. Kane's nerves tightened as he realized its meaning. Beyond it lay the swale in which was pocketed Mud Lake. Tension began to lay its hard pressure upon him—time was running out. Once more he turned to Clete Jordan. The gunman's gaze was unwavering, and he now rode with one hand resting on the butt of his pistol.

A thought entered Joel Kane's mind. Why hadn't the outlaws used bullets on Amos and him? Why hadn't they simply killed them back at the cabin, or somewhere along the trail, taken their bodies to Mud Lake, and tossed them into the slime? Why was Berryman doing it the hard way? It wasn't that the outlaw chief wished to avoid the sound of gunshots. There had been plenty of those racketing across the slopes and flats. Could it be that Berryman, in his almost fanatical desire to keep everything legal, wished to avoid direct murder and sought to make his and Amos's death appear accidental? It was splitting a hair pretty fine, but Cass was of that turn of mind. He could stand and in truth swear under oath that neither he nor any of his men ever used a weapon of any sort on the Kanes—and to his way of thinking his conscience would be clear.

It didn't really matter, Joel realized. When a man was dead, he was dead regardless of how it came to pass. But the thought did offer a glimmer of hope, a thin one to be sure, but at this point Joel Kane was ready to try anything.

Up ahead, Dobe Rivera had halted. Berryman moved in beside him, and both were looking down at the far side of the slope. Joel didn't need to be told what they saw—Mud Lake.

XI

Jordan said: "Get on up there with the others."

Joel touched the sorrel lightly with his spurs, guided him to the top of the ridge. Halting beside Amos, he looked down into the swale. The bog, its thick, oily surface gleaming dully in the moonlight, appeared to have shrunk, and he wondered if it could be gradually drying up. If and when that day came, it would be a blessing. Much good beef had been lost in its choking depths—and who could say for certain there had been no human victims?

"You still set against using a gun?" Jordan asked.

Berryman nodded. "Do it like I said, just in case."

"It's not going to be easy."

"Why not? Just stampede the horses down the slope. It's dark enough . . . they'll run right into the mud. Better cut the old man loose."

Clete did not move. "What about tracks?"

"Drag some brush. That'll wipe all the sign out."

Joel cast a covert glance at Jordan. The gunman was no longer directly behind him, and Jordan's hand was clear of the weapon at his side. Joel looked then to Amos, found his father staring at him intently. The old man raised his hands slightly, flipped his eyes. Joel looked more closely. The lead rope held by Berryman was no longer tied to the gray horse. Amos had worked the knot apart and now held the two ends to make it appear the rope was secure.

The younger Kane grinned and made a swift appraisal. The ridge, where they had halted, was barren except for small clumps of snakeweed. Farther back down the slope, however, there were considerable brush and a few cedars. Joel jerked his head in that direction, endeavoring to make Amos understand that he should follow that route if the opportunity came. The older man moved his lips soundlessly. Joel hoped it was an indication that he had gotten the message.

"What's wrong with right here?" Jordan asked. "Slope's plenty steep."

"More rocks on the far side, be less tracks to worry about," Cass Berryman explained.

Jordan shrugged. "Well, let's get at it."

Joel Kane realized he would never have a better chance to make his try. He had only a faint hope of success, anyway, but it was not in him to submit meekly to death.

"Go, Pa!" he yelled, and drove his spurs deep into the sorrel's flanks.

Startled, the big red plunged forward, straight into Clete Jordan's mount. As they came together, Joel struck out with his balled fist, smashed a shocking blow into the gunman's face.

Clete yelled as he went off the saddle backward, clawing at the hull to save himself. Instantly Joel was off the sorrel and upon the outlaw, wrenching the man's weapon from its holster.

To his left he saw Amos whirling away on the gray, dragging Berryman with him. The outlaw leader had apparently wrapped the lead rope about his wrist and was unable to free himself quickly enough to avoid being jerked off his horse. But it was only temporary. He shook loose and struggled to regain his feet. Joel, vaulting back onto the sorrel, saw Berryman draw his weapon and take hurried aim at Amos, racing down the slope. Again cruelly spurring the sorrel, Joel drove straight at the outlaw chief.

Dobe Rivera yelled a warning, and Berryman paused, threw himself from the path of the red, and tried to swing around for a shot at Joel. Joel fired hastily, spoiling Berryman's try—and then snapped a shot at the *vaquero,* who was crouched and leveling his pistol with both hands.

Rivera jolted as Kane's bullet struck him, began to stagger. Berryman was down—not hit, Joel was sure—but entangled in his own feet. He flung a glance to the slope. Amos and the gray had reached the comparative safety of the brush. He . . . Joel felt arms grip him from behind. Clete Jordan! He had forgotten the gunman. The outlaw's hands were dragging at him, striving to pull him from the sorrel, now wheeling to head down the slope. Berryman was shouting, and beyond him the Mexican was a folded shape in the moonlight.

Kane, holding tightly to Jordan's pistol, struggled to rip the man's fingers away with his free hand. He locked about one wrist and tore at it savagely, but he could not break the outlaw's grip. The sorrel, frantic now from the weight dragging at his side, began to plunge and dance nervously.

"Get away from him . . . get away!"

It was Berryman, shouting at Jordan. The redhead was standing near Rivera, pistol raised, attempting to get a clean shot. Joel hammered at Jordan's head and neck, glanced down the slope. Amos had halted and was waiting.

"Go on! The ranch!" he yelled. "I'll catch up!"

The elder Kane slapped at the gray's rump and moved

off at a trot. With his feet still bound together Amos was having a hard time of it.

Joel turned his attention again to Clete Jordan. The man was hanging onto him like a leech, and it seemed impossible to jar him loose. He looked then to Berryman. The outlaw leader had forsaken Rivera and was running toward his horse a few yards away. Kane raised his weapon, snapped a shot at the man.

The outlaw halted abruptly, and dropped to one knee. His pistol blasted a small orange spot in the silver night, and Joel saw sand spurt up immediately in front of the sorrel. Berryman would hold back no longer, Jordan or not, Joel realized.

Twisting, he renewed his efforts to knock Clete loose. Using the pistol as a club, he struck at the man's locked hands. Jordan's fingers parted, and he slipped a few inches. Joel struck again, at the gunman's head this time. The blow landed on Jordan's neck. Clete yelled and grabbed for the weapon, at the same time releasing his grasp of Joel.

Kane felt the pistol tear from his fingers as Jordan fell away and went sprawling onto the sand. The sorrel, clear of the maddening, encumbering weight, whirled and rushed off.

Joel started to pull up, to return to where Jordan lay stunned, and recover the revolver. The sharp crack of Berryman's pistol changed his thought. Bending low, he raked the big red with his rowels and plunged downgrade in pursuit of Amos.

He overtook the older man a short mile later.

Amos greeted him anxiously. "You hurt?"

Kane shook his head. "Got to keep moving. They're coming after us."

"Heard shooting. Thought maybe you needed help."

"Downed the Mexican. Lost the gun, fighting with Jordan. Too late to go back for it."

He turned and stared over his shoulder. There was no sign of Berryman and Clete Jordan—but they wouldn't lose any time. One thing, he thought grimly, there'd be only the two of them. The odds were better.

"We heading for the ranch?" Amos yelled to be heard above the thud of the horses' hoofs.

"Best place. Too far to town . . . never get there."

"Can't do much good at the ranch."

"We can fort up, hold out until Pryor and that posse get there."

"If they get there. You forgetting Bill Taney's waiting . . . maybe some of the others?"

Joel shook his head. "Haven't forgotten. We'll just get around him somehow."

They rushed on through the night. It was easy going for the horses, most of it downgrade, and even the gray was taking it with no difficulty.

From time to time Joel looked back, and finally he saw two riders silhouetted briefly on a hillock. Cass Berryman and Jordan were moving up—fast. To hold their lead, the sorrel and the gray needed to increase their pace. He glanced at the gray. The horse was doing his best. Kane swore, resigned himself to luck. They could make it, but it would be close.

He swung the sorrel in closer to Amos. The older man's face was stiff with pain. The punishment he was taking was evident, and Joel knew they should stop and cut his legs free, but it would mean nothing less than suicide. He drew his father's attention.

"Who else are we liable to find at the ranch?"

"The two you saw at the barn. Maybe a couple of others

92

who've been out, scouting up stock."

"They sleep in the house?"

"Got a place off the side of the barn. Little shack." Amos paused, then: "You were saying something about the marshal. You figuring on him for help?"

Joel checked the back trail again. At first he saw nothing, and worry instantly sprang alive within him. Had the outlaws cut off, taken a shorter route that would bring them in ahead? He couldn't recall any other road, but he'd been away ten long years, and things change . . . in the next moment he saw them, and relief eased his nerves. They had just been in a low spot, out of view. They had gained, but it couldn't be helped.

"I said . . . the marshal. You depending on him for help?"

Amos yelled his question a second time. Joel shook his head. "Hoping . . . but not depending. Expect it'll be up to you and me, Pa."

Amos bobbed approvingly. "Suits me. I reckon we can handle it."

As they drew nearer to the ranch, Joel began to have second thoughts about his father and the wisdom of his being on hand when matters came to a head. Amos was in poor condition to face any sort of desperate situation, and it was doubtful he could be of any help. But Joel said nothing until they reached the far side of the house and quietly walked the horses up to the window where he had earlier entered the structure. There Joel swung down quickly, wheeled to Amos and, after pulling the rope free of the older man's ankles, faced him.

"Pa, I was thinking. It might be better for you to ride on into town. I'll hold Berryman and his bunch here. You won't run into trouble."

Amos looked down at his son. "That means you plain don't want me around?"

"Not that at all. Figured you'd be better off."

Amos Kane shook his head. "Be better off right here with my own kin, helping fight for what's ours. And if I don't come out of it with a whole skin, I'll leastways know I did what I could."

Joel reached up, helped the older man to dismount. "Whatever you say, Pa," he replied, pride stirring him deeply. "We'll give them one hell of a run for it."

Leaning over, he quickly removed his spurs, hung them on the saddle horn, then pointed to the window. "I crawled through there this morning. Cross over and wait while I have a look at the yard."

"Berryman and Clete can't be far off," Amos said. "Keep your eyes peeled."

Joel moved off at once, hurried along the side of the house. He knew he was cutting it thin. The two outlaws would be showing up any minute, but he had to get an idea of what he'd be up against once inside the building.

Reaching the corner, he halted. Two horses stood at the corral. The body of Ben Stoyers was on one; the other belonged to Bill Taney. Kane edged a few steps deeper into the yard, trying for a better look at the far end of the house. Light showed in the window—the kitchen—and he thought he could hear voices. Taney was not alone, apparently—but who could be with him? There were no other horses.

The hostlers? The answer came to him abruptly, and, pivoting, he retraced his steps to where Amos waited. Without hesitating, he boosted himself up, started through the window. One leg inside, he paused to look at Amos.

"There a gun somewhere in one of the back rooms?" he asked in a low whisper.

The elder Kane shook his head. "Cass took them all. Afraid I might get ideas, I reckon." He checked his words, added as an afterthought: "Ben had an odd shotgun he used to hunt rabbit and quail with. Kept it in the kitchen."

Joel remembered the shotgun. Likely it was still around as Stoyers had been carrying a rifle at the cabin. But if it was in the kitchen?—he shook his head as he climbed on through the window. Nothing ever came easy.

Hesitating briefly to listen and assure himself Taney had not been disturbed, he leaned forward and assisted Amos to enter. Cautioning the older man for silence, he pointed down the hallway.

"Taney's in there," he murmured. "Somebody's with him. Maybe those two hostlers . . . couldn't tell for sure."

"Probably right," Amos said. "They won't be packing guns. Bill Taney will. How . . . ?"

"Got to surprise him. It's the only thing we can do, and we have to do it before Berryman and Jordan show up."

"They ought to be showing up soon. What do you want me doing?"

"Stay behind me," Joel said, and crossed to the hallway. Keeping close to the wall, he made his way toward the kitchen, halted just beside the doorway.

Bill Taney sat at the table, one leg thrown over a chair. He partly faced Joel and was talking to one of the hostlers, hunched against the wall to his left. There was no sign of the other stableman.

Taney would be hard to take by surprise. At the angle he faced he would see anyone in the hallway the moment of his appearance. Kane drew back to think, caught the faint sound of horses entering the yard. Cass Berryman and Jordan had arrived.

"That'll be Cass and the boys," Taney said, dropping his foot to the floor.

The hostler raised himself, peered through the dust-streaked window. "Only see two horses."

The bearded outlaw lurched to his feet. "Two?"

Crouched in the short hallway, Joel Kane prepared to lunge. He couldn't afford to let Bill Taney go out into the yard—he needed the outlaw's pistol. It would be easy to remain quiet, allow the bearded outlaw and the hostler to leave the house, and then take possession. But retaining possession without a weapon with which to fight was out of the question.

"That's all," the hostler said, moving toward the door. "Looks like Cass and Jordan . . . sure don't see anything of the Mex."

"Been trouble," Taney said, and started across the room.

Joel hit the outlaw low and hard. The man yelled and tried to turn, but the force of Kane's rush carried him to the wall, sending a shower of cans and dishes clattering to the floor. The hostler, face white, took a single glance at the sudden eruption of confusion, and bolted into the yard, shouting for Berryman.

Joel heard only vaguely. The impact had jarred him, knocked him off balance. On hands and knees, he struggled to regain his footing, to seize Bill Taney before he could also recover and draw his weapon.

Joel grappled blindly. He caught the outlaw by an arm and jerked savagely. Taney, also on his knees, lashed out at Kane's face. Joel took the blow across the bridge of the nose and recoiled with pain. Taney shouted, then threw himself forward. Joel pulled aside quickly, chopping at the bearded man's neck with the heel of his hand. Bill sagged and clawed weakly for the pistol on his hip. Kane struck him again, and the weapon, half out of its holster, fell to the floor. Joel made a grab for it, but missed as Taney kneed him brutally in the belly.

He rolled to his back and slapped Taney smartly across the eyes. The outlaw cursed. He tried again to reach his pistol. Kane, striving to get his legs beneath him for the sake of leverage, hit him once more across the face. Bill grunted, but continued to claw at the revolver. Joel, sucking deep for wind, heaved himself half around and kicked. His foot struck the pistol and sent it skittering across the floor and under the table. Taney roared, jerked himself upright. He made a lunge to recover the weapon but tripped as Amos Kane shoved a chair into his path.

The outlaw went down. Joel was upon him instantly. He had to end the fight and do so quickly. Berryman and Clete Jordan would be closing in. He flung a glance at Amos. "The lamp . . . put it out!" he yelled, and swung hard at Taney.

The outlaw jerked away, took the blow on his shoulder. Twisting, he wrapped his arms about Joel's legs. Abruptly the room plunged into darkness as the elder Kane reached the wall lamp and twisted its wick.

Joel, laboring to keep his balance, hammered at Taney's neck and head. He felt the grip around his legs slacken, so he put more strength into his efforts. Suddenly he felt himself falling, going over backward. He tried to catch himself, failed, went down solidly, his right shoulder striking the edge of a chair, capsizing it. Instantly he rolled away, avoiding Taney's groping hands. He came up against another chair and tried to brush it aside, but it was wedged against the wall. Outside, Cass Berryman was yelling something. He sounded near—too near.

Heaving with all his strength, Kane lurched upright.

Taney was a dark shape in the meager light supplied by the moon. Joel rushed in low, arm cocked. He drove a solid right into the outlaw's middle, jabbed a stinging left into his face. Taney groaned, spun about, staggered across the room and caught himself against the door frame. He hung there for a brief instant, then plunged out into the yard.

Gasping, Joel reached for the door, slammed it shut. Instantly guns began to crackle, and a dozen bullets ripped through the wooden panel.

XII

"Down!" Joel yelled, and threw himself to the floor.

Through the dust haze he saw Amos sprawl out near the table. Another blast of gunfire rocked the night and glass shattered as the window was blown into fragments.

"Pa . . . you all right?"

Amos Kane's voice was low, taut. "Those thieving, back-stabbing bastards . . . shooting up a man's place like this!"

Joel grinned. It was the first time he could recall hearing his father speak in anger. It sounded good. Staying flat, he crawled to where Taney's pistol had slid, groped about until he located it. He felt better, then. Working his way to the center of the room, he said: "We've got one gun between us. Need another one bad. Any idea where Stoyers kept that scatter-gun?"

Amos was quiet for a few moments. "Seems I recollect seeing him put it in that closet over near the door."

"Kane!" Cass Berryman's voice sliced through the old man's words. "You hear me, Kane?"

"Take a look," Joel said, "but keep down."

Amos began to pull himself across the room, his boots making loud, scraping sounds against the floor.

"Kane . . . you alive in there?"

"Try coming in and you'll find out!" Joel yelled.

A single gunshot followed. The bullet, coming through the empty window, struck high on the wall, dislodged the picture hanging there, and sent it crashing down. Amos swore deeply from his side of the room.

"Just letting you know we've got you penned up in there," Cass Berryman called. "Ain't a Chinaman's chance of you coming out alive."

"Found it," Amos Kane said in the half dark. "It was right where I figured . . . in the closet."

"Any shells?" Joel asked anxiously.

"Five . . . couple in the barrels."

Disappointment shook Joel. "Help some," he muttered.

"Scatter-gun's a mighty good weapon," Amos said. "Seen a man hold off a whole crowd with one."

Kane agreed. Nobody liked to face a charge of buckshot, but the weapon's range was limited and with only seven loads . . . ?

"Giving you a chance to come out of there!" Berryman yelled. "Both of you . . . walk out with your hands empty . . . and up. You can keep right on going."

"Get over to where you can watch the hallway," Joel said quietly. "One of them could try sneaking in through that window. I'll keep an eye on the yard."

Amos hitched his way to where he could see down the corridor. Joel crawled closer to the window, raised his head carefully, and looked out into the yard. Berryman, flanked by Jordan and Bill Taney, was standing behind the corral, only partially visible. At the barn the two hostlers crouched in the doorway.

"Kane, you hear me?"

"I hear you," Joel answered. "We'll take our chances inside."

"You're a fool. We can keep you pinned down till you starve."

"Plenty of grub in here."

"Be no trouble burning you out."

"Don't figure you ought to try. First man that tries getting close is dead."

"You can't be all over the place at one time. I've got enough help to get somebody through."

"Sure . . . just pick out the man who wants to die first. Let him start."

But Berryman was right. Joel and Amos couldn't cover every point, and, to make it worse, the north side was windowless and therefore blind. If the outlaws remembered that. . . .

"What do you think?" Amos said. "You figure we'd be smart to crawl back out that window, make a stand in the brush?"

Joel shook his head. "They'd have us cold turkey then. Our best bet's here, inside."

"Going to be hard, keeping them away from the house, if they take a notion to go circling around."

"I can see all three of them. Both the hostlers, too. Any one of them starts across the yard, I'll nail him quick."

"Kane, you coming out?" Berryman's tone was impatient. "I don't aim to wait here all night."

"Up to you," Joel yelled. "Best thing you can do is to take your bunch and ride on. You're not taking over this ranch."

"I already have," the outlaw answered.

Immediately guns opened up. Bullets thudded into the

wall, smashed through the door. Kane, risking a hurried glance, saw a dark shadow pull away from the corral and, bending low, start for the far side of the house. Resting his pistol on the windowsill, he pressed off a shot at the hunched shape.

The bullet dug sand at the outlaw's feet, brought him to a halt. Joel triggered a second shot, then ducked beneath the opening as Berryman and the man still beside him began to shoot.

Waiting until the firing had stopped, he again peered from a corner of the window. There were three figures at the corral again, two at the barn. Whoever it was that had taken it in mind to cross over had turned back. Hurriedly, Joel flipped open the loading gate of the pistol, punched out the spent cartridges. Thumbing two fresh shells from his belt, he tried to reload, then swore harshly. Taney's revolver was of a different caliber. His cartridges would not fit.

"Something wrong?" Amos asked.

"This gun . . . my shells won't work. Got three shots left."

The elder Kane groaned. "Sure doesn't put us in such good shape," he commented. "There's no reason for your being in a mess like this. I was wrong in sending for you."

"Forget it."

"No, I'm not forgetting it. Not much hope of us coming out of this alive, so I'm telling you I want you to crawl out that back window and. . . ."

"No use talking that way, Pa."

"Yes there is . . . and it makes sense. It's not right that you should throw your life away on something you don't care a rap about. Let Berryman have the place . . . I'm too old to give a damn."

"Maybe I do care about it."

Amos was silent. Finally he asked: "You mean that? You're saying you aren't here just because you feel you have to be?"

"Just what I'm saying. Ranch is yours . . . ours. Nobody's just going to up and take it away from us . . . not without a fight, anyway. Thought we'd settled all this before."

Joel paused, looked again through the window. He frowned. He could see only two dark shapes in the shadows behind the corral. Worry began to tag him, and, ducking low, he moved to the opposite side of the window for a better view. One outlaw was missing.

"Watch that hallway," he warned. "They're up to something."

"I'm watching," Amos replied, and shifted his position to one nearer the door.

Joel resumed his post at the window, kept his eyes searching the yard and the brush along its edge, alert for any movement that would betray the location of the outlaw. The hostlers, he noted, were still in the doorway of the barn.

A horse stamped wearily. The sound came from the north side of the house. It caused Joel's thoughts to swing to Eli Pryor and the posse, somewhere up on the mountain. Would they hear the gunshots and hurry down to investigate? And where would the lawman stand—with Cass Berryman? He wished he knew how to figure the marshal. If he could be sure of a fair deal from him, there would be good reason to hold out against the outlaws until the posse could arrive. But Pryor was an unknown factor. His presence could make matters worse. And their position was bad—Joel was not fooling himself for one instant about that. With a revolver containing three bullets and a shotgun that was of little use except in close quarters, he couldn't put up much of a fight. Berryman held all the cards despite the fact he was outside the house. The house, Kane thought grimly, could become a deathtrap instead of a fortress.

The room rocked suddenly with the deafening blast of the shotgun. Amos yelled, and Joel, wheeling about, saw him stiffen, then drop the long-barreled weapon. The hallway was boiling with smoke, and back in its depths there was a crumpled, smoldering heap.

"Pa!" Joel shouted and, forgetting caution, leaped across the room.

Amos Kane lay on his back. A deep stain was spreading slowly down his right chest. The old man grinned. "Ain't bad," he muttered. "I . . . I get him?"

Joel squinted again into the corridor. The haze had lifted somewhat, and he saw Clete Jordan. The charge from the shotgun had caught him straight on, done terrible things to him.

"You got him," Joel said. He rose partly and glanced out the window. Berryman and Taney were still near the corral, unaware, of course, as to how Jordan had fared. He turned back to Amos, made a quick examination of the older man's wound. It was high, just below the shoulder, and ordinarily would not be too serious. But Amos could stand to lose little blood, and at his age the shock was almost as lethal as a bullet. He would need medical attention—and very soon.

"Kane!" Berryman's voice was loud. "That's only the start . . . !"

Anger roared through Joel in a gusty blast. He spun to the window. "You're right . . . only the start! Jordan's dead . . . and it's your turn now!"

Bending down, he snatched up the shotgun, replaced the spent shell, and, thrusting the pistol into his holster, whirled to the door. Joel lunged through the opening, burst into the yard. Not slowing his steps, he aimed the shotgun from the hip, fired the left barrel at the two men crouched near the corral, then rushed on.

A yell went up, and instantly pistol shots began to fill the pale night. Bullets plucked at Kane's weaving shape, spouted sand and dust over his feet. He reached the center of the yard. Berryman was now in view, away from the protection of the corral poles.

Swinging the shotgun around, Joel released the second charge. Berryman screamed, slammed up against the corner of the pen. Joel dropped the now useless long gun and reached for the pistol. Beyond Berryman's body he could see Bill Taney, moving forward. Bill had held back, allowing Cass to take the shotgun's blast. Now, certain Kane was unarmed and helpless, he was closing in for the kill.

Joel halted abruptly, brought up his pistol, and fired. He felt a powerful force slap solidly against him, spin him half around. He knew he had been hit. Taney and he had triggered their weapons at the identical instant.

Unaccountably he was on one knee. Twisting, he aimed again at the bearded Taney, but the outlaw was sinking, pitching forward. Joel swung his attention to the barn. The two hostlers raised their arms hurriedly.

"Don't shoot! We're not armed!" one yelled in a frantic voice.

Joel waved the pistol at them. "Get a team and wagon over here! Got to get my pa to the doctor!"

One of the pair dodged back into the darkness of the barn immediately. The other turned to follow, then halted. There was a quick rush of hoofs as horsemen swept into the yard. Pryor and the posse.

Joel, battling a haziness that was creeping over him, pulled himself upright, faced the approaching lawman warily. Pryor walked his horse in close, his glance sweeping

the scene, touching the sprawled Taney and, farther over, Cass Berryman.

"Some of you take a look at those two," he called over his shoulder, and then settled his hard gaze on Joel. "What the hell's going on here?"

"You're a little late," Joel said coldly, and turned to the barn where the second hostler still stood in the doorway. "God damn it, get that wagon over here!"

The man disappeared into the structure. Pryor leaned forward in his saddle. "You haven't answered my question, mister."

"Both the others are dead . . . Cass Berryman and Bill Taney," one of the posse members said, stepping up beside the lawman.

Pryor glanced at the man in annoyance. "All right," he said irritably, then looked again at Joel. "Now . . . ?"

The rider pushed ahead. "Hell, he's been hit, Marshal. He's in no shape to talk."

"If he can stand, he can talk," Pryor said curtly.

"I don't know what's holding him up," the man said, halted before Joel. "Better let me take a look at that wound. You're bleeding bad."

Joel stared. "You a doctor?"

"Yep. Wingate's the name," the physician said, and began to pull aside Kane's blood-soaked shirt.

Joel drew away. "Forget me. I'm all right. Obliged if you'll see what you can do for my pa . . . he's inside the house."

Wingate said—"In a minute."—and, reaching into his brush coat pocket, produced a flat oilskin fold. Opening it, he obtained several pads of gauze, pressed them against Joel's wound.

"Hold that right there. I'll be back in a bit."

Beckoning to several of the posse, he started for the

house at a trot. Eli Pryor came off his horse stiffly, wearily. He pointed to the pistol in Joel's hand.

"Put that away . . . your pa? . . . you mean Amos Kane?"

Joel continued to hold the weapon. The marshal was still an unknown quantity as far as he was concerned. "You were in the bank. You know that."

"Heard you say it . . . didn't mean it's true."

Kane shook his head in disgust. "Ask Pa . . . if he's still alive."

There was a rattle in the doorway of the barn. The hostlers appeared, leading a team hitched to a light spring wagon. Kane waved them toward the house.

"Over there . . . and get a mattress . . . throw it in the back for him to lie on."

Pryor waited until the wagon had passed. He pointed then at Berryman and Bill Taney. "What about them?"

"Was either . . . ?" A shiver raced through Joel, and his knees suddenly had no strength. He sat down slowly.

Pryor immediately took a half step forward, checked when the pistol in Joel's hand came up fast. "I'm telling you again, put that iron away," he ordered. "Hell, man, I'm on your side. I've been trying to get something on Berryman for months."

Joel studied the old lawman's seamy face in the growing daylight. Maybe—just maybe—Pryor was speaking the truth. "Might have told me that sooner," he said. "Could have saved a lot of trouble . . . and killing."

"Told you? How the devil could I? Only saw you twice . . . at the bank and here."

"I was with Berryman and the others when you ran into us on the trail. Didn't you see . . . ?"

"It was dark. I didn't see anybody plain except Cass Berryman. Why didn't you speak up?"

"That *vaquero* of Berryman's was holding a knife to Pa's

throat. Would have killed him if I'd said anything."

Pryor wagged his head helplessly. "Lot more to this than I figured. You're going to have to answer some questions."

"Only thing he's going to do right now," Wingate said, coming from the house, "is climb into that wagon. Got to get him to town so's I can dress that bullet hole properly."

Joel looked anxiously at the doctor. "Pa . . . will he be all right?"

Wingate nodded. "Sure. Be fine. Lost a bit of blood, but he's a tough old rooster. He'll make it." The physician turned to the marshal. "Eli, you want the straight of things around here, go see those two hostlers. They're talking their heads off."

Reaching down, the physician helped Joel to his feet, then motioned to one of the posse members and said: "Let's get him in the wagon."

They half carried, half walked him to the vehicle, placed him on the mattress beside Amos. The older Kane grinned at his son.

"Reckon we did it, eh?"

"We did. Doc says you'll be all right."

"Sure. How about you? Looks like you've been bleeding like a stuck hog."

Joel sighed. "Felt worse . . . and I've sure'n hell felt better a lot of times."

"They told me Cass and Bill Taney are both dead. Was afraid when I saw you going through that door. . . ."

"Be about enough of that jabbering," Wingate broke in as he climbed onto the wagon seat and gathered up the reins. "Don't want you two talking yourselves to death."

Amos glanced at the medical man, grinned again at Joel. "Ain't no danger, Doc," he said. "Us Kanes are mighty hard to kill."

GUNS OF FREEDOM

I

He crouched in the bow of the dinghy and stared through the darkness toward the shore. About him the water of the Gulf rose and fell, slapping restlessly at the sides of the small craft, muting the cautious dipping of the oars. Overhead a light wind drove heavy-bellied clouds across the sky, obscuring the moon and stars.

"How far to the cove?" he asked.

"A half kilometer . . . maybe less," the old man replied.

Cain Ruby turned his head and considered the looming bulk of the *Habanero*, anchored two hundred yards distant. The big Spanish warship had not altered its position.

"Is it a deep cove with brush along the sides?"

"There is much rock. A little brush, perhaps, but mostly it is rock."

"Is it a long . . . narrow . . . bay, or one of width?" Ruby asked again.

The old man shrugged. "It is only a small place."

A shallow inlet—and wide open. Cain Ruby shifted angrily. "God's uncle!" he muttered. "Nothing about this damned thing goes right!"

Girard, the third man in the dinghy, rested his oars. He laughed softly. "Didn't bargain for the whole Spanish navy when you took on this chore, eh, Cain?"

"No more than I bargained for you," Ruby said curtly.

"Seems you're saddled with both."

"Seems . . . just row!"

The quiet whisp of the oars slicing through the black

111

water resumed. Ruby again looked ahead. Through the darkness an irregular, gray blur was taking shape.

"I see the shore now," he said to the old man, returning to Spanish. "I would say it is less than half a kilometer . . . will the others be there?"

"It was so arranged."

That's probably fouled up, too, Cain Ruby thought. From the moment they had reached the designated point off the Pinar del Río coast where the *Felicity*, sailing them up from New Orleans, was to rendezvous with the Cuban scout, matters had gone wrong.

The scout had been hours late. Spanish patrols had prevented his pulling away from shore at the appointed time. In the subsequent haste to make up lost minutes, Jess Lockwood, upon whom Cain was depending heavily, had slipped and fallen into the dinghy. He had suffered a broken leg in the process. It was a blow, but there was no turning back, and, with only Gavin Girard, Ruby had completed the rendezvous.

They started for the shore as the *Felicity* pulled away, and a short time later had become aware of another ship. It proved to be the *Habanero*, one of the many gunboats patrolling the seas as the Spaniards sought to maintain their grip upon the island. Now, almost in the shadow of the huge ship, guarding the bay they hoped to enter, they were carefully making their way.

He could see the silhouettes of the men on watch aboard the *Habanero*. They were scattered along the rail every fifty feet or so. More were in the rigging. At that moment a truth dawned on Cain Ruby—the *Habanero* was there by intent, not accident. Somehow the Spaniards had learned of their coming, were possibly also aware of their mission—but how? It had been a well-guarded secret. Only he, Girard,

Jess Lockwood, and the members of the New Orleans combine who hired him were in on the plan to slip ashore, work inland to the Spanish fort, the Montaña Sangre, and blow it to rubble with a few well-placed charges of explosives. Nor was there anyone on the island who knew the precise reason for their coming; it had been said only that they were making a visit to size up the situation for the merchants.

"You get the feeling we were expected?" Girard drawled in his soft way. "Battleship like the *Habanero* has no reason to lie off a small cove like this one."

"How would they know?" Cain Ruby replied irritably. "I didn't talk . . . and Lockwood's got a tight mouth."

Girard waited a minute, then said: "Meaning maybe it was me . . . ?"

Ruby moved his shoulders slightly, continued to stare at the shore, gradually becoming more distinct in the darkness.

"Well . . . it wasn't," Girard said. "Fact that I hate your guts much as you hate mine means nothing. My neck's on the block same as yours . . . and you're forgetting the members of the combine . . . my own father included. One of them could have let it out."

Cain Ruby said nothing. Regardless of how—the secret had apparently been leaked, and there was nothing to do but make the best of it.

"Keep rowing," he said, and looked at the old man crouched beside him. The Cuban wore a thin shirt and dirty cotton drawers. He was shivering from the cold, and in the weak light his face was sad and deeply lined.

"How are you called?" Cain asked in Spanish.

"Escobar."

"From where do you come?"

"The village of Esperanza. It is not far from the cove. Do you know the place?"

"No. I am not acquainted with this part of the island."

"It was a fine village," Escobar said.

"Does it no longer exist?"

"It is there but as a ghost. A fine village but the Spaniards have ruined all things."

"I am sorry," Cain Ruby said. "Perhaps the day of liberation will come soon, old one."

"Perhaps."

Cain Ruby's mind dropped back to that morning—weeks before—when he had paused in Jackson Square to hear Narciso Lopez speak. The fiery Venezuelan general was preparing to embark upon his second invasion attempt of the island in the hope of overthrowing the Spanish crown. His first expedition, undertaken that previous year of 1850, had terminated in disaster. Now, with stronger financial backing and greater public sympathy, he was forging a repeat effort. His declared intent was the reason the combine, an organized group of wealthy Louisiana merchants and ship owners, had decided to put a scheme of their own into operation. They, too, wished to see the Spanish stranglehold on Cuba broken—but for a less aesthetic purpose. Their lucrative trade with the Pearl of the Antilles had been suspended completely and indefinitely by Spanish edict. To further guarantee their monopoly, the Spaniards had declared a blockade and flung a bristling ring of warships around the island. They had also reinforced their military garrisons on land. The wealth of Cuba was for the Spanish king alone, they said, and they were ready to fight for every pound of it.

The side result of such suppression was a steady and effective reduction of the Cuban people to the worst kind of vassalage. They tried feebly to overcome it. Minor uprisings and miniature revolutions sprang periodically across the island, but to no good end. The Cubans were too disorganized, too fearful of bloody retribution, and too poorly equipped to offer any opposition of consequence. They lay helpless under the heel of the Spaniards, prisoners and slaves in their own land. Narciso Lopez dedicated himself to changing that. A determined, sincere man, he had the courage, if not the good judgment and cunning, so necessary to make a success of such a venture. Thus, when he had made known his design for a second invasion, the combine, writhing under reduced profits because of the Spanish proclamation, came up with a plan of their own. They wanted Lopez to succeed, yet they entertained little confidence that he would. Likely the project would be only an echo of the 1850 fiasco in which he lost many men and barely escaped with his own life. The Spaniards were strong on both land and sea. If he did manage to slip by their gunboats with the ships he had wheedled, he would be faced by a formidable land force under the command of General José Enna, the ruthless military consort of Don José de la Concha who governed the island for the throne.

The Louisiana merchants concocted a means by which they felt they could insure Lopez's success. The hive of military strength on the island was the fort known to the Cubans as the Montaña Sangre. To them it was an infamous symbol of oppression, of merciless slavery and utter degradation. The stories that seeped to the outside world relating the torture of Cuban men, the abasement of Cuban girls and women within its high, well-guarded walls, chilled the hearts of the most hardened. Built by forced labor under the brass-studded whips of the Spaniards, it was said that every stone in its massive bulk represented a Cuban life, that the good, red blood of a thousand patriots had gone into the mixing of the mortar.

The Montaña Sangre must be destroyed, the combine

declared. Its destruction would shatter the Spanish army from within, smooth the way for Lopez and his invading soldiers, and guarantee victory over the crown. It was the combine's plan. They chose Cain Ruby to fulfill it.

At the first meeting he had asked why they had selected him. Gaston Deveney, spokesman for the aggrieved group, had been blunt. "Your reputation along the waterfront is known. We also know how you feel about the Spaniards."

Cain Ruby had grinned wryly, and equally blunt, countered: "How much is it worth to you?"

"Ten thousand dollars . . . gold."

It was a lot of money, badly needed, but Ruby knew how to press his advantage when he realized his opponent in bargaining was at a disadvantage. He had looked at the strained faces of the men gathered in the smoke-filled room: Deveney, Sturgis, Gavin's white-bearded father, Edwin Girard, pig-eyed, paunchy Joseph Clinton, the one-time slaver who continually dug at his yellowed teeth with a gold pick, Antoine DuRique, Wade Stevens, and a few more.

"Not enough," he had said.

"There is more," Deveney had said hurriedly. "We will pay off your bank notes . . . those being pressed for settlement. And we will take care of the repair of your ship."

That had been the clinching argument—had he been inclined to refuse. The *Island Queen* had been attacked by a Spanish gunboat and blasted into a helpless wreck of smoldering splinters. Not only was the ship almost beyond salvaging, but it had cost him a cargo in which he had invested every cent he possessed. It had plunged him as deeply into debt as it had sent his hatred for the Spanish soaring skyward. There had been no reason for the attack other than that he had sailed too near the island.

He had accepted the merchants' proposition and final

arrangements were quickly made. It was most important the Montaña Sangre be destroyed prior to Lopez's scheduled landing. The combine would furnish him with transportation to within a safe distance of the island, making arrangements with some of the Cuban liberation forces, with whom they were in contact, to meet them and afford proper assistance. The same ship, the *Felicity*, would return after ten days and nightly stand off shore to receive him and his party when the task was completed and transport them back to New Orleans safely.

They would supply one man; he was to select another. Their choice was Gavin Girard. He would go along to aid in whatever manner possible but particularly as a representative of the combine who would verify the destruction of the fort and thereby make the payment of Cain Ruby's fee possible. There was also one man now on the island upon whom he could rely—an American, Saxon Carver. He was a partner of Joseph Clinton—had been trapped there and unable to leave because of the blockade. He would prove an invaluable assistant as he knew well the country and its people.

Cain had accepted the aid thrust upon him with no comment. He had already settled on the *Island Queen*'s first mate, Jess Lockwood, as his man and knew he would have no worries there. Gavin Girard and Carver were a different matter. Carver he knew not at all, and, as for Girard, he entertained the usual opinion of a hard-working, self-sufficient man for the wastrel son of a doting, rich father. He had encountered Gavin on occasion in the gambling halls along St. Charles Avenue and in the bars and brothels of Gallatin Street, and their dislike for one another had been mutual and instantaneous. Girard would be as an albatross about his neck, Cain decided, and accepted the younger man's presence with poor grace.

A chain clanked on the deck of the *Habanero*. Ruby turned to look, at the same time hearing Escobar speak.

"*Señor* . . . something occurs on the warship."

"I hear."

"They put a boat over the side."

Ruby listened to the faint squeal of pulleys, the dull thuds. He glanced over his shoulder at Girard. "Ship your oars."

Gavin ceased rowing. Cain listened into the void. The lap of the sea, the cautious sounds on the *Habanero* were remote, barely audible. The world around them was a black cloak, the sky above still thick with clouds. He heard a faint splash.

"They have seen us, I fear," Escobar murmured.

"It is possible they only suspect."

"One thing sure . . . they've put a boat out," Girard said. "We swim for it?"

"If we have to," Cain Ruby replied, straining his eyes to locate any motion in the blackness alongside the warship. "Water around here's alive with sharks."

"As soon take my chances with the sharks here than the ones at the bottom of the chute at Morro Castle," Girard muttered. "Be where we'll end up, if they catch us."

Ruby made no reply, his gaze still locked on the shadows. He thought he saw movement, but was not sure. He shifted his eyes, gauged their position. They had come abreast the *Habanero*, were now drifting shoreward slowly.

"Row," he whispered. "No noise . . . !"

He heard Girard shift. There was a slight ripple in the water as the long paddles bit deeply. He felt the dinghy slip forward, increase speed, saw the creamy roll surge from beneath the bow.

"Not too fast . . . !"

The Spaniards appeared at that moment. They were little more than a blur, moving into the open water in front of the warship. They were pointing for shore on a direct line.

"Starboard," Cain Ruby said softly. "Put some water between us."

The dinghy veered gently. Such altered course would bring them to beach above the designated cove where they were to meet Carver and the Cubans, but it did not matter. They could double back once they were on land.

He continued to stare into the darkness. He could see the blur that was the Spanish boat, but he could determine none of its details. It did seem, however, that the craft was moving away from them.

Girard's dry chuckle reached him, grated on his nerves. "The merchants all figured you were asking too much for this job. Way it looks now, they won't have to worry about it. I'd say your chances for collecting anything are mighty slim."

"Quiet," Ruby muttered.

I'll collect, he thought. *I'll get it all, along with that extra thousand I've got coming from Antoine DuRique, one of the combine members.* Annette, he had said, was his daughter's name as they stood before a large portrait in the DuRique mansion. She was on the island visiting a sister and brother-in-law—the René Gayardees. They owned a large plantation near the village of San Rafael.

Three months ago, DuRique had said, communication from Annette had ceased. He feared something was amiss, and with the projected invasion by Lopez and its accompanying strife in the offing he feared for his daughter's safety—if, indeed, harm had not already befallen her. Cain would receive a thousand dollars, if he would find her, bring her back with him. Ruby had agreed. It would be an inconvenience, yes, he realized, as he studied the fragile beauty in the portrait—a march through the jungle with a frail woman unaccustomed to the slightest hardship was not a chore to be looked forward to—but a thousand dollars was something he could not afford to turn down.

He had not mentioned the matter to Girard. After he had located the girl and made the necessary arrangements, he would break the news to him. He doubted if it would make any difference to the man; likely he would welcome the opportunity for displaying some of his vaunted charm to Annette DuRique. It didn't matter, anyway. Cain Ruby would do as he damned well pleased.

He swung his attention to the shore, less than two hundred yards distant now. "Straight in," he said in a low voice.

Girard obediently corrected course. Beyond his bowed shoulders Cain Ruby could see the high bulk of the *Habanero*. The warship had not moved. He brought his eyes back to where he had last seen the boarding party. There was no sign of them. He continued to search the darkness.

"The Spaniards!" Escobar said suddenly, and sat up.

Cain saw them at the same instant. They were astonishingly near and bearing down fast. Apparently they had cut about and had been running parallel to the shoreline. An oar splashed. Ruby heard a muffled curse. Abruptly a voice yelled into the night.

"*¡Aquí! ¡Aquí! Delante. . . .*"

Muskets crashed, blossoming bright orange in the blackness. Leaden balls smashed into the dinghy, sent up showers of splinters. Escobar muttered, sank into the bottom of the boat. Cain Ruby rolled the Cuban to his side, peered at him closely. Escobar was dead. The bullet had torn away half his face. Cain jerked himself upright.

"Overboard . . . quick!" he shouted, and threw himself backwards into the water.

Water closed over Cain Ruby. He went deep, drove himself away from the shadow of the dinghy with a quick kick. Lungs bursting, he rose to the surface. Immediately ahead he saw the curving shape of the Spanish boat. A half a dozen marines, muskets poised, were etched against the night.

He filled his lungs, sank below the surface. The Spaniards' dinghy glided over him like a dark shadow. Drawing in his legs, he lashed out suddenly, shot upward, both arms outstretched, hands reaching. He burst from the water in a shower of drops, fingers clawing for the gunwale of the boat. Yells greeted his unexpected appearance, and a musket discharged close by. He caught the side of the small craft, threw his weight against it, plunged back into the water. More shouts lifted as the boat tipped, spilling its complement of soldiers. He was aware of struggling shapes spearing through the wet darkness around him and immediately kicked out, propelled himself away from the confusion.

He came to the top a dozen yards nearer to shore. Treading water, he looked back. The Spaniards' rowboat was bobbing, bottom side up, on the surface. Soldiers were thrashing wildly about, yelling, endeavoring to climb aboard.

Cain Ruby twisted around, struck out for the shoreline, mindful of sharks. After a few strokes he paused, glanced to left and right in search of Gavin Girard. He could see no sign of the man. He considered that for a moment, and then continued on. Girard could take care of himself.

His feet touched gravelly bottom. At the same instant his hands came up against the worn, sea-washed surface of rock. Pulling himself to a standing position, half out of the water, he listened. All was quiet. Even the Spanish marines had stopped yelling. Moving slowly, he climbed onto a slab of flat rock and stretched out, breathing heavily from his exertions.

"Ruby?"

Girard's guarded voice startled him. He stirred, sat up. "Here. . . ."

"Got the boat . . . give me a hand."

Keeping low, Cain eased off the slab, made his way toward the sound of Gavin's voice. He located him in a small backwater. There was a thin stand of brush near its end, and together they dragged the small craft into its scanty cover.

Girard pointed to the body of Escobar. "What do we do with him?"

"Leave him there . . . until we find the others," Cain Ruby replied. He swung his eyes to the open water, to the distant, dark shadow that was the *Habanero*. "Can't hang around here for long. They'll be putting another party over the side."

He reached for the water-tight sack suspended about his neck. It contained a pistol, along with a supply of powder and lead. He examined the contents closely. No moisture had entered. He retied the oilskin pouch, thrust it into a pocket of his black cord breeches for future use, and shoved the weapon under his belt. "Better have a look at your gun," he said.

Girard fingered his ornate, silver-mounted revolver. It was of the latest design. "Wet. Have to depend on my knife . . . if we run into trouble."

Ruby grunted, felt for his own blade. It was still in place inside his left boot—along with a quantity of water. He sat down, removed his footgear, drained it. Faint sounds were coming from the *Habanero*.

"Let's find that cove," he said, rising. "Carver and the

Cubans ought to be there."

He dropped back from the edge of the water, walking quietly as possible over the loose rock, with Girard a few paces behind. A quarter hour later he halted, seeing the shallow, half moon of a cove to their left. Gavin moved up beside him. Together they listened to the stillness. There was no sound except the gentle lapping of the sea along the ragged shore.

"Ought to be it," Gavin murmured.

Ruby nodded, angled toward the bay. They reached the water, halted. Immediately a voice came to them from the rocks.

"*Señores*. . . ."

Cain Ruby's hand dropped to his revolver. He waited out a long moment, then said—"How are you called?"—in Spanish.

"I am called Ramiro Aramo."

Tension slipped from Ruby's tall frame. It was one of the names given him by Deveney. "Come forward."

A slight but muscular man materialized in the darkness and walked toward them. He was young with deep-set eyes looking out from beneath a shelf of thick brows. A thin beard covered the lower half of his face.

"You are welcome to my country," he said, extending his hand. "The gunshots. There was trouble?"

Cain Ruby nodded. "Speak in Spanish if you wish. The tongue is known to us."

Aramo smiled. Abruptly he sobered. "Escobar? . . . were there not to be three of you?"

"Only two," Ruby said, feeling it unnecessary to go into detail concerning Jess Lockwood. "Esbobar is dead. A ball from a Spanish musket."

Ramiro Aramo looked toward the *Habanero*. "He was a

good man. But many good men are dead. Did the sharks . . . ?"

"No. He is in the boat. A half kilometer from here."

Aramo lowered his head. "I will see to him. Please wait here."

Ruby studied the Cuban. He had not spoken of Saxon Carver or of the other Cubans who were supposed to be here. Suspicion stirred through him.

"You are alone?"

Ramiro Aramo said: "I am alone."

"There were to be others. We were told so."

The Cuban frowned. "You were told many would meet you?"

"Perhaps not many, but several."

Aramo shrugged. "I know nothing of this."

"Have you seen an American . . . one called by the name of Carver?" Girard asked.

"I do not know the name."

The suspicion that gripped Cain Ruby strengthened. He stirred impatiently. "You don't seem to know much about anything," he muttered in English.

The Cuban nodded, smiled faintly. "I am Ramiro Aramo," he said quietly. "Of that I am certain. I am also certain three Americans were to arrive at this cove. From New Orleans they would come in a ship of the name *Felicity*. Miguel Escobar was to guide them ashore. Later we were to do as requested."

"Is it known by you who sent us?" Girard asked.

"Men of wealth who have interest in the island. I know only the name of one . . . Deveney. It was he who prepared us for your coming."

Gavin Girard glanced at Ruby. "Seems to be the right one. . . ."

Cain said: "Maybe." He studied Aramo. "The American . . . Carver. You have not heard of him? You were not told of his presence?"

"It was not mentioned. He is to be one of us?"

"That was the plan."

Again Aramo shrugged. "This I cannot comprehend. Perhaps he will join with us later." He hesitated, looked toward the water. "I go to take care of Escobar. You will remain here."

Cain Ruby motioned at the *Habanero*. "What if the Spaniards come? Where shall we meet you?"

"They will not come. They have respect for the dark."

Ramiro Aramo turned, disappeared swiftly into the night. Ruby waited until he was gone, then beckoned to Girard.

"Let's move."

Gavin pulled himself to his feet. He frowned. "Move . . . the Cuban said to stay here."

"I heard him. We're not doing it his way. We'll wait in those rocks. I'll be no sitting duck for him, if he comes back with a half a dozen soldiers."

They crossed to the opposite side of the cove to where a massive upthrust of boulders formed a low mound. Crawling over the rim, they settled in a bowl that provided a natural fortress.

Gavin Girard lay back against the cool granite, shook his head slowly. "You don't trust this Aramo much."

"I don't trust him at all . . . yet."

Girard sighed. "Fact is . . . you don't trust anybody."

"Can't afford to."

Off in the jungle a bird set up a sudden racket, flapping its wings and cawing harshly. Girard listened for a time, then swore wearily. "Be glad when this little fandango's over. Can think of a lot of places I'd rather be."

Cain Ruby grunted. He drew his revolver, began to clean it with a handkerchief. Girard considered him in the half light.

"Money mean so much to you . . . so much you'll risk your neck for it? I'm here because I have to be. With you it was different."

Cain shook his head. "Unless he's a fool, a man never does anything without a reason. I had the best one of all . . . money."

"Gold's not all that important."

"Wrong!" Ruby cut in impatiently. "Only somebody who's never had to scratch and sweat for it would make a statement like that. Whether you realize it or not . . . cash money is the most important thing in the world today. If you've got it, you can do anything. If not . . . you're nothing."

"You had it . . . or so I heard."

"I had it," Ruby admitted in a bitter tone. "Made my pile and was making more when the damned Spaniards blew me out of the water."

"But . . . just one cargo."

"Every cent I had was sunk in it. I lost everything."

Girard smiled. "See now why this job's so important to you. While you're drawing pay, you'll be getting back at the Spaniards, too."

"Why not? I've got a private axe to grind same as your father and all the other merchants in the combine. They're not doing this because they love Cuba . . . they're thinking about the money they're losing because of the blockade. I understand that. Man looks out for himself."

"Voice of the cynic?" Girard asked.

"Call it what you like, but I've lived long enough to learn

a few things about this life. Nobody drops anything good in your lap. Nothing's free. You fight for what you get."

"There are things called ideals. . . ."

"Meaning Lopez? Scratch deep enough and I expect you'll find he's not half as interested in freeing the Cubans as he is in becoming head man on this island."

"Could be you're right. And could be he just wants a scrap. Seems generals are like that . . . always on the lookout for a war."

"Wars are for fools," Ruby said, staring out to sea. "No cause is worth fighting for."

"Again the words of a cynic."

Cain Ruby shrugged, his somewhat square face suddenly cold and withdrawn. It was easy for Girard to be glib, a man without eyes never knows what it is to see. Ruby had never known his father, could scarcely remember his mother; existence for him along the waterfront, for as long as he could recall, had been a matter of staying alive by whatever means he could find at his disposal. It had been an educational if brutal experience, one that had enabled him to claw his way out of the derelict rabble and eventually become the master of his own ship. It was a period of high profits, and he plied the seas regularly, buying from the islands, selling on the mainland. Then had come his great opportunity. He had invested all he had in a cargo of fine silk, spices, crystal and teak—only to have the Spaniards destroy it all in a blast of cannon.

It had been a bitter blow. He had stood to make a round quarter million dollars on the cargo—instead, he came up broke. But he would sail again now, thanks to his deal with the combine and to the one he had made with Antoine DuRique. With the *Island Queen* again seaworthy and eleven thousand in gold in his pocket. . . .

"¿Señores?"

At Aramo's soft summons, Cain Ruby's thoughts came to a halt. He raised himself slightly, peered over the rim of rock toward the cove. The Cuban stood at the edge of the water.

"*Señor* Ruby?"

"Answer him," Girard prompted.

Cain searched the area beyond the Cuban with slow, careful eyes. He appeared to be alone.

"Over here," he called.

Immediately Aramo crossed the sandy flat and climbed down into the rocky bowl. He glanced at Ruby and Gavin Girard curiously, having his understanding of the change in position. But he said nothing of it.

"All is ready."

"Any sign of the Spaniards?"

"There was none."

"We heard sounds on the *Habanero*. Thought maybe they were making up a search party."

"This I also hear. They would not come. . . ."

"I know. They have respect for your freedom fighters and the dark."

Aramo's face stiffened. He stared at Ruby as though endeavoring to understand the meaning behind the tall man's words. Abruptly he smiled, waved it off. "It is best we go. Soon will come daylight. There will be safety in the jungle."

"Soldiers?"

"There are many. They roam the island as packs of wild dogs."

Ruby nodded, got to his feet.

Gavin Girard looked at him questioningly. "What about Carver? Aren't we waiting for him?"

"He didn't show. We'll go without him." Ruby turned to Aramo. "How far to the horses?"

The Cuban lifted his hands, allowed them to drop in a

gesture of despair. "There are no horses."

"What?" Cain Ruby shouted in exasperation. "Why the hell didn't you get . . . ?"

"I had them, *señor*. Four fine animals. But the soldiers came to the village where they were hidden. They were discovered and taken away. We must walk."

Again Cain Ruby swore. Would bad luck never end? Without horses they were faced with days of marching . . . and time was short.

"My failure is regretted," Aramo said. "But such is only temporary. The village of Cabezón is not of great distance. It is my hope to obtain animals there."

"That will help," Girard said, taking some of the edge off Ruby's sharpness. "It is of importance that we accomplish the task we were sent to do very soon."

Ruby frowned, wheeled angrily to Girard.

Ramiro Aramo came to attention. "This task of which you speak," he said, "it is of special nature?"

Girard shrugged, looked away. "Yes."

"I was not told of this."

"You will be," Ruby said. "In time. Let's go."

The Cuban did not take his eyes from Ruby. "It is my thought that you place little trust in me."

Gavin Girard laughed. He reached out, clapped Aramo on the shoulder. "Let it not disturb you, my friend. He is one who trusts only God."

"*¡Hola!*" a voice broke in from beyond the rocks.

The three men wheeled. A squat, heavily built individual in dark clothing and a sweat-stained Panama hat stepped into the open. His thick mustache laid a black crescent across his mouth.

"It's Carver," Gavin Girard said, sliding his knife back into its sheath.

Cain's taut shoulders relaxed. He glanced at Girard as Saxon Carver moved through the rocks toward them. "Never told me you knew him."

Gavin shifted, laughed. "Don't recall you ever asking," he said, then added: "It's a casual acquaintance and not a cordial one."

III

Carver climbed down into the hollow. He smiled, nodded to Girard, gave Ramiro Aramo a brief glance, and settled his attention on Cain.

"Expect you're Ruby."

"I am. How long have you been standing out there?"

Carver's brows lifted at the blunt question. His shoulders lifted, fell. "Not long. Would've been here sooner but got held up." He looked again at the Cuban, his small eyes sharp. "Who's he?"

"Aramo. He's taking us inland."

Carver leaned back against the rocks, took a long cigar from his pocket. "Won't need him. I know my way around," he said lazily.

Ruby's manner was still cold. "Get out of sight if you're going to light that weed."

Only Carver's eyes betrayed his awareness of Cain Ruby's hostility. He shrugged, squatted. Scratching a lucifer into life, he held it to the tip of his cigar and puffed. Exhaling a cloud of thin smoke, he ducked his head at Ramiro. "Like I said . . . no use of him coming along."

"I'll decide that," Ruby said. "You ready now to move out?"

"Any time," Saxon Carver said, rising.

Cain motioned to Aramo, and in single file they left the rocks and struck for the edge of the jungle. The Cuban walked at a steady pace, and not long after the sun broke over the eastern horizon in a broad fan of yellow light, bringing with it almost immediate heat. Aramo did not slow the march, however, but pressed on. Two hours later, when they came to a small, fast-flowing stream, he finally halted.

"We shall drink and rest for a while," he said, dropping to his knees beside the water.

Ruby and the others satisfied their thirsts, lay back to recover breath and ease their aching muscles.

"What happened to the horses we were getting?" Saxon Carver asked. "Going to be hell if we have to do all our traveling on foot."

"Spaniards beat us to them," Ruby replied. He glanced to Aramo. The Cuban was quietly studying Carver. "How much farther to that village, Ramiro?"

Aramo roused hastily. "Five kilometers . . . less, perhaps. Do I go too fast?"

"No," Ruby said, and closed his eyes.

They were well inside the jungle. Dense growth closed in upon them from all sides, and sunlight broke through here and there with effort. Birds sang from the thickets, and the hum of insects was a monotonous sound on the hot, still air.

"I would ask a question," Aramo said. "In truth, does General Lopez plan to invade the island?"

Cain Ruby considered the implications of a reply. Finally he said: "That is his plan."

The Cuban's features showed immediate interest. "Then it is so. When will such occur?"

Again Cain gave Ramiro's words thought. Lopez had made no secret of his intentions; it was only the plan for the

131

destruction of the Montaña Sangre that was being guarded. "The fifteenth day of this month," he said finally. After a moment he added: "How did you hear of this? It is said the blockade has cut all communications from the mainland."

"Word was sent Peréz-Rosario by the man, Deveney. It told that such invasion was imminent, that also you and other men would arrive to assist."

"That all he said . . . that we would assist?"

"No more was told to us."

"Give him the good news," Saxon Carver drawled. "Tell him we're to blow up the fort."

Anger rushed through Cain Ruby. Girard cleared his throat, laughed softly. "Guess our little secret's out, Cain."

"You're a fool," Ruby said, glaring at Carver. "We're trying to keep it quiet. Fewer who know about it, the better."

Saxon Carver sat up slowly. His face was stiff. "Go a bit easy on the strong words. I don't take kindly to that kind of talk."

"Then keep your mouth shut!"

The eyes of the two men locked, held. After a long minute, Carver looked down. He drew a long-bladed knife from his belt, took an oil stone from his pocket, and began to whet the blade methodically.

"This is true?" Ramiro Amaro's voice trembled. "You come to destroy the Montaña Sangre?"

It was useless to deny it. Ruby nodded. "That is our task. It must be done before the landing of Lopez."

The Cuban seemed not to hear the latter words. A half smile was on his lips. "At last the day has come. A sword is to be driven into the belly of the Spaniards." He lifted his gaze to Ruby. "We will owe you much. It is a debt that can never be repaid."

"You will owe me nothing," Ruby replied flatly. "My pay comes from New Orleans."

Aramo's moist eyes did not shift from Cain Ruby's features. "It is understood, but the debt nevertheless will exist. All Cuba will be grateful."

Ruby touched Saxon Carver with his still angry glance, came back to Ramiro. "Now that it is known to you what is in our minds, it must be kept as a secret."

"I shall do so. But there are things you will need."

Cain nodded. "A plan of the fort. I would talk with someone who has been inside. And we must have gunpowder and fuse."

"Those things can be provided. Peréz-Rosario will tell you of the Montaña Sangre. He was one of those forced by the Spaniards to labor in the building of it."

Girard rolled to one elbow. "You speak often of Peréz-Rosario. He must be a man of greatness."

"It is so. He is an ancient one, and very wise. He does not fight the Spanish with machete or gun, but with thoughts and words. He is the soul of Cuba who teaches that the struggle for freedom must never end."

Cain Ruby's tone was faintly sarcastic. "He another Lopez . . . or one of the original Cubans?"

"There are none of the original natives. Not a single descendant lives today."

"What has become of them?"

"The Spaniards killed all, when they colonized three hundred years ago. A new Cuban has risen to call the island his land."

"They're Spaniards, then . . . ?"

"At one time such was so. Now they love Cuba as their own. In the beginning the crown promised to them independence. Those promises have been dishonored. Thus we fight."

"Spaniard against Spaniard . . . in reality," Gavin Girard observed.

"No, my friend," Aramo said quietly. "Cuban against Spaniard. There are three peoples on the island . . . the Spaniards from Spain, who control our country and its wealth . . . the blacks who are slaves, and the new . . . the Free Cubans. I and my family are of those. So also is Peréz-Rosario. We, as the generations before us, fight to throw off the Spanish *garrote*. My small son, if it is not accomplished in my lifetime, will take up the struggle."

Cain Ruby stirred, bored by the recital. "A long time to squirm under another's heel."

"It has become a way of life," Aramo said. "We know little else. But we do not lose heart, although we may grow weary. Always there are the Peréz-Rosarios to give us heart."

"Perhaps the time is near when such will end for you," Gavin Girard said gently. "With the fort destroyed, it will be easier for General Lopez. It is possible he can drive the Spaniards into the sea."

"And make for himself a fine kingdom," Ruby added dryly. "Thus you will have a new enemy to fight."

Aramo considered that soberly. After a moment he said: "Will General Lopez bring many men bearing arms?"

"He will have many. There are also soldiers of Quitman and Gonzales. Combined it will make an army of a thousand men, perhaps more."

"Quitman and Gonzales?" Ramiro echoed. "Of those I have heard nothing."

"They are in this with Lopez. Each has a ship and an army. They will unite and march together."

"It is as we have long dreamed," Aramo murmured. "Feeling on the island is strong. Joaquín de Aguerro had many patriot recruits, all with weapons, when he returned to the Bien Refugio and issued the Declaration of Freedom. Such was on a day known to you . . . the Fourth of July."

"The Fourth?" Girard said, surprised. "That is our Independence Day."

"So also we would make it ours. De Aguerro said as much. There are many things we have patterned after your country, *señor*. We hope the day comes when we, too, can stand proud before the world as free men as did your people beside your great General Washington."

Cain had heard of Joaquín de Aguerro and his Liberation Society. The man had inspired an uprising on the island a little more than a month previous. Rumor said his band of insurrectionists were now roaming the jungles, creating havoc among the Spanish soldiers. Other reports declared him dead, or captured and suffering horrible torture in the dungeons of Morro Castle.

"Where is de Aguerro now?" he asked, interested in the truth.

Aramo shook his head. "This I do not know. Perhaps he leads many Free Cubans to plague the Spaniards. There has been no certain word . . . you would seek him?"

"He is not important to me. It is Peréz-Rosario. Do you know where he is to be found?"

Ramiro Aramo moved his shoulders. "It is a thing no man can say. He lives in the jungle . . . never for long in one place. The Spaniards seek him continually."

"Then how can we . . . ?"

"It shall come to pass. Word of our desire will travel swiftly. We shall be told."

In the silence that followed only the steady scrape of Saxon Carver's knife upon the oil stone could be heard.

Girard broke the hush. "With Peréz-Rosario in hiding, I

would say your revolution goes badly. Yet Lopez has said that the island seethes with rebellion."

"In spirit only," Aramo said sadly. "We have but little with which to fight."

The stropping sound ceased. Carver looked up. "Waste of time, anyway. You will never drive the Spaniards out. Too many of them."

Ramiro's face was solemn. "It may be so, but always there will be a hope. Many who were *pacíficos* now fight actively."

Girard said: *"¿Pacíficos?"*

"Those who do not war openly with the Spanish but help those who do."

Ruby glanced to the sky. The sun was well on its way. He got to his feet. "Let's go. We need those horses."

The others rose, and the party resumed the trail, much easier now as they dropped off a long slope. Masses of vivid flowers were everywhere, thrusting upward through the tangles of vines and ferns like colored spears. The grass was lush, the trees tall and plentiful. It reminded Cain Ruby of New Orleans—and turned his thoughts to new channels. He pushed forward to Aramo's shoulder.

"Do you know well this district of Pinar del Río?"

"I know all Cuba," Ramiro answered proudly. "It is my country."

"Do you know of a plantation owner of the name René Gayardee? It was said his place is near the village of San Rafael."

"Such is true. A very fine plantation, although I have not visited it of late. These people are your friends?"

Ruby said: "Not exactly. Will it be an inconvenience to stop there?"

"It will be simple. It is on our way."

Ruby dropped back into line. It was a bit of good luck—the Gayardees being on their route. He could pause there long enough to advise Annette of his plans to return her to New Orleans. She could make herself ready, and, after the Montaña Sangre business was finished, he would pick her up on their way back to the coast. In that manner she would be exposed to less danger and fewer rigors on the trail. It would be difficult for her at best, he realized, recalling the portrait that hung in the DuRique mansion.

It was an excellent likeness, the Frenchman had assured him. He tried to recreate the portrait in his mind's eye. She had dark brown hair—almost black, he thought. Her eyes were blue, wide set, and complemented by full brows and thick lashes. Her lips had been set to a perfect bow—too perfect, perhaps—and her chin, if small, had been firm. She had been dressed in what appeared to be a velvet gown of black, trimmed in purest white. It had been cut low at the neck to reveal her high, arching breasts and accent the slimness of her body. Now that he gave it thought, Annette was a most beautiful woman. He tried further to visualize her, making her way beside him through the jungle, crawling over brush, fording the innumerable streams—fending off myriad of persistent insects, but somehow the picture would not focus. He sighed. He could expect trying moments and considerable delay—not to mention an endless procession of womanly complaints. But for a thousand dollars he could stand it.

Ramiro Aramo slowed his pace noticeably. Ruby glanced ahead. The Cuban was studying several plumes of smoke visible in the sky above the jungle.

"Soldiers?" Cain suggested, moving to the younger man's side.

Aramo was plainly worried. He shook his head. "It is

near Cabezón. Of that only I am certain."

"Perhaps it is just a field being cleared."

Aramo agreed, continued on, but now he moved at a faster pace. They were following a narrow, almost indiscernible trail that crossed a slight depression. When they reached the opposite edge, they cut right, gained a somewhat higher plateau. The filmy streamers became more pronounced as they hurried on.

Shortly they transversed a hardwood forest, heavily scented by countless bright flowers and broke then into a small valley that had been cleared. A cluster of huts had stood in its center; all had been reduced to smoking, smoldering ruins. The wailing of women, the shrill cries of children reached them at that moment.

"Have a care," Ramiro warned.

They edged toward the desolated settlement, skirting the field and keeping within the dense growth. As they drew nearer, sounds arising from within the stricken village became louder. They could hear the shouts of men, coarse laughter, an occasional burst of profanity. Through it all came the periodic screams of women.

They came to a halt behind a limestone building that had weathered the torch. Most of the racket seemed to be coming from its interior. There were no rear windows or door facing them, and they were unable to look inside.

Ramiro Aramo dropped to his knees. He motioned to Ruby. "It is best you wait here. I shall go to the front and see what has happened."

"We stay together," Cain Ruby said, and beckoned to Girard and Carver.

Crouched low, they silently moved to the opposite end of the building and paused at its corner. A dense clump of brush several yards to one side offered a screen from behind which they could view the plaza around which the village had been erected. One by one they darted across to its protective cover.

"Great God!" Girard breathed, as they peered through the thick foliage.

A dozen or more broken, crumpled bodies—men and boys—were heaped into a grotesque pile in the center of the square. Arms and legs and bloodied heads protruded at odd angles, and here and there a dusty portion of a torso was visible. Moving about beneath the pall of smoke that hung low over the village and paying no attention to the pyramid of death were several uniformed soldiers.

Cain Ruby recoiled at the frightful scene. Girard muttered unintelligibly—and then Ramiro Aramo lurched to his feet.

"*¡Los asesinos!*" he cried in a wild, choked voice. "It is Maspera and his assassins!"

IV

Cain seized the Cuban by the arm, forcibly dragged him down. "No," he snarled. "Nothing you can do."

There were women inside the limestone structure. Screams were issuing from its open door, but they could not see what was taking place. Other cries rose from the brush beyond the plaza. Across the way a young girl darted into the open. She covered three steps when a soldier appeared, overtook her. He swept her off her feet, carried her back into the shadows.

Just beyond an older woman staggered into the clearing. Weaving uncertainly, she collided with two uniformed men angling toward the stone building. She fell to her knees, tried unsuccessfully to rise as the soldiers stood by watching, finally collapsed, and lay face down in the dust. One of the men moved up to her. With the toe of his boot he rolled the woman over. He drew his pistol, pointed it at her head. Transfixed by fear, she stared up at him. The Spaniard laughed, jammed his weapon back into its holster. Turning, he rejoined his companion, and they continued on.

Again they halted, their eyes now on the door of the limestone structure. Two more soldiers emerged. They were dragging a naked girl between them, each supporting her limp body by an arm. Her long hair was dragging on the ground, and her bronze skin bore numerous thin welts—the marks of a quirt. Laughing and joking, the soldiers moved toward the shrubbery just beyond Cain Ruby and the others.

"Dead," Girard muttered.

Ruby nodded grimly.

Close by Ramiro Aramo choked back a deep sob.

"Can't we do something?" Girard asked in a hoarse whisper.

Cain said: "It's too late."

"We can make those bastards pay. . . ."

"What good would it do? We'd be fools to jump twenty or thirty well-armed soldiers."

"We could sure as hell square things with a few of them."

Cain Ruby shook his head. "Would only jeopardize the job we've come to do."

"And maybe knock you out of ten thousand in gold."

The muscles of Cain Ruby's jaw hardened. "Have it your way," he murmured, "but we're not getting into this. Too much at stake."

"They're pulling out," Saxon Carver said, pointing at an officer striding into the plaza.

Over to their right Cain could hear the two men who had dragged the dead girl into the brush moving about. They were still laughing, tossing obscene observations back and forth. He saw Aramo go tense again.

"Do nothing," he warned in a low voice.

A whistle shrilled three times in short, imperative blasts. Soldiers began to move from the shadows and from the limestone building and assemble in the square. Some were drawing on portions of their clothing and buckling down weapons. Others were eating, and several carried long-necked flagons of wine or rum.

The officer who had skirled the summons stood apart from his men watching them assemble. He was a tall, rapacious-looking man, arrogant in his splendid blue uniform.

"That Maspera?"

It was Saxon Carver who answered Ruby's question. "That's him. Hernando Maspera."

"Takes a brave officer to turn his men loose on helpless people like these."

The two soldiers, either ignoring or not hearing Maspera's whistle, were still in the deep brush carrying on their raucous banter. The officer blew again. Abruptly the laughter ceased.

"We ride!" one of the pair shouted. "Hurry!"

There was a loud crashing in the shrubbery. Ruby crouched lower, realizing the two would pass only a few paces away. He lifted his arm to caution the others. At that moment Ramiro Aramo leaped upright and charged the soldiers, knife flashing in his hand. There was a startled oath, a dry, scuffing sound.

"God damn him," Ruby breathed in a raspy voice and,

rising, plunged after the Cuban.

One of the Spaniards was down, blood spreading across his back. Aramo was locked to the other as they struggled for possession of the knife. Cain Ruby closed swiftly. He snatched up a rock, smashed it against the soldier's head, driving him to his knees. Aramo, eyes flaming, struck hard with his knife.

The thud of marching feet in the plaza reached Ruby. He grasped the Cuban by the shoulder, whirled him about roughly. "Come," he snapped, and headed back to where Gavin Girard and Carver were hidden.

Anger was boiling through him, matched by a strong worry of what would come next. They reached the clump of brush, dropped into its shadow. Cain flung a glance to the plaza. Beyond the pile of bodies Maspera and his men were moving toward their horses at the far end of the clearing. The two soldiers were not yet missed, but when the command to mount up was issued and empty saddles were noted . . . ?

"Head out . . . the way we came," Ruby said in a barely controlled voice. "Place will be crawling with soldiers in another five minutes."

Immediately Girard pivoted, started off through the thick growth, followed by Carver and Aramo. Keeping a close watch on Maspera and his men, Cain Ruby brought up the rear. They darted across the open ground, gained the side of the limestone building. Girard turned to Ruby.

"Which way?"

Ignoring him, Cain Ruby grasped Aramo's arm, spun the Cuban about. "What the hell you trying to do?" he demanded in a savage tone. "Get us all killed? I told you to stay put . . . and, when I give an order, I want it obeyed!"

Ramiro Aramo made no reply. Ruby, breathing heavily from anger, realized he was speaking in English. "You think

I would not like to take vengeance on the soldiers?" he continued in the more formal Spanish. "It would be a great pleasure, but such we cannot afford to do. A more important job faces us."

"I regret . . . ," the Cuban began.

"Regret is of no value. I cannot take chances," Cain Ruby broke in. "If it were not necessary that I keep you as a guide. . . ." His words broke off as his glance settled on Saxon Carver. "Such is not necessary," he said. "There will be no need for you to remain with us. Carver knows the country. He can guide. . . ."

"Don't know how to find this Peréz-Rosario you want to see," Carver said. "I know this country, sure, but not that. Better hang on to the Cuban."

Ruby swore softly. He looked at Ramiro's stricken face, nodded. "All right. The next time. . . ."

"There will be no second time, *señor*," Aramo said quietly. "On this you have my word. It was only the sight of so much death, so much brutality. . . ."

A burst of shouting lifted from the village plaza. Ruby glanced over his shoulder. He could see nothing beyond the fringe of brush, but he could hear the pound of running feet.

"Lead out . . . hurry," he said to Aramo.

The Cuban moved off at once, going deeply into the thick shrubbery. He pressed hard for a full quarter hour, then slowed to a walk. "There is no danger now," he said.

Ruby mopped at the sweat accumulated on his face. Anger still tugged at him, and he turned to the Cuban. "This must not happen again. It is understood between us?"

Ramiro Aramo lowered his head. "It is understood. I have given my word."

"Good . . . who is this Maspera?"

"The vilest of dogs. A captain in the forces of General

Enna and a devil with no equal. The band of men he leads are known as the *asesinos*. They are special soldiers, cruel and ruthless."

"Why would they destroy a village such as we have seen?"

Aramo shrugged. "Often there is no reason . . . only one to keep fear alive. It is possible there were *pacíficos* among the villagers. It is Maspera's way of punishment."

Gavin Girard spat. "Punishment . . . murder a whole village?"

Ramiro was silent for several moments. "This is no uncommon thing. The soldiers have been slaying our men and boys and ravishing our women for hundreds of years. It is a way of government, of politics."

"A great political system," Girard said wryly.

"Seems to work. Got to admit that," Saxon Carver observed.

Ruby frowned, gave the man a wondering glance, and then looked away. They were beyond the range of sounds rising in the clearing now, and he wondered if they had found the bodies of the two soldiers yet.

"What are we doing about horses?" Carver asked.

"It will be necessary that we walk to San Rafael," the Cuban said. "If fortune is with us, we shall there obtain the animals."

San Rafael? That was the settlement near which lay the plantation of René Gayardee—and where Annette DuRique would be found. Vague alarm rose within Cain Ruby. What if the *asesinos* had passed that way—had struck there? The thought of the girl in the hands of Maspera and his men sent a chill throbbing through him. "How far to San Rafael?" he asked.

"More than a day, *señor*," Aramo replied.

"It must be done in less," Ruby said grimly.

V

The morning turned gray and misty as the sun climbed slowly into an overcast. It was hot.

"There will be rain," Ramiro Aramo said as they pushed on through the tangled depths of the jungle. "I fear we shall have difficulty."

"Been through storms before," Ruby replied, urgency turning him short and ill-tempered.

The Cuban said no more, simply hurried on, picking a trail through the wild, lush growth with skill. From time to time, however, he glanced skyward as though fearful of what lay in store for them.

As the hours passed, the heat increased until it became a stifling, throttling force that restricted breathing and hampered their pace. There was not the smallest breeze and the forest transformed into a simmering cauldron through which they labored. Sweat soaked clothing, plastered their bodies, and, to make the moments more disagreeable, swarms of stinging flies and gnats hovered about them in persistent, ravenous clouds, clogging their nostrils, settling on their lips, and feasting on exposed skin.

They felt no hunger, but there was no satisfying thirst, although they stopped often at the streams that crossed their path. Eventually walking became sheer drudgery, painful and exacting. Late in the morning it began to look as though the terrible heat would defeat them, cause them to abandon the forced march for rest, and then abruptly the clouds opened, and rain spilled forth.

Joy was short-lived. At first, there was a hint of coolness, but soon a sweltering blanket of humidity enveloped the land and discomfort was more intense than ever. Cain Ruby, face bared to the hammering drops, slogged wearily on through the downpour. Having grown up in Louisiana and later plying the seas in the *Island Queen*, rain was no stranger to him, but never had he encountered one so ill-timed and frustrating. Each moment was precious, and he begrudged their loss with a deep, consuming anger.

Gradually the storm built itself into a fierce, driving gale. Raindrops splashed at them with relentless fury, and the valley across which they were traveling became a vast, ankle-deep lake.

Aramo, his slender shape bent against the blasts, turned to Ruby. "It will be wise to find shelter," he shouted above the keening wind.

Cain Ruby's face was a mask of helpless resignation. He nodded. "Where?"

"There are cliffs on the far side of this valley. In some can be found caves."

Ruby signified his approval, and they moved on.

They reached the low bank of buttes a short time later. Aramo led them to a gouged-out hollow halfway up the nearest. It was a small chamber, scarcely ten feet in diameter, but it was dry and beyond the violence of the storm. There was no relief from the heat, however; it rose in steamy clouds from the jungle to hang low in a smothering mist over the land.

In the comparative comfort of the cave they stripped, wrung the water from their clothing, and, after spreading it about to dry, they settled down to rest.

"It is good," Ramiro Aramo said, lying back. "There is much hard walking yet ahead."

Ruby, impatient with the delay, was forced to agree. Under ordinary conditions midday on the island, when heat was at its peak, was no time for extensive physical activity. Complicated by a storm such as raged outside the cave, travel was out of the question.

There was a slight motion at the mouth of the hollow. A cavy, terrified by the torrential downpour, paused momentarily in its quest for shelter. Saxon Carver, again idly whetting his knife, raised his arm swiftly as though to hurl the sharp-pointed weapon. Instantly the bedraggled creature bolted into the nearby brush.

Aramo's dark eyes studied the man. "You would kill the little cavy, *señor?*"

Carver nodded. "Was too quick for me."

"For what purpose? We are not beset by hunger. It would have been difficult to cook him, if we were."

Saxon Carver honed deliberately, the scrape loud in the confines of the cave. "You need a reason, *amigo?*"

The Cuban lay back again. "Always there should be a reason to kill," he said.

"Somebody should tell that to Maspera," Girard commented. "And to the rest of the Spaniards."

"The *aesinos* are the worst of all," the Cuban said. "They are men apart. I would say even General Enna knows moments of nervousness where they are concerned. It has been said that Maspera is responsible to the crown."

Girard shifted his attention to Cain Ruby. "You think he knows it was we who killed those two soldiers?"

"Possible. He'll know it wasn't someone of the village."

"But he never saw us . . . doesn't even know we're around."

"Doubt that. By now he's been told that a party landed on the coast. He'll put two and two together and come up with an answer."

"He could not have followed in the storm," Aramo pointed out.

"Perhaps not, but, when it's over, he'll start hunting."

"And this island's not big enough to hide from a man like that," Saxon Carver said.

There was a long minute of silence. It was finally broken by Gavin Girard. "Cain, for what it's worth now, you were right back in the village. There wasn't anything we could do. Couldn't see it then."

"It is so," the Cuban agreed. "I acted as one of foolish impulse. It is to my sorrow. . . ."

"Forget it," Cain Ruby said, and closed his eyes.

Cain Ruby awoke shortly after noon. Disturbed, he leaped to his feet and crossed to the mouth of the cave. The rain had ceased, but the world beyond the hollow was a green, overloaded sponge. Wheeling, he roused the others and began to draw on his clothing.

Aramo, first to the entrance of the shelter, shook his head doubtfully. "It will not be a journey of ease."

"Can't be helped," Cain Ruby snapped. "We have slept much too long."

The Cuban shrugged in his customary way and stepped into the open. The soil on the slope was loose and grease-slick. Aramo's feet went out from under him, and he fell hard. His head made a soft thudding sound, when it struck.

Ruby was at his side immediately. He helped Ramiro to a standing position, peered into the man's swarthy face. "You are hurt?"

"It is nothing. But, as you see, great care must be used. There will be many such accidents unless we travel slowly . . . and the earth is not always so soft as here."

They started down the grade in the thick mud, slipping, sliding, and always hard put to maintain their footing. When they reached the floor of the valley, they found themselves knee-deep in silty water. The soil had reached its saturation limit and could absorb no more. But wading was not too difficult, only irritatingly slow.

They continued on for an hour, gradually climbing out of the low country and working upward to a tableland that spread out before them in a broad plain. Patches of blue sky had begun to appear between the banks of sullen, gray clouds, and Aramo, wise to the way of the elements, remarked that they would see no more rain that day.

"Good," Girard muttered at low breath. "Much more and this island would sink."

Ramiro Aramo smiled. "It is the way of it in Cuba. In certain months we have many such storms. Often they are worse, as when the strong winds sweep in from the sea. Today it was bad, but I have seen it when no hut can stand, when even the rock houses tremble. . . ." The Cuban hesitated in stride. He raised a hand for silence.

Ruby, about to voice a question, checked his words.

"What now?" Girard asked in a hoarse whisper.

"Do you not hear it?"

The quiet of the jungle, broken only by the steady dripping of the drenched trees and undergrowth, was no longer absolute. Now could be heard a new sound—a distant, deep-throated rumbling.

Cain Ruby stared questioningly at Aramo. The Cuban was solemn. "A river. I fear it has become a thing of great violence."

Again they moved on, traveling at a slow trot as though anxious to discover the source of the impending and possible obstacle. They were not long in reaching it. It was an awesome sight. Louisiana was laced with many streams, all occasionally riotous within their channels, but, when they halted beside this wild torrent, Cain Ruby realized he had never really witnessed the turbulence of which a river was capable.

"We'll not be fording this one," Saxon Carver said, squatting down with his back to a palm.

Cain watched the raging flow slashing and tearing hungrily at its banks. Great chunks of soil were breaking off, whirling away in the surging current. Angered anew by the seemingly endless delays that plagued them, he wheeled to Aramo. "You have said you know this country. There another place where we can cross?"

"I know of none," the Cuban replied. "Perhaps it is as well we wait. To drown would not be difficult."

"No time to wait." Ruby was thinking not only of the Montaña Sangre and the need to dispose of that matter before the arrival of Narciso Lopez, but of the safety of Annette DuRique as well. From the moment he had looked upon the rape of Cabezón village, an uneasiness had grown within him.

Aramo shrugged, glanced upstream. "I have seen at times where a tree has been felled by the storm. Or the river cuts from the roots all support. Thus a bridge is made. If it were possible to find one such. . . ."

"We'll look for one," Cain Ruby said abruptly, and started off along the river's edge.

Aramo forged out ahead of him. Carver, grumbling deeply, and Gavin Girard, maintaining his silence, followed. They were fortunate. Less than a kilometer below their starting point they came upon a palm that had been toppled by the wind. It lay diagonally across the stream. The fronds were a considerable distance from the ground, since it had not fallen completely, but it did offer the means by which they could gain the opposite side. The ten-foot drop was of no consequence.

Once over they continued on through the harsh heat. With sundown a slight lessening in its intensity became ap-

parent, but it was not sufficient to bring any noticeable relief. They marched steadily past midnight and on into the
early morning hours, halting only occasionally for brief pe-
riods of rest.

"We shall be there by sunrise," Ramiro Aramo said later
in response to Ruby's inquiry. "The storm has cost us much
time."

"You plan to lay over there a bit?" Girard asked. "I'm
needing some food."

Cain nodded. "Got some personal business to attend.
You can eat while I'm doing that."

Saxon Carver showed immediate interest. "What kind of
personal business?"

"You'll know, when it's time," Ruby answered. "Aramo,
there a good chance we can get horses in San Rafael?"

"It is to be hoped," the Cuban said, but his tone carried
no real conviction. With the Spanish soldiers plundering the
villages at will, nothing could be anticipated.

They crossed a rocky hog-back, dropped into a
rain-drenched valley. With its breadth behind them, they
came again onto a ridge with the first streaks of dawn
brightening the sky. A light, cooling breeze sprang up, fan-
ning their fevered bodies, and some of the dragging weariness faded from them.

"Where can be seen those trees," Ramiro said, pointing
to the far end of the valley stretching below them, "we shall
find the Gayardee plantation. Beyond it, but a short distance, is the village of San Rafael."

Cain Ruby heaved a sigh. It had seemed during the long,
tedious hours of the preceding night that Gayardees' and
San Rafael were impermanent goals, that with each tor-
turous step taken, both receded farther into the distance.
Now, at last, they were in sight.

"At the plantation I will halt," he said to the Cuban. "You will lead the others on to the village. Find them food. Get horses if possible. I will join you there."

"It shall be as you wish," Aramo said, and pushed on down the gentle slope.

They reached the band of trees that formed a natural wall around the plantation. Leaving the trail, the Cuban led them in a direct line across the fields, all of which appeared neglected and untended to Cain Ruby.

"Does not Gayardee farm his land?" he asked, moving in beside Aramo.

The Cuban's face was clouded. "It is not to be understood. But I have not been here for many months. The fields were high with cane, then."

They left the cleared ground, ragged where the jungle's stealthy repossession laid its mark, and shortly broke again into an open area. A large house stood on the far side. Beyond it were various smaller buildings—all appearing forlorn and deserted in the early light.

"Something is wrong. Of this I am certain," Ramiro murmured, coming to a halt.

Cain Ruby looked closer. The anxiety he had kept so carefully submerged during the hurried march crowded to the surface. Heedless of possible ambush by Spanish soldiers, he walked nearer to the bulky, two-storied main house.

He pulled up short, a grimness settling over him. As at Cabezón—they were too late. The inside of the structure was a charred ruin. Maspera—or someone like him—had been there.

VI

In the deep hush that followed Girard voiced the obvious. "Soldiers have been here. . . ."

"Likely they have struck San Rafael, also," Aramo said heavily.

Cain Ruby was trying not to think of Annette, but the remembrance of her kept slipping in and out of mind. He told himself he should not care too much—that the Montaña Sangre's destruction should be his first consideration, but it was a losing battle. Slowly he moved toward the ruined structures.

"Ought to be somebody around . . . somebody who can tell us what happened," he said, thinking aloud.

"The fire is old," Aramo broke in gently. "It was a time ago. A month, perhaps two . . . see how the laurel already grows in the sheds? It is best we go to San Rafael. There we can learn of the Gayardees."

"If there is still a San Rafael," Cain said tonelessly, and they moved on.

He felt the curious, wondering glance of Gavin Girard but offered no explanation. Again he cautioned himself; he must not become too upset over Annette DuRique. She was a stranger, no more than a figure in a portrait—and of secondary importance. He would get ten thousand in gold for the Montaña Sangre; if he was to do any worrying, it should be over the fort.

They heard sounds of life in the settlement before they reached it. Somehow that eased the dread within him, but that quickly vanished when they entered the plaza and glanced around.

"It is as I feared . . . the *asesinos* have been here, also," Ramiro Aramo said in a dragging voice.

It was evident in the blackened scars of burned huts, in the absence of men, in the furtive faces of women who peered fearfully from crudely built shelters. Motioning for the others to follow, the Cuban crossed the square and angled for a small hut squatting at the edge of the jungle. He halted before it.

"This is where lives a friend. If he has survived the *asesinos,* he will tell me all we wish to know."

Aramo drew aside the palm fiber curtain that hung over the hut's entrance. "Juan! Juan Rodriguez!"

A woman's tired voice replied: "He is not here. Go away. Leave me in peace."

"Where is he, mother? It is Ramiro Aramo."

There was a length of silence. Then: "Ramiro? It is truly you?"

"Yes. Where is Juan?"

"Dead. Like many others, dead."

Aramo was shaken by the information. He stood quietly at the entrance to the shelter, head bowed, eyes on the ground. Finally he shrugged. "It was Maspera?"

"The same. They came a time ago. Only a few of the men escaped into the jungle."

Again the young Cuban was still. After a moment he asked: "What of the plantation? Where are the Gayardees?"

"Also dead. There was trouble of some sort with the Spanish . . . a matter to which they were opposed. Thus all were destroyed."

Cain Ruby was a hard man. Growing up on the New Orleans waterfront and, later, knocking about from one port of call to another, he had witnessed brutality and death in many forms, but the sheer, senseless cruelty of the Spaniards in their dealings with the islanders was beyond belief. A deep core of anger began to build within him, and he had a better understanding of the Free Cubans.

"Ask her about a girl who stayed with them," he said to Aramo.

"A young woman who lived there . . . what of her?"

"The blessed Anna?" For the first time the old woman showed a spark of interest.

Ruby nodded. "Her name is Annette. They could have called her Anna."

"She is the one, mother."

"Gone . . . the bleeding heart be praised! She was here in the village, tending the sick when the plantation was attacked. Thus we were warned in time. With several of the young men and women she fled."

Relief eased the tension that gripped Cain Ruby. "Where is she now?"

Ramiro repeated the question.

"When told the Gayardees were dead, she chose to go with Peréz-Rosario and those who camp with him. It was best. Maspera looked hard for her. He would have her for his own devil's pleasure."

"Where, then, is *El Profeta?*"

"I know not to be exact. To the east, I have heard. Perhaps it is where the river meets the lake."

"I remember the place. Do you have food to spare? My friends and I have not eaten for many hours."

"There is only dried mutton and meal cakes."

"For such we will be grateful."

"It is nothing. Come inside and fill your needs. I am not well and move but poorly."

"Thank you, good mother."

Girard reached into his pocket, obtained several coins. He offered them to Aramo. "Pay her with these. Expect she could use some cash."

The Cuban shook his head. "There is nothing that she can buy for there is nothing to sell. Also it would be an insult. Among my people a friend is one with whom all things are shared without cost."

Aramo entered the hut. He and the woman continued their conversation in a low tone. Carver moved up beside Ruby.

"What's this about a girl?"

"Has nothing to do with you," Cain replied.

"The hell it doesn't!" Carver said harshly. "Anything connected with this deal is my business."

Gavin Girard's features were stiff, reflecting his resentment. "She a friend of yours?"

Cain stared off across the plaza. There was no point in keeping the matter quiet any further. Annette still lived, so they would eventually know. He shook his head.

"Never met her. She's DuRique's daughter."

"DuRique . . . the merchant?" Carver asked.

"The same. She's been living here with relatives . . . the Gayardees."

"So?"

"I agreed to take her back to New Orleans."

Gavin Girard smiled crookedly. "For a price, of course."

"Rest of the combine know about this?" Saxon Carver demanded, frowning.

"I never mentioned it. Could be DuRique did."

"But probably didn't. Doubt if they'd be in favor of your taking on a second chore that might interfere with what they're paying you to do."

"It won't interfere."

"Seems it has already. And once you've found her, you'll have to look out for her. . . ."

"My responsibility," Cain Ruby said. "You're not involved."

"Like hell I'm not! You don't even know for sure where

she is. Could lose a lot of time looking. . . ."

"The old woman said she was with Peréz-Rosario," Girard observed. "And we've got to find him."

Cain shrugged. "If she is, there's no problem. If not, I'm on my own. You two can head back without me, when the job's finished."

Girard yawned lazily. "Once we blow that fort, this island will be alive with soldiers hunting for us. Best we stick together."

Ruby favored Girard with a glance, now opening his shirt in deference to the barbarous heat. He was beginning to like him; beneath the veneer of indifference there was a man. "Can't ask you to stick your neck out for me," he said.

"Not for you," Gavin replied, "for the girl. Always a sucker for a woman in trouble."

"*Señores,*" Ramiro Aramo's low voice broke in hesitantly, "I have food."

They turned to the Cuban. Ruby accepted a handful of the stringy, dried meat and several small cakes. He bit off a chunk of the mealy biscuit, munched its grainy goodness hurriedly. The others took their share, began to eat.

"What of horses?" Ruby asked after a few moments had passed.

"There are none," Aramo replied. "The Gayardees had several. They were taken by the soldiers, when they stripped the plantation."

Saxon Carver swore in disgust. "More walking."

Ruby nodded. "And we're losing time standing here." He faced Aramo. "Know where to find this Peréz-Rosario?"

"If he is at the place the old woman mentioned."

"How far?"

"One day. No more."

Cain Ruby groaned silently. Another day lost.

VII

They moved on, bearing eastward and soon getting into a more dense and less frequented section of the island. The heat was again oppressive. Beneath their boots the earth was sodden from the previous rain, and moisture still clung to the vines and brush. After the first hour beyond sunrise the sticky, wet atmosphere closed in upon them, and there was no escaping its sapping drain. Gnats and stinging flies were with them once more, and to increase their problems the heavily salted mutton they had eaten set up a burning thirst, forcing them to pause at every opportunity to ease the craving in their throats. But they pushed on tirelessly, prodded by Cain Ruby who would not permit a halt of any duration. Late in the morning they ran across a squad of Spanish cavalrymen and were compelled to lie in hiding in a partially submerged field of broad-leafed palmetto. It was a miserable quarter hour, but the soldiers eventually passed on, and they resumed their journey.

At high noon they stopped to rest. In their condition, Aramo pointed out, it would be best to wait while the sun was at its hottest, and then continue. They would thus be in better shape to travel faster—and it would make little difference at which time they would arrive at the lake. Once there, it would be a matter of searching about until they found the camp of Peréz-Rosario, anyway. The leader of the Free Cubans was constantly on the move, often making and breaking camp three or four times in a single day. It was the only means by which he could avoid falling into the hands of the Spaniards, always on the prowl for him.

At three o'clock they took up the march again. The jungle had become even more arduous, and they made slow progress. Late in the afternoon, worn and clothed with sweat, they halted once more to ease their aching bodies.

"Never should have started this without horses," Saxon Carver grumbled as he stretched out along the edge of a small stream.

Aramo paused in the act of bathing his face. "A horse would be of little use here. The way is too difficult."

"Soldiers we saw were riding."

"They must keep to the trail," Aramo explained patiently. "A thing we are not required to do. Because of such we have seen few of the enemy."

Carver drew forth his knife and stone, began to strop the glittering blade. The monotonous rasping was loud in the hush. "Good rider can take a horse anywhere."

The Cuban resumed his bathing. Gavin Girard stirred irritably, brushed at the sweat clouding his eyes. "Can't you forget that damned knife?" he snapped.

Saxon Carver ceased his whetting. "It bother you, boy?"

Girard came upright in a sudden move. His jaw was clamped shut, and anger brightened his eyes. Cain Ruby waved him back. "Save your breath," he said wearily.

The overpowering heat, the savage, silent jungle—the endless miles were getting to them, turning their nerves raw, building the minor irritations and resentments into towering incidents.

Ruby pulled himself to his feet. At least, while they marched, there was less opportunity for friction. "Let's go," he said.

Still ruffled, Girard and Carver and, last of all, Ramiro Aramo arose and moved onto the trail. About them the forest was vivid with flowers, heavily scented with thick, almost sickeningly sweet odors. The birds were quiet, but the drone of ever-present insects was a low-pitched litany on the weighted air.

"We are coming near," Aramo said a short time later. "It is soon we will see the lake."

He stopped abruptly. Ruby swung his glance to the path ahead. A figure loomed before them—a great, broad-shouldered bull of a man with one arm missing and a white rag stretched diagonally across his head to cover his left eye. He held a rapier in his one hand. A pistol was thrust into the waistband of his soiled drawers, and for a brief moment it seemed to Cain Ruby that they had dropped back a half century to Jean LaFitte and Galvez Town.

"*Hola*, Pablo!" Aramo cried, and rushed forward with outstretched arms.

The giant's swarthy face broke into a wide grin. "Ramiro! It is you?" His voice boomed deep in the hush.

The pair embraced, Aramo clapping the big man soundly on the back several times while being whirled about as a child in a circle. Finally it was over, and Aramo turned to the others. "This is Pablo Quintana. He is one of us . . . so much so that he has given his arm and one eye to the Spaniards."

"But I have collected many times for both," Pablo laughed. "And I shall collect more! One day it will be the greatest prize of all . . . the black heart of Hernando Maspera! I shall hold it on the tip of my rapier and wave it under the nose of de la Concha!" The huge Cuban paused, glared at Cain Ruby and the two men standing beside him. "And who are these *ingléses*, my Ramiro? Why are they here?"

"Good friends from New Orleans. They come to fight the Spaniards."

Quintana advanced a long stride, his single eye darting over the three. "Fight! With what? They are but lightly armed. Will they use sticks and stones?"

Ramiro tapped his forehead meaningly. "The mind, great friend. They will accomplish with the mind. You shall see. Where is *El Profeta?* He is well?"

"He is well," Pablo replied, nodding his shaggy head. "He sleeps now. Twice this day I was required to change the camp. There were soldiers on horses. . . ."

"We met them but a short time ago."

Quintana drew up sharply. "In which direction did they ride?"

"To the north."

"Ah, it is well. Since the uprising in Puerto Principe, they have been as plentiful as flies on a dung heap. I have need to watch with care."

"Pablo stays at the shoulder of Peréz-Rosario," Aramo explained. "He is what you call in your language a . . . a. . . ."

"Bodyguard," Girard supplied.

"A bodyguard. No other man in Cuba knows the island as does he. A thousand secret hiding places are stored in his brain. He is the reason the Spaniards have not been able to capture *El Profeta.*"

"It is so," Pablo said proudly.

"Once they were taken unawares. Pablo permitted them to do so in order to draw the soldiers from where Peréz-Rosario lay hidden. They gouged out his eye to make him speak, but he would not. He only laughed. Later he escaped. Now the soldiers would like to capture him almost as much as they would Peréz-Rosario."

"But they are as oxen seeking the fox," Quintana said scornfully. "I play with them as the cat with a mouse. And sometimes I prick them . . . so . . . with my blade, just to remind them Pablo Quintana can yet fight."

"We must see *El Profeta,*" Aramo said then. "Will you lead us to him?"

"Of a certainty. Come, it is but a short distance."

He wheeled, amazingly light on his feet for a man so large and incapacitated. Aramo and the others moved in behind him. Ruby heard the younger Cuban voice the question that was on the tip of his own tongue.

"A girl . . . of the name of Anna. Is she with you here?"

"The angel? Oh, yes . . . she has been with us since the *asesinos* slew her people and burned their plantation. A wondrous one . . . this Anna. Why do you ask?"

"My friends would have words with her. It is a matter of privacy."

"It would have been better had they brought to her medicine and bandages," Pablo growled. "Those things she has need of. Words she does not."

Quintana led them down into a narrow gully overgrown with scarlet poincianas and other brilliant blossoms. He turned sharply right moments later, climbed a sight rise. Where it leveled off, he stopped. "We have arrived," he announced, his solitary eye dancing merrily.

The Cuban shook his head. "I see nothing, Pablo."

Quintana laughed in child-like glee. "Is it not proof that I have no equal? Is it no wonder the Spaniards tear their hair in rage?" He moved forward a dozen steps, pulled aside a screen of brush. Only then was the encampment of Peréz-Rosario visible. "Come," he said, "I shall lead you, Ramiro. With my one eye I see better than do you with two!"

Aramo smiled, slapped Quintana on the backside. "It is not difficult to understand why *El Profeta* trusts none but you to care for him, big one."

They entered the clearing. In the center was a small cooking fire over which a blackened iron pot had been suspended. Coals glowed beneath it, but there was little smoke rising from the especially selected wood. More of Pablo Quintana's talents, Cain Ruby assumed.

On the far side were two palm-thatched lean-tos. Each had a square of stained canvas hanging over its entrance. The one to the right drew back, and two young women emerged. One was small, dusky-skinned, and strangely beautiful in a quiet, madonna-like way. Unquestionably she was a Cuban. The other could only be Annette DuRique.

But there was a vast difference in this and the carefully groomed, stylishly clothed girl of the portrait. She was dressed in a patched and faded shirt, ragged pants, both many sizes too large for her slim body. Her hair had been clipped to shorter length for convenience's sake, and her face, devoid of cosmetics, looked creamy and firm. Only the eyes were the same: soft, ethereal, blue as a morning sky beneath dark, full brows.

She smiled at Quintana. "You bring us visitors."

"They are friends," the Cuban explained. "They would speak with *El Profeta* . . . and with you, small angel."

"With me?"

Ruby stepped forward. "I'm Cain Ruby. Been commissioned by your father to take you home."

He watched the girl closely, expecting some sign of relief, of welcome. Her wide-set eyes flickered briefly as though the mention of her parent stirred something within her.

"Is my father well?"

"Worried . . . he doesn't want you here when the invasion starts."

She looked at Ruby with stronger interest. "Then Lopez is finally coming?"

"Soon. Main reason I'm . . . we're here. Got a job to do. When it's finished, we'll all head back for New Orleans.

There'll be a ship waiting for us."

The Cuban girl moved closer to Annette, timidly sought her hand. Annette smiled reassuringly at her, returned her attention to Cain Ruby. "My home is here now," she said. "I shall stay."

He stared at her in disbelief. Anger lifted slowly within him. "You don't know what you're saying," he said quietly. "We'll talk about it later."

"As you wish," she replied, "but the matter is settled."

"Not by a damn' sight!" Ruby exploded, abruptly losing his temper. "You may be the grand lady to everybody around here, but to me you're just a spoiled brat . . . and you'll do as I say!"

Annette's eyes sparked. Patches of color showed on her cheeks, and her lips set to a firm line. "It is I who decides that," she said stiffly, and turned to the girl beside her. "It is time to prepare the food, Margarita. Come." She paused, looked again at Cain Ruby. Her anger had not cooled. "You wished to talk with Peréz-Rosario. He sleeps now, but will awaken soon."

Simmering with frustration, Ruby watched her move off, graceful and poised despite her shapeless garments, and with the girl, Margarita, she began to put together the evening's meal.

He wheeled about, stalked to where Gavin Girard and Carver were sprawled in the shade at the edge of the clearing. He realized he had put on a scene with Annette, but he couldn't have cared less. She would be going back with him—even if it involved carrying her across his shoulder.

Girard grinned up at him. "Got yourself a problem?"

"Nothing I can't handle," Cain snapped, and settled down beside him.

VIII

Saxon Carver took his knife from its leather sheath, spat on the oilstone, and began his senseless whetting. He felt Cain Ruby's hard glance, paused. After a moment he shrugged, put the blade aside, and lay back. Pablo had disappeared, and Ramiro Aramo had wandered over to the fire and was conversing with Margarita. She was Peréz-Rosario's daughter, the Cuban had informed Girard. Annette stirred the contents of the kettle with a long-handled spoon.

Beyond them Pablo reappeared abruptly, bringing with him two hollow-cheeked men. "More friends for the cook pot!" he sang out jovially, and departed to again resume his post.

The newcomers nodded unsmilingly at Ruby and his companions and, hats in hand, advanced to the fire. Annette greeted them reassuringly and both squatted near the kettle of steaming food, now savoring the clearing with the fragrance of boiled meat and vegetables. Aramo said something to Margarita, to which she nodded, and immediately the young Cuban circled the preparations, halted beside the two men and began to speak. Cain Ruby came to attention.

"Ramiro!"

Aramo hesitated, turned, and crossed the clearing to the Americans. "Yes, *señor?*"

"It will be wise to guard your tongue," Ruby warned, his voice still showing traces of anger. "Tell those men nothing of the Montaña Sangre."

Ramiro frowned, hesitated briefly. "I shall not tell of your plans, if you wish," he said. "But there is no danger. They are loyal followers of Peréz-Rosario."

"Perhaps. But no risk must be taken. Repeat to them

what you said to Pablo . . . only that we are here to fight the Spaniards."

"So it will be. I intended to ask for exploding powder. It is possible they can procure such for us from a supply hidden on the island."

"Good. Make no explanation as to what purpose it will be put, however."

"It is understood," Aramo said, and returned to the fire.

Gavin Girard slapped at a beetle slowly crawling up his leg, grinned at Ruby. "Nothing changes for you. Wouldn't surprise me any if you backed off telling Peréz-Rosario what it's all about."

Cain shrugged. "Too late to be taking any chances," he said, and settled in the cooling shade.

His eyes were heavy, and it felt good to relax, simply to turn loose and not plan, not to think of anything. Off in the jungle birds sang gaily to the low hum of insects; the air was sweet with the odor of flowers mingled with the earthy smell of wood smoke and cookery. It was a strange land. A paradox. Here, in a small square of the universe no larger than the ballroom of a Louisiana mansion, was peace and calm and utter beauty—yet it lay in the very heart of throbbing violence and death. It was odd—difficult to understand.

Cain Ruby awoke with a start. A figure towered over him—a tall, gaunt man with long white hair and flowing beard. His face was lean, his nose sharp and drawn to a scimitar-like hook; his large mouth was firm, yet kindly; his eyelids were shrunken, crinkled shutters. Cain realized that he was blind, that the lids were tightly clamped to mask empty sockets from which the eyeballs had been torn. He was dressed in shirt, shapeless drawers, and handwoven fiber sandals.

"I am Peréz-Rosario!" he boomed in a resonant voice.

"You are welcome in my camp!"

Ruby drew himself upright, accepted the man's extended hand. Girard and Saxon Carver followed, and then all stood by, curiously affected by his talismanic personality.

"Ramiro has told me of your mission. Your aid to our cause puts all Cubans in your debt. But you hunger. First we shall eat . . . then will come the time for speaking."

Guided by Margarita, the sightless prophet of the island wheeled about and stalked to the fire where Annette was spooning portions of the stew into gourd bowls. Coffee had been brewed, and Pablo had dragged up a log upon which a folded mat had been placed for Peréz-Rosario. There were no signs of the two newcomers; evidently they had eaten and departed.

Cain Ruby, flanked by Girard and Carver, took a position in the half circle and dipped into the meal. The stew, a mixture of vegetables laced with chunks of lean meat, was well seasoned and tasty. In addition, there were meal cakes, berries and, of course, the thick, black coffee.

Pablo was the first to finish. He put aside his bowl, drew himself to his seven foot height, and slapped the rapier hanging at his hip. "I go now to watch for jackals," he said. "I would not wish to disappoint them, should they come."

Peréz-Rosario smiled toward the dark giant. "Go with God, friend Pablo," he said.

Quintana spun about and strode into the brush.

Peréz-Rosario listened to his footsteps. "The heart of a lion, the gentleness of a lamb. There is but one Pablo in this world."

"He is devoted to you," Aramo said.

"He is devoted to Cuba," *El Profeta* corrected. "I am but the symbol."

There was a stillness in that last hour preceding darkness. The heat had dwindled, and a faint breeze was slipping down the narrow passageway of the gully where Pablo Quintana had established the camp. Birds were throwing their final songs into the sky, and from somewhere in the far distance a cow lowed. The moment was almost pastoral—and could easily have been so had not the inescapable awareness of danger hung so threateningly over all.

"Is it not a time of beauty, these last minutes before the night comes?" Peréz-Rosario said quietly. "I no longer have eyes to serve me, yet I remember. The softness of shadows, the cool touch of wind, the joy of living things . . . these things I feel and cannot forget. Is it not strange that such exists in a world scarred by death . . . for that is where you are, my friends . . . in a world of death. You have entered a land where we mourn the birth of a child, knowing he is destined for a life of slavery and pain. We are merry at the arrival of death, since we know escape has come at last to one of our people. But during that span of life, however lengthy or brief, we fight, we hope, we struggle. And to share our burden you have joined with us. Ramiro tells that you have in mind to destroy the Montaña Sangre . . . God give you strength in that design! The walls of the Montaña Sangre are a hideous curse . . . a revilement that encloses us in a pit of hell."

Peréz-Rosario had risen to his feet. Drawn face tipped to the fading light in the sky, his figure loomed starkly against the darkening background.

"In truth, those blooded rocks do not confine only a square of our land . . . they encircle the island . . . the whole of it! They pin us helpless to a cross of fear . . . they shut out the world beyond. They imprison more than the body . . . they imprison the spirit, the will to live, the need to think. They throttle the souls of men . . . and world over . . .

symbolize tyranny and intolerance and man's refusal to respect his fellow beings. The walls of the Montaña Sangre
. . . a curse in the sight of God! May He grant you the
power to level them forever!"

In the closing night Peréz-Rosario's florid words rang
like the notes of a silver-throated bell. Cain Ruby glanced
around. Except for himself and Saxon Carver, all present
seemed caught up by the Cuban leader's flamboyant ora-
tory.

"We will do our best, Holy One," Ramiro Aramo said in
a voice that trembled.

Peréz-Rosario lowered his head. "No more can any man
do. It is my shame that I can offer little except comfort.
Since the day Joaquín de Aguerro arose to challenge the oppressors, I have been forced to hide. No longer can I move
among my people. They are compelled to seek me out."

"What of de Aguerro?" Aramo asked. "Does he still
fight?"

The prophet's shoulders sagged. "De Aguerro failed," he
said, sinking onto the log. "He and all that are left of his
army . . . three, perhaps four, men . . . are somewhere in the
jungle, fleeing for their lives. The remainder were murdered
by Colonel Lamery."

"Such will be bad news for General Lopez," Cain Ruby
said. "His plan was to unite with de Aguerro and other insurgents when he landed."

"None is left," the Cuban leader said. "None . . . Joaquín
de Aguerro was betrayed from the beginning. A priest,
faithless to the sanctity of the confessional, revealed to
Lamery what was told to him of the proposed uprising. He
gave names of all men involved. They were arrested and ex-
ecuted. Only de Aguerro and those who happened to be
with him escaped. As for the other insurgent armies . . . they

do not exist. The flame of freedom burns low at this sad hour."

Ruby stared into the fire. The rumors Narciso Lopez and all New Orleans had heard were false. Such was certain now. To many they had been suspect from the start, but most, including Lopez, had wanted to believe them. The destruction of the Montaña Sangre took on greater importance in Cain Ruby's mind. With no rebel force to support him Narciso Lopez would need assistance on a grand scale.

"Can you not send messengers . . . tell the men in hiding of Lopez's coming?" Girard suggested. "They could gather at a place, go then and join the invasion army."

"You forget the Spaniards," Peréz-Rosario said. "They are everywhere, lurking in the jungle like wolves. The island is over eight hundred kilometers in length. Our only means of communication is by word of mouth. And there are those among us who spy for the Spanish . . . traitors to our cause. It would be difficult."

"If but a few came, they would be of help to Lopez," Cain Ruby said. "He will need all who are willing."

Peréz-Rosario rubbed his thickly veined hands together. "To be sure . . . and it shall be done. Tomorrow I will send messengers. Yet I fear it will be to small purpose for, as I have said, matters are at low tide for us. Only hope lives at this hour . . . the one flame that does not die. Viva and his forty thousand soldiers could not crush it. Nor could those who preceded him. Even the evil O'Donnell with his ladders to which he bound helpless men such as Joaquín de Aguerro . . . men who rise and, standing alone, defy the oppressors. . . . in itself their individual rebellion is hopeless, since they are quickly overpowered, but so long as they continue to voice defiance, the flame of freedom cannot be extinguished."

"Unless you run out of Cubans," Saxon Carver said dryly.

Cain Ruby scarcely heard the facetious, if true, remark. His eyes were on Annette as he wondered at her reaction to Peréz-Rosario's philosophy. She had found a place behind the log and, arms locked about her knees, was looking into the dwindling fire. She was more the Annette of the portrait now—her face serene, her eyes deep-shadowed and thoughtful. Could she believe in the theory the Cuban prophet was expounding—a fatalistic faith in which men died in a fanatic demonstration of their desire to preserve a nebulous ideal? It was inconceivable that anyone with her background could accept it, yet her features reflected no denial.

To Cain Ruby's practical mind it was senseless, a hope being sustained on the cold bodies of countless dead men. Death in itself meant nothing; all that mattered was there were those who dared rise and flaunt the invincible enemy. That they fell immediately and were crushed into the dust was of incidental note. Vaguely he heard Peréz-Rosario's voice, rising and falling.

"In your land a hundred years ago or less, your people faced the same difficulties as we . . . many times the task appeared hopeless. But you did not lose heart, and in the end right and justice prevailed. It shall be so with Cuba. The day will come when the tyrants are overthrown, and we will walk as free men upon the earth."

All of which means nothing to me, Cain Ruby thought. *I am here on this island for two purposes . . . to destroy the Spaniards' fort and return Annette DuRique to New Orleans. Beyond that, I have no interest. It is a cruel thing that has befallen the Cubans, but they cannot expect me to assume their troubles.*

He glanced toward The Prophet. Peréz-Rosario had stopped speaking. "It was said by Ramiro Aramo that you

171

could give me details of the Montaña Sangre. I would like to learn all possible about its arrangement."

The old Cuban moved his head up and down. "Yes, I was one of those forced to build it. I know it well. I was a young tutor at the time, and it was there I was crippled. In the. . . ."

"It is time for sleeping," Margarita interrupted quietly. "The morning will be soon enough for that."

Peréz-Rosario raised his shoulders, allowed them to fall in a gesture of resignation. "It is the voice of my keeper. Will the morning be satisfactory?"

Cain Ruby hesitated. Another day—but the night was upon them, anyway. "It will be satisfactory."

El Profeta rose to his feet. "When will General Lopez arrive? Is this known to you?"

"On the fifteenth. Such was the date agreed upon."

"He will strike first at Havana?"

"No. He will come in three passing vessels. They mount no large cannon."

"But Havana is the heart of Cuba! To attack the Spaniards there would light a flame that would sweep the island like wildfire!"

"It is also a well-defended port. The Spaniards have many gunboats defending it."

"Yet we must show the people. . . ."

"Papa!" Margarita's voice carried a note of stern reproach.

The tall frame of the Cuban relented. With one hand resting on the shoulder of his daughter, he wheeled, started for his lean-to. "Until the morning," he said. "I regret I have no comfort to offer you other than my fire. But sleep well, knowing you are not in danger. Pablo will let no harm come to you."

Ruby watched him limp slowly into the shadows. Annette arose. She smiled impersonally to all, turned, walked to her quarters. Ramiro Aramo absently reached for a handful of branches, tossed them onto the almost dead fire.

"It is difficult to understand your *El Profeta*," Girard said, stretching out on the warm earth.

Ramiro smiled. "From the beginning of time such men as he were not understood."

"His thoughts are hard to follow."

Again Aramo smiled. "It is said the Yankee thinks with a bloodless mind, the Cuban with a bleeding heart. A difference is to be expected."

"I would say he is a mite addled," Saxon Carver observed bluntly.

Anger flushed Aramo's face briefly, and then he looked away. "He is the soul . . . the will of Cuba. Without him we are nothing. There would be no resistance, not the smallest of desires to fight against the Spaniards."

Carver wagged his head. "Your people hang their hopes on smoke. The Spanish have this island in their pocket. They will not give it up."

That could be true, Cain Ruby thought. *It takes steel and powder and lead . . . and a lot of men to win a war. Ideals alone have never yet done the job.*

IX

Despite the primitive accommodations Cain Ruby slept well. An active man, tough in both body and mind, he was accustomed to taking his rest when and where he found it expedient. Rising shortly before dawn, he made his way to the fire and helped himself to a gourd full of still lukewarm coffee. Moments later he was joined by Gavin Girard, Carver, and Ramiro Aramo. And then, finally, the entire camp was awake with the two women going about the task of preparing breakfast.

Peréz-Rosario, tall, remote, ate his meal in absolute silence, and then settled himself on the log to discuss the business at hand. "You would hear of the Montaña Sangre," he said. "I shall tell you."

Cain Ruby smoothed a small area in the soft soil and selected a sharp twig. "It is necessary that I know where the guards are stationed. Also the arrangements of the gates and where is stored the ammunition."

Annette crossed nearby at that moment, touched him with her glance. She looked weary, as though she had not rested well. Perhaps she had done some thinking during the night—possibly had changed her mind about returning to New Orleans with him. He hoped so. He disliked the thought of forcing her.

"In the beginning," Peréz-Rosario intoned, "there was a mountain. A small one and nothing like those in Oriente Province where the Pico del Tarquini thrusts its head high into the clouds . . . but a mountain, nevertheless. The Spaniards decided a fort should there be built . . . one to which the soldiers could retire, if ever Havana, the key to the island, were invaded by a strong army. It should have sufficient strength, they said, to withstand a determined siege and hold out forever if need be."

Cain Ruby stirred impatiently. He caught Girard's eye, saw him smile, shrug. Peréz-Rosario was a man from whom words flowed fluently—and endlessly. The detailing of the Montaña Sangre was destined to consume considerable time. Cain sighed quietly, sank back.

"So the small mountain was chosen. First a square one hundred and fifty meters in length of sides was marked. Upon those lines were erected walls four meters in height, two in thickness. Such were built of rock carried on the backs of Cuban men driven to labor. Later cactus and thorn bushes were planted along the base."

Ruby, now listening carefully, traced a square on the smooth surface he had prepared.

"Thus the walls are now complete. At a distance no greater than five meters inside the walls a fence was erected. It is of logs, sharpened at the tips, which were hardened by fire. It was the thought that an enemy able to breach the outer walls by unforeseen strategy would find himself trapped between the two high barriers and discover himself at the mercy of the defenders. Meanwhile, as the walls and fence were being built, other men hollowed out the mountain, shoring the sides with stone and wood, creating a large underground room. Here ammunition, food, equipment, and all such supplies would be stored. It is as a circle within the square, *señor,* with the sides touching at four points."

Cain inscribed the circle. The powder magazine was there, below ground. That was usual. The problem would be gaining entrance.

"Where are the gates?"

"There is but one in the walls . . . to the north side and in center," Peréz-Rosario said. "The fence has two, one a short distance from the main gate, the other across the compound, opposite."

Ruby made these additions to his map.

"When the underground room was completed, quarters for the soldiers were built. These are of wood and in the shape of low-roofed halls. Other structures were also erected such as stables, kennels, prisons, dining rooms, and sentry huts."

"These stand above the underground room?"

"They cover the area."

The Montaña Sangre was made for destruction, Cain Ruby thought. *All I need to do is place a charge of explosive in the magazine. It will set off the stores of gunpowder and blow the fort to hell.* "During the night . . . where are the sentries?" he asked.

"Two men guard the main gate. Also on the catwalk that was built inside the wall there will be others who pace back and forth."

Cain studied the lines he had drawn in the soil. The details of the fort were well established in his mind. He erased the marks with the tips of his fingers. "How may the underground chamber be entered?"

"There are many doors. Perhaps one most suited to you is within a small hut twenty meters or less inside the main gate. Thus you will find it unnecessary to go deeply into the fort. An entry way in the south wall of the hut opens into a tunnel, leading underground. The hut serves also as quarters for the sergeant of the guard."

"Will many men be inside the hut? Do you know this?"

"Only one, possibly two. Also there are dogs. The Spaniards use the animals for hunting Cubans as they do with escaping slaves."

Cain Ruby did some rapid calculating. "Therefore, it can be expected that we will encounter six or perhaps eight guards."

"And a few dogs," Girard drawled.

Peréz-Rosario nodded. "There are also patrols who police the area. They are engaged mostly in the preservation of order among the soldiers, however, and are not involved in routine guard duty."

"Are the gates locked at night?"

"To be sure. It is closed with the coming of darkness and barred. That one in the fence I cannot say. My thought is that it is not. It serves more for emergency purposes."

"The main gate will be the problem," Cain Ruby said, more to himself than the others. "A man will have to go over the top, let himself down, and get rid of the guards. Only then can he open it. . . ."

"And there'll be soldiers walking the catwalk," Girard reminded.

"Not much to worry about there. Men on sentry duty generally walk a specified distance. In this case each one probably marches from his corner to the center of the wall, reverses and goes back. We'd pick the moment after they'd turned, then make our move."

"Do you discuss something the nature of which I may be of service in solving?" Peréz-Rosario asked.

Cain realized he had been speaking in English. He smiled, said: "Your pardon, *señor*. We do not intend to be impolite. We were considering the difficulties of the gate. The solution has been reached."

The Prophet said—"Very well."—and lapsed into silence.

Ruby tossed the twig he had been using as a marker into the fire and glanced around. Annette had finished whatever she had been doing in her lean-to, now stood behind Peréz-Rosario, listening. Margarita was sewing at a garment of some sort, using a bone needle and coarse white thread. Pablo was the only absent member.

"It is good," Cain said. "No more information will be necessary. I am obliged."

The aged Cuban leader lifted his head, shrugged. "It is a small thing to do for men so brave." He drew himself up-

177

right. Annette stepped to his side quickly. "I shall rest now," he said as the girl led him toward his shelter. "Awaken me if you have need."

Gavin Girard waited until the old man was inside his lean-to. Then: "Think it can be done, Cain?"

"Good chance. We'll go in during the early morning hours while it's still dark. One of us will go over the gate and open it."

"A job for me, *señor*," Aramo cut in eagerly.

Ruby frowned, studied the younger man. "Your job's to take us there . . . no more."

"But I wish to be of greater assistance."

"We leave one man at the gate," Cain Ruby continued, making no reply. "He can put on the guard's helmet so the sentries on the catwalk won't get suspicious. We cross over to the opening in the fence and do the same thing. I'll go on to the guard hut. Once I'm inside, it will be simple to take powder and fuse and go down into the magazine. I'll set the charge and get out fast. You and Carver will cover me until I'm in the clear."

"Sounds simple enough," Girard said.

"Big problem will be to keep it quiet . . . no noise or disturbance of any kind. Can't afford to attract other guards."

"If you will permit . . . ?" Aramo began hesitantly.

Cain turned inquiringly to the Cuban.

"Would it not be better for two men to enter the hut? It is not known for certain the number of sentries who will be in attendance. Also, there is the matter of dogs."

Ruby smiled. "This second man you mention, I assume, would be you?"

"It is my hope."

Cain Ruby considered the suggestion. After a moment he smiled again. "It is agreed, Ramiro. You will be with me."

178

Carver got to his feet, stretched, yawned. "When do we pull out?"

To Aramo, Cain said: "How far to the fort from here?"

"Three hours at most."

"We'll leave at midnight," Ruby said.

X

Cain Ruby turned to the clearing. It lay hot and silent in the mid-morning sunlight. He could hear Margarita, reading to Peréz-Rosario in his shelter, her voice little more than a low murmur. Far to the south a gun boomed; one of the warships firing a cannon for some reason, he guessed, and had a moment's wonder as to Narciso Lopez.

Annette came from her lean-to. She carried a small basket under her arm and, not looking at him, headed into the jungle. Cain gave her full consideration and then on impulse followed. She glanced up as he drew alongside. He smiled, shook his head, and they continued on.

Shortly, she halted before a dense stand of tall pipestem cacti, sank to her knees, and began to probe about in the shadow of the sweet-smelling night bloomer.

"This the way you keep up your food supply?" he asked, hoping to break down her cool reserve.

"I'm looking for *cobrizos*," she replied stiffly.

"*¿Cobrizos?*"

"A small herb. Pounded into pulp and mixed with fat, it makes a good salve for wounds."

"Don't you ever get any real medicine?"

"There was a little at the start. It didn't last long. The native remedies are all right."

179

"It's a hard way to live," he said.

"Perhaps. But it has its rewards."

She found the plant for which she looked, began to dig away the moist earth that imprisoned it. Cain studied her intent features, noted the way her dark hair hung about her neck and cheeks. A portion of one ear was exposed, and the line of her jaw was softly curved—yet firm and stubborn.

"About yesterday," he began hesitantly, "expect I said some things I shouldn't. If you feel you have an apology due, I'm offering it now."

She paused, looked up at him. "And you are a man who does not apologize often. I should be flattered."

The irony of her words stirred him slightly. "Have it your way," he said curtly. "It doesn't change things. You're still going back to New Orleans with me."

Annette resumed her digging. "It's too hot to quarrel," she murmured.

"It's for your own good," he continued. "I think you overestimate your duty here. I don't mean the necessity for it. This revolution's been going on for centuries. Probably will continue for a few more."

"The suffering will also continue."

"And you think you ought to shoulder the needs of all of those who get hurt. That's wrong. Don't you realize you have other obligations . . . obligations to your father . . . to yourself?"

"Obligations are something you owe someone who deserves . . . and wants them," Annette said quietly. She picked up one of the tubers, brushed soil from it, and dropped it into the basket. "As for myself, I have answered that before. I have a life of usefulness here."

"Meaning such is not true in New Orleans?"

"Not in any way that matters. You should understand

that, but, being a man, I guess you can't. You take the world for granted. You do what you wish, when you wish."

"I do the things expected of me, and that I find necessary."

"That's what I mean. Here on the island I am given the same privilege. In New Orleans . . . or anywhere else on the mainland . . . such isn't possible because I am a woman. There I must do only those things approved by society."

"Possibly, but this is no life for you. Someday the Spaniards will catch up with Peréz-Rosario. It will mean death. Worse for you."

"And you may be killed tonight at the Montaña Sangre, yet no one denies you the right to take the risk."

"It's entirely different."

"Different?" she echoed scornfully. "That's a man's usual reply when he can find no honest answer. Why is it different? Haven't I the right to convictions, too? Why is it you may believe in something and I cannot?"

He stirred, ill at ease and slightly angered. "Anybody's a fool to believe in hopeless causes."

"Why are you here?"

"Money . . . and nothing else," he said bluntly. "For the cash I'll collect when I've done a job."

Her eyes registered vague shock. For a long moment she stared at him, and then finally looked away. "Yours must be a lonely world," she said. "But to live in it is your right. I prefer my own here on the island where I can follow a hopeless cause . . . as you term it."

Temper claimed Cain Ruby abruptly. "God's uncle, girl!" he shouted. "What's the matter with you? Can't you see you're making a mistake?"

"It's no mistake," she said calmly, resuming her digging. "Our ideals are poles apart, and, if we argued until doomsday, we could never reconcile them. Now . . . I must work."

Ruby wheeled, strode back to the clearing. Aramo met him. The two Cubans had returned, departed again. They had obtained a small amount of gunpowder—not much but enough to work with. They had also provided a short length of fuse. The curtain was down on Peréz-Rosario's lean-to, and Margarita was making preparations for the noon meal. Girard and Saxon Carver lolled in the shade. Beckoning to Aramo, Cain Ruby crossed to where they lay.

"Want to get things settled," he said in a quick, clipped way. His conversation with Annette had turned him edgy. The three men hunched before him. "Tonight I'll handle the gunpowder. Ramiro, you will be with me. Girard will stand at the main gate. Leaves the fence gate to you, Carver. Understood?"

Carver and Girard nodded. Ruby turned to the Cuban. Ramiro was frowning.

"You don't have to do it," Cain Ruby said. "Now's the time to make up your mind."

"It is not that I wish to change, *señor*," Aramo said hurriedly. "It is only that you speak the English words so fast I cannot understand!"

Ruby's manner softened. "Doesn't matter. If you wish to be with us, you need only to do what is told you by me."

He then reviewed carefully the proposed operation from the beginning, discussing all phases, the job expected of each man, the time element, the chances for errors and slip-ups. When he concluded an hour later, there were no uncertainties. Only unexpected contingencies could upset the scheme—and against such he would take all possible precautions.

Shortly after the noon meal Pablo Quintana entered the

clearing. He brought with him three men. Word of Lopez's coming had been passed on to several others who had chanced by, Pablo told Peréz-Rosario, and these were carrying the news on to the west. There were quite a number of men hiding in that area, rumor said.

"Is there any estimate of how many men can be expected?" Cain asked Quintana.

"*¿Quién sabe?*" Pablo replied with a shrug of his great shoulders. "Perhaps ten, perhaps hundreds. They are scattered because of the *asesinos*."

It won't matter, Cain thought. *If I can destroy the fort, along with its supplies and the men who will be inside sleeping, I'll be helping Lopez more than any rag-tag Cuban army ever can. With a little luck I should be able to wipe out about half the Spanish forces.*

He strolled off toward the stream, deciding a few hours' rest should be next in order for him, if he were to be in fit condition for the night's work. It was some cooler by the water, and he would be a distance away from the camp and the flow of conversations that were taking place. He glanced at Annette as he moved by, saw her raise her eyes, grave and thoughtful, to him. But she said nothing, and he maintained his own close reserve.

He found a grassy spot and stretched out. Again he went over the plans for the destruction of the Montaña Sangre, looking for anything that could bring disaster. He could discover no flaws, but he was not deceiving himself; he had laid down a hard and fast scheme on the basis of second-hand information. It could be things were different from what Peréz-Rosario had outlined. If so, changes would have to be made, but he would not worry about that now—but later, when the time came.

XI

When Cain awakened, it was almost sundown. He could hear Pablo Quintana's voice, excited and urgent, coming from the camp. Instinctively he felt for his pistol. Assured of its presence, he arose, quickly crossed to the clearing. Everyone was moving about hurriedly. A stranger was speaking to Peréz-Rosario. Cain Ruby stepped from the brush, question in his eyes.

Quintana whirled to him. "Make haste, *inglés!* The soldiers come!"

Annette was at the thatched shelters. In swift, competent motions she yanked the curtains free. Spreading them on the ground, she began to pile on the possessions that must be saved. Margarita was assisting Peréz-Rosario. Elsewhere Aramo, Carver, and Gavin Girard were doing their bit.

Pablo Quintana placed his foot against the kettle, capsized it, extinguishing the fire. Wheeling, he said something to the man who had brought the warning. The elderly Cuban hurried off into the jungle, apparently to watch for the oncoming soldiers. Everything in the clearing was motion, yet there was no confusion. It was evident the little group of patriots had been through the experience many times before.

"Is it Maspera?" Cain Ruby asked, touching Pablo's muscular forearm.

"A patrol of regular soldiers. If you would help, see to the women. Time is short."

Ruby wheeled to Annette. She was in need of no assistance. Two sacks had been made of the canvas squares. Annette now had thrown one across her shoulder. Margarita had taken up the other.

"Where will they go?" Cain asked Aramo.

Annette threw him a sharp glance as if to warn him of

184

the futility of entertaining any further consideration of her return to New Orleans. He ignored the look.

"Only Pablo will know. Perhaps he cannot say for certain. It will be necessary to lose the Spaniards. He may try many places."

"Go! Go!" Quintana's insistent, low breath commands broke across the clearing. "We must make haste!" He seized the kettle by the bail, swung it to his side. Steam issued in thick vapors from its interior, but he seemed not to notice that it was still hot.

"Where will you take them?" Cain Ruby asked, again touching the Cuban's arm. There was a faint note of anger in his voice.

Quintana said: "To the place of the falling water. I have no time to describe directions, *inglés*. Ramiro knows of it. He can bring you there." The burly giant whirled away. "Let us go, my little chickens . . . the jackals nip at our heels."

Annette and Margarita, each carrying a bag and supporting Peréz-Rosario between them, started across the clearing after Pablo. Halfway the island prophet turned. "God be with you, my friends," he called back. "May He give you strength to pull down the walls of infamy."

Beyond the camp Pablo's voice pleaded from the jungle. "Come . . . come . . . we must hurry. There is no time for talk."

Cain Ruby watched the women guide Peréz-Rosario into the concealing brush. In the abrupt silence that descended upon the clearing, he turned to his men.

"We, too, are ready," Ramiro said, anticipating Cain's question. "Let us depart. The Spaniards. . . ."

"Take the shortest trail to the fort," Ruby cut in brusquely. "I want to finish the job and get the hell out of this country."

185

The Cuban gave him a puzzled glance, then turned and struck off into the sultry twilight. They marched steadily, relying entirely upon Aramo's sense of direction. Now and then birds, settling down for the night, skittered out from under their feet, winged off into the jungle. Once a cavy darted across the trail near Carver, jarring a curse from the man's lips and sending his hand streaking for the revolver at his hip.

They were jumpy, Cain Ruby realized, and he did not like it. The sudden approach of the soldiers, the hurried dismantling of the camp, and the subsequent flight into the forest of Peréz-Rosario had shaken them. To know danger was always so near, death so imminent, set a man to thinking. Had not the old man, passing through the jungle, accidentally noticed the Spaniards and rushed to warn Pablo, likely all would be dead at that moment, or on their way to the torture chambers of the Montaña Sangre.

Ruby pushed up past Carver and Girard to Aramo's shoulder. "There is no need now for haste. We are far from the clearing."

Ramiro slackened his pace. Some of the rigidity faded from his body. "It is so," he said. "We shall have time in the darkness. It was only that my hatred burned so fiercely as I thought of the soldiers . . . and *El Profeta* and those with him scurrying into the jungle as frightened fowls."

"They will be safe. Pablo can handle the Spaniards."

"Even the lion sometimes fails," Aramo said. He shook his head, and Cain saw the Cuban's hands tighten into hard fists. "I pray the day is not distant when my people will never again be forced to hide from any man!"

"Such a day could be nearer than you think," Cain Ruby replied. "You have brought the things we will need?"

It was a means of changing the subject, an attempt to

still the boiling currents flowing through the young Cuban. He could see the bag of gunpowder hanging at Ramiro's waist.

"Yes. The exploding powder is here," Aramo said, touching the sack. "Also inside there is fuse and a quantity of lucifers wrapped in oilskin."

"Good. If rain comes, place the bag inside your shirt. It must not get wet." Ruby dropped back to Saxon Carver. He pointed to the man's revolver. "You're a little quick reaching for that thing."

Carver shrugged. "Damn' rabbit . . . I almost. . . ."

"Forget you've got it. Job calls for quiet. If you have to use anything, use that knife you've been keening."

Carver's lips pulled into a half smile. "Expect I'll do as I please."

"You'll do what I tell you," Cain Ruby snapped.

"All depends."

"Meaning what?"

The smile had faded from Saxon Carver's lips. "That I'm not sticking my neck out no more than makes good sense. You're the bucko who's getting paid big money for this job. I'm here to see that it's done."

"You're here to help . . . same as I am," Gavin Girard said, coming into the conversation.

Cain Ruby said—"Aramo."—and pulled to a stop. He faced Carver. "You want out?" he demanded, anger threading his tone. *If this bastard's going to be a problem,* Ruby thought, *I'm dumping him here and now. I've had all the trouble I can swallow. All the setbacks I aim to take. Three of us can do this job . . . Girard, Aramo, and me. Three are all I figured on in the first place.*

"Never said that," Carver murmured. "Just don't like somebody riding me."

"If you figure it that way . . . pull out . . . turn back right now. I don't need you."

Carver's head came up quickly. "I'll stay," he said. "Don't pay no mind to me."

"You'll stay," Cain Ruby said, "if you take orders and do what you're told. Agreed?"

"Agreed," Carver mumbled.

Ruby motioned to Ramiro Aramo, and they moved on. Around them the jungle was in complete silence, filled with deep pockets of darkness where pale starlight failed to touch. Somewhere a dog barked, the sound hollow and somehow one of loneliness.

"*¿Señor?*"

At Aramo's low whisper Cain Ruby brought himself back to the moment. He moved to the side of the young Cuban.

"We are there," Ramiro said, pointing.

Ruby followed his leveled finger. The forbidding bulk of the Montaña Sangre loomed before them.

XII

Peréz-Rosario had described it well. Rising from the mountain's slope, it appeared squat and ugly in the half light, a massive, monstrous barricade of threatening mien at the base of which a broad band of impenetrable cacti and bristling thorn bushes grew in close conjunction. As Ruby had been told, there was no entry except by the gates.

"They are to the right," Ramiro Aramo said in response to Cain's question.

The Cuban moved off silently, leading them deeply into the fringe of brush which bordered the cleared area on all sides. Their first test would be the crossing of that barren fifty-foot-wide strip. They halted opposite the gates. They were the same height as the walls, a heavy double affair swinging in to the center. They were shut. The fort was in darkness, insofar as they could determine, and entirely quiet. Motion at the two corners visible to them and a distance along the walls marked the assigned beats of the sentries as they paced to and fro on the catwalk.

"Drop back," Cain Ruby said, finally satisfied with what he could see. "We'll hold off until the sentry is almost to the gate, then run for it."

"How about the guard on the adjoining wall?" Gavin Girard wondered.

"Corner will block his view."

They retraced their steps through the brush to a more practical position. Watching the sentry, they delayed until he had halted, pivoted, and started his return to the gates.

"Now," Ruby said, and sprinted across the open ground.

Breathing hard, they gained the shadows lying along the very edge of the thorny growth. Pausing only a moment, they began working their way toward the gates. Halfway they heard the sentry on his return trip. Only his helmeted head was visible to them as he mechanically trod the catwalk.

When they came to the end of the brush, they stopped. The gates reared before them. Cain studied the high, pointed logs. Scaling the high panels would have to be done quickly. It must be accomplished during the moments when the men on the platform had wheeled and were marching to their corners. Most particularly, it all had to be carried out quietly and in such a manner that the guard, or guards, standing inside would hear nothing.

"I'll go over," Girard murmured, pulling off his boots.

Aramo's features mirrored his disappointment. He started to speak, but Ruby silenced him with a wave of his hand. Gavin would be better for this particular job.

"Ready," Girard whispered into the warm darkness.

Ruby nodded. "If there's two guards . . . signal. I'll come up, and we'll go over together." He listened into the night. "Sentries are coming back . . . when they turn, up you go."

They pressed against the gates, scarcely breathing. Cain put an ear to the tightly fit logs; he could hear nothing. It was possible there would be no inner guards, that only the ones on the catwalk were on duty. He rode out the moments, marking the measured tread of the soldiers on the platform. The thud of heels ceased almost in unison. There was a slight scraping sound, and then again the regular strike as the guards began their retreat.

Ruby and Saxon Carver rose quickly. They locked their hands together, formed a step. Girard placed his foot upon it, reached upward, pulled himself to the top. Drawing his body parallel, he clung there.

"Nobody below," he whispered, and dropped from sight.

Cain took a deep breath. Luck was with them. This might mean other things were different, too, however. Peréz-Rosario could have been wrong—and changes may have taken place. He shrugged. It was too late to worry about it now. He would simply have to meet problems as they arose.

The gates separated in the center a narrow distance. One by one they slipped inside, froze. The rap of the approaching sentries sounded uncomfortably near. Cain glanced up. The catwalk upon which the soldiers trod was only an arm's length above.

Gavin Girard took his boots from Ruby, drew them on. He pointed at the guards, now pivoting, whispered: "We get rid of them?"

Ruby said: "No . . . men farther down might get suspicious. Won't be hard to stay out of their view. Keep the gates closed . . . but don't drop the bar."

Cain Ruby was eyeing the opening in the inside fence, thirty or forty feet to their right. It was offset and did not directly face the main entrance. No guard was in evidence. " 'Luck," he heard Gavin murmur, and, turning, he saw the man grin at him. Nodding, Ruby motioned to Aramo and Saxon Carver, and together they crossed the alley-like area between the two barricades and reached the inner gate. It was open, propped wide by slanted stakes driven into the ground, and unattended.

"Your post," Cain said to Carver. He pointed to a nearby hut. "Keep your eye on that . . . it's where we'll be. If we run into trouble, come fast."

Peréz-Rosario had been right about where the guard's quarters were. They were exactly where he had said they would be. A lamp burned inside, and Cain could see the shadow of a man's bowed head against the rear wall. The sergeant of the guard, no doubt—and apparently asleep. There was no positive indication that he was alone.

Elsewhere in the sprawling fort all was quiet. Cain glanced at Aramo, crouched beside him. The skin on the young Cuban's face was stretched taut, and his eyes held a hard glitter. "Come," Ruby murmured, and moved off along the fence.

There was no danger now of being seen by the men on the catwalk; the high poles protected them from view on that side. They needed only to keep their attention on the hut and on the narrow street that apparently circled the camp itself. Likely there would be guards patrolling it and the similar avenues that criss-crossed the area in which the barracks and other structures lay.

They reached a position directly opposite the building. Ruby halted, motioned for Aramo to remain. Low to the ground, he hurried to the side of the hut. Crowding up close, he listened. He could hear the rasp of deep breathing. Working his way to one of the open windows, he peered in. There were two guards. One lay stretched on a bench; the other, whose shadow Cain had noted upon the wall, was slumped in a chair, head dropped forward on his chest.

Ruby signaled Aramo. The Cuban came immediately, and they eased their way along the side of the hut to its entrance. The door was open to any breeze that might pass, and they entered silently. Cain pointed to the soldier on the bench and turned toward the one in the chair.

At that precise instant the man came awake. He saw Cain Ruby before him. His eyes widened in surprise, and he lunged to his feet. Knife in hand, Cain closed with him, aware that he must prevent any outcry. He thrust hard, felt the guard wilt, heard his soft moan. Holding onto the man, Ruby lowered him into the chair. He spun to Aramo. The Cuban was sliding his blade into its sheath. The guard on the bench had not moved. The only change was the dark stain spreading over his chest. Ruby stepped to the window and glanced out. The sentries paced their weary beat on the catwalk; the fort was still a dark, hushed void.

Turning, he reached for the bag of gunpowder hanging from Aramo's waist. The young Cuban drew back, appeal in his eyes. Impatient, Cain said: "All right. Get at it."

Ramiro brushed past him hurriedly, opened the door in the rear wall. A dark passageway slanted downward. Cain halted the Cuban with a whisper, handed him one of the lamps that stood on a table. Ramiro nodded and with the explosive in his left hand, the light in his right, started for the depths of the underground chamber.

Ruby dropped back to the window. Because of the buildings to the south of the hut, a full view of the fort was impossible, and he could see only that area which lay between the structures and the fence. All seemed quiet and in order. The sentries were in their positions, and he could hear no sounds of anyone on the streets.

From the tunnel came faint noises as Ramiro put things in readiness. The plan was to open at least one keg of gunpowder—more, if there was time—and spread its contents about thickly. Such would heighten the immediate explosion and spread the fire. Aramo would follow that idea. But it was taking time—too much time. Ruby stepped to the inner door. "Hurry," he called in a hoarse whisper.

The Cuban's reply was not intelligible. Cain resumed his post at the window. So far it had been easy, and that, somehow, disturbed him. It was inconceivable that with all the unrest on the island, the Montaña Sangre would be so inadequately guarded.

A pistol shot echoed through the night. Cain leaped to the door, glanced out. The sound seemed to have come from the main gate. Immediately shouts lifted. Ruby whirled to the tunnel.

"Ramiro!" he yelled, and rushed back to the door. Shadows were converging on the hut. He could hear the pound of running men.

"*¡Alerta! ¡Alerta!*" a voice cried through the darkness.

Aramo appeared. The sack of gunpowder still hung at his waist. There had been no chance to use it. Ruby swore—but there was no time left.

"Something's gone wrong," he said. "Got to get out of here."

He plunged through the doorway into the open, the Cuban at his heels. Immediately a man shouted—"*¡Aqui!*

¡Aqui!"—from the shadows alongside the hut. Cain Ruby whirled, saw the crouched figure of a soldier, and then braced himself to meet a dog leaping for his throat.

XIII

Cain threw up his arm. He met the snarling brute with his knife, thrusting it deep and hard into the writhing body. He felt razor-sharp teeth graze his wrist, heard the brittle clack of powerful jaws snapping together. He was aware of two soldiers rushing in, of Ramiro Aramo hurling himself at both. A musket discharged, the deafening blast adding to the confusion. He shook free of the dog, whirled to aid the Cuban.

He saw a man break clear, struggling to bring his long-barreled weapon into play. Cain leaped, caught him around the waist, and bore him to the ground in a threshing tangle. Wrenching his right arm from beneath the squirming soldier, he drove his blade into the man. He struck again and, as the Spaniard's muscles went slack, rolled to his feet. Over to their left dogs barked frantically, and men shouted questions into the darkness as they drew nearer. Ruby flung a glance toward the fence—where the hell was Saxon Carver? He spun about. Aramo, knife glittering dully, stood over a prostrate soldier.

"Come on," Cain Ruby hissed, and raced across the open ground to the shadow of the fence.

They halted. Ruby looked back at the hut. The Spaniards were almost to it. "Carver!" he called in a hoarse whisper.

There was no response. Ruby and the Cuban, bent low, rushed for the opening in the fence. Reaching it, they again paused. There was still no sign of Carver. Cain Ruby swore savagely. The man had run out on them. Most likely that was what the shooting had been about.

Motioning to Aramo, Cain moved on to the opening and looked toward the main gate. The two sentries were standing at the edge of the catwalk, staring in the direction of the hut. Ruby took careful aim at the one to his left, squeezed off a shot. The man buckled, fell heavily. The other yelled, started to back off along the platform. Cain dropped him with a second bullet from his revolver.

Behind them, on the opposite side of the fence, Cain heard a fresh burst of shouting. The soldiers, attracted by the gunshots, had changed course. He waited no longer. With Ramiro at his side, he broke from the darkness along the fence, ran for the gates, standing slightly ajar. At least, Girard had not failed. He had everything in readiness.

They gained the log panels. At that instant Cain Ruby saw the figure of a man, lying close against the rocks. He frowned, swerved aside. Dropping to his knees, he rolled the man over. It was Gavin.

Girard's eyes opened. He managed a grin. "Glad you . . . made it."

Cain raised Girard to a sitting position, supporting him with his arm. He looked down at the blood-soaked front of his friend's shirt. The sound of the approaching soldiers had grown in volume. They were only moments away. "Got to get you out of here," he said. "Spaniards."

"I will halt them," Aramo said, and hurried off into the night.

Ruby gathered Girard into his arms, rose to his feet. Standing the wounded man upright, holding him to prevent his falling, Cain twisted about, took Girard onto his back, and started for the jungle at an unsteady run.

"No . . . use . . . ," Gavin protested weakly. "Carver got me . . . good."

Cain slowed, not certain he had heard correctly. "Carver?"

"Carver . . . warned the Spaniards . . . working with them . . . he . . . and Clinton . . . put his knife . . . in me. I shot . . . missed."

There was a roar and flash of an explosion back at the gates. Ruby, startled at first, realized then what Ramiro Aramo had meant. He had halted the oncoming soldiers with the bag of gunpowder. It would only do minor damage to the wall, but it would delay pursuit for a few precious minutes. The young Cuban came running up.

"I will help," he said, extending his hands.

Ruby shook him off, and they plunged on through the darkness, Cain staggering across the uneven ground with his burden as he struggled to reach the safety of the jungle. Aramo hung back, glancing now and then toward the fort, alert for the first soldiers to break through the smoke and dust.

They reached the brush, ducked into it. Aramo caught up to Cain Ruby. "I will stay, lead them in a different direction."

"Forget it," Cain said, breathless and angry. "Get us somewhere out of sight."

The hammering in Cain Ruby's heart came not only from the physical strain he was undergoing but from what Girard had told him as well. Saxon Carver had betrayed them—sold them out. He had been in league with the Spaniards all along—had come on the mission, not to aid in its success as he professed, but to ensure its failure. It all added up now. Clinton and Carver, heavily involved in some manner with the Spaniards, did not want to see the crown overthrown. They had fooled everyone, even the other members of the merchants' combine. "The black-souled bastard," he muttered bitterly. "Damn him to everlasting hell!"

"This way, *señor*," Ramiro Aramo's voice cut into his bleak thoughts. "It is a small stream. Walk with me in it. They will use the dogs, and we must take care to leave no trail."

Ruby followed the Cuban into the shallow water, stumbling over the smooth stones that lay beneath the surface. They continued for a good quarter hour, and then Aramo turned abruptly from it, led the way to a small hill thickly overgrown with cacti.

"Here we will be safe for a time." He stepped forward, slipped his arms under Gavin Girard's shoulders, and helped lower the man to the ground.

Girard groaned weakly. He saw Aramo, grinned. "*Hola, compadre* . . . it is good . . . you made . . . it."

"Never mind the talk," Ruby said harshly. "Save your wind. Soon as I patch you up, we'll head for camp."

"Yes, *señor*," Ramiro added. "Then all will be well. Anna has great skill with wounds."

Girard shook his head. "Don't josh me . . . I know where I stand. Carver . . . put his blade . . . in me . . . good."

"Carver!" Cain Ruby ground out the name as though it were an evil word. "I'll see him dead for this!"

Gavin winced as a spash of pain wracked him. He swallowed hard, said: "Cain . . . get word to my . . . father. Clinton . . . they've got to know . . . about him."

"They'll know," Ruby said, his jaw set. "I should have guessed. . . ."

"Cain . . . ?"

Ruby bent lower to catch the faltering words.

"My pistol . . . give it to . . . Ramiro. He . . . can use it."

"Sure."

"Tell . . . Peréz-Rosario that. . . ." Girard's voice faded. His body went slack, and whatever it was he intended for the Cuban patriarch to know was forever lost.

Ruby stared down into the man's blanched face for a long minute while hatred seared through him. From the tail of his eye he saw Aramo cross himself, wished he, too, might have a means for expressing his feelings. After a time he reached over, removed Gavin's revolver and pouch of bullets and powder, and handed them to the Cuban. "You heard him," he said, his throat tight. "Wanted you to have these."

Ramiro took the weapon, fondled it reverently. "I shall do credit to him, a good friend. That I swear."

They buried Gavin Girard on the hill, doing as good a job as they were able with no tools save their knives and bare hands. Before they had finished, the sounds of the Spaniards now searching the jungle came to them. They completed their task hurriedly and struck off at once, going deeper into the tangled growth. In only a short while daylight would break across the land, and it would be more difficult to hide from the soldiers.

"We will go to Peréz-Rosario's camp," Ruby said. "There must be new plans made. Pablo told me they would be at a place called the falling waters."

"I know of it. It is some kilometers from here."

"That is good. It is necessary that we use care. We do not want the Spaniards to follow us."

"Have no fear," the Cuban replied. After a moment he asked: "You will again try to destroy the Montaña Sangre?"

"I shall," Cain Ruby said, his voice firm. "It is now a thing that must be done at any cost."

It had turned into a personal matter, somehow. Perhaps it was because of Gavin Girard; it could be his hatred for Carver—or possibly it was something far larger than both; he was unsure which. He knew only that he must pull down the Montaña Sangre, that it was his enemy now—a living enemy. They would clash, and one or the other would survive.

Aramo nodded understandingly. "It is an anger that grasps a man forcefully, holds him tight. It now possesses you as it does many of us."

They pushed on, climbing into an area of low cliffs. Ruby caught the sound of rumbling water as it dashed against rocks, knew then the meaning of the term Pablo had used—a waterfall. They topped a rise.

Ramiro paused, said: "There is the place."

They moved down into a narrow ravine, again ascended a hill, and came out onto a narrow plateau. The first thing to greet their eyes was the lifeless body of Pablo Quintana, sprawled on the sand.

XIV

Cain Ruby reacted instinctively. He seized Aramo's arm, dragged him into the shelter of the nearby brush. "Have care! There may still be soldiers."

They peered through the foliage. Pablo's massive body was scarred with blade and bullet wounds, the blood from which had dried to a dark crust. Beyond him lay two soldiers—evidence of the desperate struggle in which he had engaged as he sought to protect his beloved *El Profeta* and the two women.

That thought stirred fresh worry in Ruby's mind. Where were they? What had happened to them? Ruby considered that grim question. No sounds came from the camp, a short distance to the left of where Pablo lay. He could see the tops of the lean-tos. They appeared undisturbed.

With Aramo crouched at his side, Cain rode out a long five minutes, and then he could wait no more. Rising, pistol in hand, he moved slowly toward the clearing. He drew abreast of Pablo, paused. Reaching down, he plucked the rapier from the dead man's stiff fingers. Unconsciously he tested the steel, checked the balance. It was a fine blade—and it had belonged to a good man. Keeping the weapon, he continued on, hearing a small note of grief slip from Ramiro's throat as he knelt briefly beside Quintana. There were no other sounds in the stifling silence. Even the birds were hushed. It was a deserted camp.

Nothing had been touched. Cain saw the worn, leather-bound book from which Margarita often read to her father. The pallets were spread smoothly in the shelters; two or three simple articles of clothing hung from the brush where they had been put to dry. Annette's pitiful supply of concocted medicines was in her lean-to. He noticed a shawl, the blackened kettle with its long-handled spoon. Everything was there, in its place. The camp was complete—except there was no sign of life.

"It is possible they hide in the jungle," Aramo said hopefully.

"I think not," Ruby replied soberly. "Pablo has been dead for many hours. By this time they would have returned and taken their possessions." He stared off into the dense green beyond the clearing. "They are captives," he said finally.

The Cuban sighed heavily. "I fear it is so."

Immediately Cain Ruby started for the edge of the jungle. "There will be a trail," he said. "A sign of sorts."

They began to skirt the fringe of rank growth, examining the ground, the shrubbery. Almost at once Ramiro sent up a low summons. "Here . . . blood is on the leaves."

Ruby hurried to the Cuban. The evidence was plain. Someone wounded had brushed against the waxed foliage of a coral bush.

"An injured person." Aramo said. "A soldier who escaped death at the hands of Pablo but was sorely wounded."

"Perhaps. It could be Peréz-Rosario . . . even Annette or Margarita."

"Such I would doubt," Ramiro said, shaking his head. "They will wish to preserve the women for their own use. And *El Profeta* will be saved for torture."

Cain Ruby glanced ahead, pushing aside the clamoring apprehension that gripped him. His eyes picked up a second dark smear. Hurrying forward, he looked more closely. "This is the way," he said, and moved on.

Aramo was quickly at his shoulder, and together they began the search, following the path left by the soldiers and their prisoners. A broken branch. Low plants trampled underfoot. Another blood stain.

"They do not go to the Montaña Sangre," Ruby said, noting the direction taken. "Where will this lead?"

Aramo shrugged. "There are many camps. It is a way of holding the people in control."

They lost the trail a short time later, spent a full half hour probing about. Aramo located it finally—another dribbling of blood—and they pressed on.

"The wounded one forces them to travel slowly," he said. "Soon we will overtake them."

Cain Ruby was silent. The memory of Cabezón and the

horror wrought by the soldiers were again filling his mind. He recoiled inwardly at the thought of Annette, of Margarita, being subjected to such barbarity. He quickened his step, rushed on. Aramo, hard put to keep up, tugged at his arm.

"¡Señor! So great a hurry is not good . . . we shall lose the trail."

A man's deep shout broke the hush. It was followed by another's laugh. Cain Ruby halted abruptly. The sound had come from somewhere to their right. Ruby brushed at the sweat collecting on his forehead and trickling into his eyes. Silently he began to move forward.

Aramo, angling more to the side, hissed softly.

Cain turned to him.

"Here. They can be seen."

Ruby veered, joined Ramiro. Through a corridor-like opening in the forest he saw two soldiers. Their backs were to the trail. They were watching something in the brush. Cain suppressed an urge to shoot them where they stood. There could be more.

"It is no camp," Aramo whispered. "It is likely they would have marched this far after the attack . . . and now pause for rest."

Ruby's face was a bleak mask. Raising his pistol, he checked its loads. Taking it into his right hand, he tightened his grip about Pablo's rapier, held in his left.

"I shall strike from this side. You will circle about, come from the opposite."

Aramo frowned. "We do not know how many soldiers are there."

Cain Ruby swung to the Cuban. "Is it a matter of consequence?"

"No, it is not," Aramo said quickly. He glanced at the ornately scrolled weapon that had been Gavin Girard's. His slender fingers stroked the handle. "This time I am their equal. I am ready."

Ruby said: "Look for me at the edge of the clearing. When I can be seen, it will be the signal to begin the fight. Use the pistol but take care not to hit the women or Peréz-Rosario."

"It is understood," Aramo said. "Go with God, *señor*."

Cain moved silently into the brush. Shortly he reached the small clearing in which the Spaniards had halted. On his knees, he studied the camp. Five soldiers, one a sergeant, were in sight. Two were standing, the others sprawled nearby in the shade. Anxiously he searched farther. Relief flooded through him when he saw Annette. She sat off to one side, ankles and wrists bound securely. A short length of rope encircled her waist and was affixed to a small tree. She appeared unharmed. He frowned, continued his probing. Where were Margarita and Peréz-Rosario?

Three more soldiers strode into the clearing. One carried his helmet under his arm. Leaning their muskets against a low, bench-like shrub along with others, they sat down. The one with the bared head allowed his gaze to settle upon Annette.

"It is a misfortune that she must be saved for the captain," he said. "The little Cuban died under me."

Cain Ruby drew back stiffly. Margarita—poor, timid Margarita. The worst had befallen her. He stifled his anger, felt relief for Annette. At least, she had escaped a similar fate. She was being held for some captain. He wondered if they were speaking of Maspera.

The sergeant sat up. "I shall be glad when we are rid of her. She stirs the blood too much, and I am not a man with great will power. It is always that way with me when there is a French woman."

The soldiers laughed. A large, red-faced man with pointed beard and drooping mustache tugged at his ear. "Where the captain is concerned, I am careful to obey his orders with exactness. I would prefer to face alone a hundred of these howling Cubans and their machetes than the captain when he is angered!"

There was more laughter. The sergeant bobbed his head, said: "True! And most particularly when it is over a woman he has taken a fancy for!"

Cain Ruby, deadly calm, turned his attention to other matters. He must locate Peréz-Rosario. He must learn exactly where he was being held to avoid endangering him.

"You will not have to resist yourself much longer, Sergeant," one of those who had just entered the clearing said. "The captain and his men are not far distant. By this hour Santiago will have delivered the old blind one to the fort and given word to Maspera that we wait here with his tender pigeon."

So it was Maspera. Ruby knew he could delay no longer. At that moment the officer could be approaching the clearing—likely was, if the words of the soldier were accurate. One worry had lifted; others of the party had taken Peréz-Rosario on to the Montaña Sangre. There was only Annette to think of.

He drew himself to a crouch, glanced again at his pistol, and took a firmer grip on Quintana's rapier. He considered the soldiers. *Put my bullets into the men nearest the muskets,* he thought. *Maybe they'll fall into them, block the others. The sergeant's got a pistol. Take care of him next.*

Cain Ruby pulled himself upright. Unnoticed at the fringe of brush, he leveled his pistol at the man chosen to be the primary target. He pressed the trigger. The jungle resounded with the sharp blast. The soldier jolted from the bullet's impact, came half way to his feet, and stumbled into the muskets. A startled yell broke from the others. They leaped to their feet, looked wildly about. Ruby drew a bead on the sergeant, sent him sprawling across the first.

At that moment Ramiro Aramo burst from the screen of brush behind which he had hidden, revolver thundering. Ruby plunged into the open, ran the rapier through a man struggling to get to his musket. He jerked the blade free, wheeled, fired point-blank at a soldier slashing at him with a knife. A gun exploded close by, and he felt the breath of the ball as it plucked at his arm. He spun again, stabbing with the rapier. The soldier wilted, yelled, sank away. Across the clearing Aramo was a raging madman, his keen blade flashing in the sunlight, his pistol, empty now, a death-dealing cudgel. Two of the Spaniards were yet alive. On hands and knees they were crawling for the safety of the brush. Ramiro surged after them.

Cain turned, ran to Annette. He slashed the cords that bound her wrists and ankles, the rope that linked her to the tree. Her face was pale, drawn, but she managed a faint smile. Suddenly, overriding all other sounds, Ruby caught the hammer of oncoming horses. It would be Maspera, attracted by the shooting. He pulled Annette to her feet, shouted at Aramo.

"Hurry!"

Whirling, he raced for the edge of the clearing, dragging the girl behind him. They reached the brush, flung themselves into it. Cain could hear Aramo over to the side, crashing headlong through the dense undergrowth. The Cuban had gotten clear. Annette stumbled, fell. Wordless, he jerked her upright, rushed on.

XV

There was no time to choose a direction in which they could flee. There was no time to speak with Ramiro Aramo. There was only time to plunge blindly through the brush.

Behind them Maspera shouted commands. "Encircle! Encircle! Fan out and encircle! Fools . . . they are gone from here. Look to the jungle!"

Off to their left a horse galloped madly by, a reckless action over such difficult terrain. Cain could hear the soldier cursing. From the opposite side a yell went up. "This way! Here are signs of passage!"

Aramo, sweat glistening on his swarthy face, breath coming in deep gulps, swerved to join Annette and Cain Ruby. "There is a ravine . . . I will lead you."

Cain, holding tightly to the girl's hand, veered from his headlong course. Horsemen were moving in from both sides now, as well as up from the rear. Fortunately, the thick undergrowth was slowing them.

"Dismount! Search well beneath the bush!"

Maspera's voice was a harsh shaft slicing through the confusion. Ruby felt Annette dragging at his hand with every step. She could not continue the frantic flight through the clawing jungle much longer.

"How far?" he called hoarsely to Aramo, a dozen steps in front of them.

"A small distance," the Cuban replied, looking over his shoulder. His expression changed to one of alarm. "*Señor* . . . behind you!"

Ruby released Annette, whirled. A soldier, off his saddle, was unexpectedly near. Face tipped down, he was scanning the brush. He had not yet noticed them.

Cain pushed the girl toward Aramo, cut to one side.

"Keep going," he whispered. "I will catch up."

He dropped to a crouch, hiding himself in a stand of large, white flowers. Shifting his pistol to his left hand, he gripped Pablo's rapier in his right. He dare not risk a gunshot. The report would bring Maspera and the remainder of the *asesinos* down upon them instantly.

He shuttled a glance to Annette and Ramiro. They were almost gone from sight. He swung his attention back to the approaching Spaniard—no more than fifteen paces away. Tensely he waited in the heavily scented bush.

Ruby allowed the man to get little more than a stride from him, then rose upright. The soldier halted abruptly. His eyes flared with surprise, his mouth fell agape.

"*¡Madre de Dios!*" he exclaimed, and dragged out his saber.

Rapier poised, Cain Ruby lunged. The clash of the blades was loud, and he realized the sound would be heard. He parried, rushed the man, bore him back into the underbrush. The soldier swore again, drew a slim dagger from his belt. Lips parted in a hard grin, he bore in, slashing at Cain's belly. Ruby leaped away, escaping the razor-sharp weapon by only a breath.

The Spaniard continued to surge forward, pressing his advantage. Cain went to his heels. He saw the look of triumph rise in the man's eyes. He spun, checked, and with elbow stiff extended the rapier. The Spaniard, victim of his own momentum, impaled himself on the blade. He gasped in pain, sank to the ground.

Ruby wrenched the rapier clear, wheeled off into the high grass to his left. He could hear more soldiers advancing, moving in an orderly, closely spaced line. With a shock he saw they would intercept Annette and the Cuban, if they were permitted to continue. Deliberately, he drew his pistol and fired at the nearest. A yell lifted.

"This way! They go this way!"

Cain Ruby turned, headed off into an opposite course, heedless now of the racket he created, relying upon it, in fact, to draw the Spaniards away from the ravine for which the girl and Ramiro hurried. A hundred yards farther he halted. Maspera's men were in full chase. He grinned bleakly. All he need do now was to devise an escape for himself. He looked around. There was little concealment available except the brush itself—and no safety lay there. The soldiers, converging in almost shoulder-to-shoulder rank, would not bypass him. He moved on, now traveling as quietly as possible.

The twisted, vine-wrapped stump of a dead tree caught his attention. The tall hardwood had been snapped by one of the hurricanes that periodically lashed the island. The trunk had buckled near center and now formed a triangle with the ground beneath it. A broad-leafed parasite vine had taken over the skeleton and entirely clothed it in green.

Ruby reached it in quick strides. He threw a glance to his back trail. He could see none of the soldiers, but the noise of their coming was plain. He found secure footing on the stub of a shattered limb and hurriedly drew the leaves of the parasite about his body.

In only moments the Spaniards broke into view. Peering through his screen of foliage, Cain watched them work nearer, poking, probing, slashing at the bushes and other shrubbery. None was mounted, and their search was diligent. He caught their voices, listened to their comments. They were still convinced those they sought were yet ahead.

Scarcely breathing, Cain Ruby watched them move up to the base of the dead hardwood. They paused there briefly, finally continued on. Cain felt his taut muscles release. He caught himself abruptly as a second group of Spaniards appeared. It was Maspera and several of his officers. Deep anger rolled through Ruby as he remembered again the ravaged village of Cabezón, heard once more the cries of the helpless people.

"A fortnight's leave in Havana for the man who brings to me the French woman! A fortnight . . . and a month's extra pay!"

The Spaniard was directly below. Ruby got a better look at the man. Lean, arrogant, he had close-set eyes, cropped beard, and a thin-lipped mouth.

A cheer went up from the soldiers at their captain's offer. One of the men at Maspera's shoulder said something, and they all laughed.

Cain Ruby swore silently. It would be easy to drop from the tree, drive his blade into the Spaniard's heart—and rid Cuba of a criminal who scourged without pity and reason. Easy and simple—if there were not other things to consider. At that moment it was out of the question. There were still Lopez and the Montaña Sangre—but the day would come when he would call the officer to account just as he would Saxon Carver.

He watched the party pass on in wake of the searching soldiers. He remained on his perch until there was no doubt they had gone, and then climbed down from the tree. He wasted no time but turned his face toward the ravine. Finding the trail quickly, he soon reached the narrow cleft that Aramo had mentioned. It was thickly overgrown, and a small, shimmering stream cut a path along its rocky floor. There were no signs of Annette and the Cuban, but he knew they would be somewhere within the confines of the gash, watching for him.

After cooling his parched throat at the brook, he pushed

on. He had covered a short distance, when Aramo's hushed voice, coming from halfway up the right hand bank, halted him. "*Señor* . . . we are here."

Ruby swung immediately up the steep slope, found them waiting in a small cave. The relief Annette DuRique felt at his appearance was evident in her eyes. "We were beginning to worry," she said hesitantly.

Cain shrugged. "Had to lead them off. Things got a bit tight," he said, and let it drop there.

Aramo asked no questions, simply sat in silence. Cain Ruby regarded the girl. "About Margarita. From what I heard, I assume she is dead. Do you think so? If not, I'll go back."

"She's dead," Annette replied, holding herself very still. "The soldiers . . . carried her into the jungle. Later they joked. . . ."

"Never mind. Peréz-Rosario was taken to the fort?"

She nodded. "With a soldier Pablo wounded."

Cain considered that. It further complicated his plans for destroying the Montaña Sangre. The Cuban leader would first have to be rescued.

Annette said: "Ramiro told me about the failure. I'm sorry."

"And Girard?"

"Yes. I'm sorry about him, too, Cain."

He looked at her, surprised. She had never called him by his given name before. He liked it, and in it he thought he saw a softening in her attitude toward him.

"Will you try again?"

"Job's still got to be done."

"Because of General Lopez?"

"What else?" Ruby demanded, then added: "Well, maybe there are a few other reasons. Guess I could name a couple.

. . ." He stopped, stumbling uncertainly over words.

Aramo, his face solemn, leaned forward. "Perhaps for Pablo Quintana . . . and for Cuba and all like him who have died. It is no disgrace to love justice, to desire to avenge the cruel wrongs men have done."

Ruby shifted impatiently. "You sound much like Peréz-Rosario. To me it is a job for which I will be paid."

Aramo settled back. "I understand. What is it we must now do?"

"Leave here. Go to where I can find help . . . a half a dozen good men."

"What of exploding powder and fuse?"

"I will use the Spaniards'. You said there were many barrels in the magazine. What I have need of now are men."

Aramo thought for a minute. He nodded finally. "I know the place. The village of San Cristóbal. It has many *pacíficos* living there who will aid us."

"How far from here?"

"Three kilometers. No more."

"Good. Let us start."

Ramiro frowned, turned his eyes to Annette. "Would it not be wise to rest further?"

Cain Ruby said—"No."—in a quick, blunt way. He was thinking of the girl as well as his own need for haste. "Maspera is near. He will discover that he has overshot us and turn back in this direction. We should not be here." He glanced at Annette. "Can you travel?"

"I will keep up," she said.

XVI

Gaspar Rodriguez, he said his name was. He stared down from where they lay on the crest of a hill, overlooking San Cristóbal, and shook his head. "It has been such for seventeen days."

"A long time," Cain Ruby observed.

"A long time," the old man agreed.

"How, then, is it in the village?" Aramo asked.

"Food is scarce. Many suffer. And there is sickness. I fear the Spaniards shall have their way."

Ruby studied the cluster of poor huts. It all began, Rodriguez said, when a company of soldiers had marched into the village over two weeks past. The officer in command had demanded the surrender of the man, or men, responsible for the deaths of two of his soldiers. He had been respectfully refused. The Spaniards had then withdrawn, formed a tight ring around the settlement. They would remain there, the officer stated, and no one would be permitted to enter or leave the village until his demands were met—even if it meant starvation for every person in San Cristóbal.

It was becoming just that, a helpless village trapped in a circle of steel, slowly dying of want. Several men had attempted escape. They had been killed for their efforts. To make it more unjust, it was not known by the villagers who had killed the soldiers. Perhaps it was someone from another settlement. This was explained to the *comandante*, but he would not believe it. Many suspected that no soldiers had been murdered at all, that the Spaniards had trumped up the charge as an excuse for wiping out the village. Such would serve as a lesson to all *pacíficos* and an example to other villages who harbored them.

Cain thought over Rodriguez's story. "If no man can

leave the settlement, how is it you know all this?"

"A brave young girl brought the word. She pretended to give herself to one of the soldiers. He smuggled her through the line of sentries. She escaped him and ran to the village of Villareal where I was visiting with my daughter and her family."

"You are of San Cristóbal?"

"All of my life. I was born there. I hoped, also, to die there. It just happened I was in Villareal when the Spanish came."

Annette, silent through the conversation, now spoke. "Is there much sickness?"

"Yes, my lady. It grows worse, especially among the small ones."

Cain Ruby stirred irritably. The need to strike again at the Montaña Sangre was urgent. The day when Narciso Lopez and his army, backed by ex-Governor Quitman and Ambrosio Gonzales with their troops, would make a landing on the island was fast drawing near. Every effort must be made to cripple General Enna's forces before that moment arrived.

Now, balked in his hope to obtain help from the men of San Cristóbal, he faced more delay. And pushing on to another village would mean further loss of time. He turned to Rodriguez. "How many men are in your settlement?

"Twenty, I would say. Perhaps less."

Ramiro Aramo glanced at Ruby in surprise. "You think to go there, anyway? There are other places."

"Such would require time."

Aramo continued to stare at Cain Ruby. After a moment he smiled faintly, shifted his attention to Gaspar Rodriguez. "Old one, you have lived in San Cristóbal all your life. Is there not some way we can safely enter?"

The Cuban stroked his beard. He nodded. "There is a way," he said. "At the rear of the village stands a *precipicio*. The Spaniards keep no sentries at this point for there is no way up. It is very steep. But a man, with care, can descend. I must warn you, it is not possible to escape by such route, only to enter."

Ruby signified his understanding. "A problem to be faced, if such becomes necessary. However, I think it is likely we can break the ring of Spaniards."

Rodriguez's faded eyes brightened. "You will do this, *señor* . . . for San Cristóbal?"

"Not for San Cristóbal . . . for myself," Cain Ruby said gruffly.

Again Aramo smiled in that quiet, secret way. Rodriguez shrugged. "The reason does not matter. It is the doing of it that is of merit."

Eleven thousand dollars' worth of merit, Cain Ruby thought. *Besides, I can't let Peréz-Rosario die in the blast. The Cubans need their blind* El Profeta. "Before it is begun, there is a favor I would ask," he said, facing Rodriguez.

"You have but to ask."

"The lady with us . . . I wish her to be taken to a place of safety."

"No," Annette broke in quickly. "I'll be needed in the village."

"Can't let you endanger yourself. If this thing goes wrong. . . ."

Her eyes met his, locked. "We've been all through this. It is my decision to make . . . I will go."

He moved his hand despairingly. "Have it your way," he grumbled, and motioned to Rodriguez. "Lead us to the cliff. We have little time."

"It is not far," the old Cuban replied, worming his way

back from the crown of the hill. "We must circle wide to avoid the soldiers. Such will require no more than one hour. Follow, please."

They met no opposition during the brief journey. The Spaniards seemed content to hold their places in the ring they had thrown around the village. Ruby caught an occasional glimpse of them, once or twice heard their voices as he and his party threaded in and out of the brush.

The cliff would not be easy to descend. He saw that immediately when Rodriguez halted on its rim, and they looked down the forty-foot escarpment.

"In the days of my youth," Rodriguez said plaintively, "I entered many times by this means. It was a great adventure. Now I have misgivings. It appears no longer possible."

"Is there a path?" Ruby asked.

"No, but to your right by that large rock is where I made my way down."

Cain moved to that point, studied the almost vertical slope. It could be done. There were projecting bits of stone, a few tough shrubs that would afford ample, if precarious, footing, and, where there was barrenness, a man with a knife could gouge out footholds. "Is it possible for the Spaniards to see us?"

Rodriguez wagged his head. "Trees and brush hide the cliff from the village."

"Can we be heard?"

"That is a different matter. We must use care. The soldiers are no more than fifty meters to either side."

Cain Ruby nodded, moved to the edge. "I shall go first. The lady will follow. Then Rodriguez. Ramiro, you will come last."

He wanted to keep Annette close to him. In so doing, he could prevent her from falling, should she slip. Aramo, bringing up the rear, would serve as a lookout and give warning if any soldiers made an unexpected appearance below.

"No one will speak until we have descended," Cain said, and started down.

He clawed his way around the boulder, paused to let Annette catch up, and moved on. They had no difficulty until the mid-point was reached. There it became necessary to hollow out small cups in the sun-baked surface. He feared the sound of the digging and muffled it as best he could with his body. Finally it was done, and all passed safely to the next level. Numerous small shrubs studded the surface here, providing them with secure footing, and soon they were on the jungle floor. Ruby held them there for a full five minutes, unsure whether they had been heard or not, and he was taking no chances. When it became apparent their arrival had passed unnoticed, he faced Rodriguez.

"Take us to where I can talk with the men."

"My hut will serve well for such purpose," the Cuban said. "Come."

He led them through a narrow strip of tall cane to a small shelter that stood at the extreme edge of the settlement. They waited at the rear of the thatched structure while Rodriguez made a swift survey for soldiers. Finding none, he returned, motioned for Cain Ruby and the others to come forward and enter.

"I shall summon the men," he said, and moved through the open doorway.

Annette followed. At Ruby's frowning glance she paused. "There's no reason for me to remain. I'll see what I can do for the sick."

She did not wait for his approval. Ruby swore helplessly.

She was taking a great risk. She could be recognized, and Maspera was searching for her, willing to reward any man who brought her to him. He wheeled to Aramo, half angered. "Overtake her . . . warn her to move about with care. She must not be noticed by the soldiers."

Ramiro departed immediately. Cain Ruby moved to the rear of the hut, sat down on a crude bench that stood against the wall. He allowed his eyes to rove. The shelter contained the barest of necessities, a small table made from scraps of lumber, a second bench of tree limbs similar to the one upon which he sat. A thin pallet of goatskins placed in one corner served as a bed. There were no cooking utensils, no store of food.

Moved by pity, Cain shook his head. Existence for the Cubans under Spanish domination was elementary as well as cruel. Small wonder they longed to throw it off, become their own masters. He heard a faint noise outside the hut. His hand dropped to the handle of his rapier, fell away when he saw it was Gaspar Rodriguez. The elderly Cuban had two men with him. He led them to where Ruby sat.

"My friends, Osmundo and Pedro Aragon," he said, bowing ceremoniously. He faced the Aragons. "The valorous one of whom I have spoken."

They shook hands gravely, their dark, serious eyes dwelling upon Ruby intently.

"Where are the others?" he asked.

"They come," Rodriguez replied. "I thought it best that all not move this way at a single moment. There are no soldiers in the village, but such commotion would perhaps attract them."

The remainder of the men of San Cristóbal began to appear shortly thereafter, slipping silently through the doorway in singles and in pairs. Ramiro Aramo returned, took up a stand where he could watch the clearing. To Cain's questioning look concerning Annette, he nodded.

Ruby turned to Rodriguez. "All are present?"

"All are here."

From the back of the hut a voice in deep disgust said: "An *inglés*. We are fools. They are little different from the Spaniards."

"That you do not know, Eduardo Chávez," Rodriguez replied, shaking his finger angrily. "Would you judge him unjustly? Hear him out."

There was a moment of silence, and then another voice said: "Yes. We will hear him."

Gaspar Rodriguez brought his attention back to Cain. His lined face was sad. "You will forgive them, *señor* . . . in their hearts is little hope. Speak to them of your plan."

XVII

Cain Ruby allowed the room to hush. He placed his glance on Eduardo Chávez, the dissenter. "No, I am not like the Spanish. They are my enemies. I have been hired by men of importance on the mainland to do them great damage. Thus I am here."

Chávez said: "What is the nature of this harm you will visit upon the Spaniards?"

"I will destroy the Montaña Sangre."

This was a quick murmur of conversation. Chávez moved forward a few steps. "It is a brave thought," he commented. "But little is accomplished by words."

"They are not idle words," Ramiro Aramo broke in. "An attempt has already been made by this man. It failed because of treachery. I, myself, was there. I speak knowingly."

Again there was an excited run of low voices. Pedro Aragon, his round face glistening with sweat, lifted his hands for silence. "Why do you tell us of this? What do you want of us?"

"Before such can be accomplished, there is something that must be done."

"And what is this?"

"The soldiers have captured your *El Profeta*. He must be taken from the fort before it is destroyed. I do not wish to kill him, also."

There was a long moment of stillness. Finally a voice, filled with disbelief, said: "*El Profeta* . . . he has become a prisoner?"

"It is true," Aramo said, and hurriedly gave an account of the deaths of Pablo Quintana, Margarita, and the capture of Peréz-Rosario. When he was finished, the room was again hushed.

"I have need of six men to aid me in this matter," Ruby said. "Such will enable me to get inside the fort, release Peréz-Rosario, and permit me to set my charges of explosive."

Aragon lifted his shoulders, allowed them to sag. "We are willing to assist, but how can this be done? We are prisoners ourselves . . . in our own village."

"I have a means," Ruby said. "Will you listen?"

"We will listen," Aragon said.

Cain Ruby nodded. He glanced around the room at the faces turned to him. What he would tell them first they would find hard to accept. But it was the truth. "The Spaniards mean to destroy your village," he said. "It will happen if you sit, as you do now, and, if we break their ring and your families escape, the soldiers will still come back and burn your huts to the ground in revenge. You must understand this."

"It is so," Rodriguez said. "No longer will there be a San Cristóbal."

"At least, not until the Spaniards are driven into the sea!" a young Cuban said. "Anyway, the land will remain. One day we can return and rebuild our homes."

"Yes . . . even better ones . . . homes of wood and rock."

Ruby said: "Then it is agreed. Now, have you weapons?"

The young villager answered. "Only knives and machetes. There are no guns."

"They will suffice, perhaps better than muskets. Listen well to what I have to say. If I am wrong, tell me so, for your lives may depend on it. As we came around the village with Rodriguez, I took note of the Spaniards. They are spaced three or four meters apart. It is a tight loop, but it is also a thin one. There are no soldiers behind the line. Thus, if we remove the men on sentry duty, the ring is broken."

"But so near are they? To kill one will bring notice from the men on either side, will it not?"

"Such is not my plan. We will kill eighteen or twenty . . . depending on the number of men we have . . . at the same instant."

Ruby waited for his words to be absorbed. When the murmuring had ceased, he continued.

"Tonight with darkness, we will move on the Spanish line. We will be three meters apart. In that way it will be one against one. We shall advance together so that all may strike at the same moment. Surprise will be with us since the soldiers expect no resistance from you. When you have slain the guard assigned to you, take his musket and ammunition and run to the center of our force. We will gather there and move ahead into the jungle."

"Away from the village?" someone questioned. "Would it not be better to take refuge among the huts?"

"No . . . we must draw the soldiers away. When they follow us, that will be the time your women and children can escape."

"Are we not to fight the soldiers . . . besides those we kill at first, I mean?" It was the young Cuban again.

"Yes. When we pull off into the jungle, we will set an ambush. It must be far enough from the village to allow the escape. I suggest you choose several of the older men, and your priest, to supervise the removal of the families."

"We cannot hold the Spaniards for any great time," Osmundo Aragon said doubtfully. "I count nearly forty of them."

"It will not be necessary," Ruby replied. "Ten minutes should be enough, if the women and children are ready. The signal for them to depart can be when they hear the sound of gunfire at the ambush. They will know then the Spaniards have left their positions, that it is safe for them to scatter into the jungle. Now, all is said. I will wait while you consider."

Eduardo Chávez moved forward. "It is not necessary to consider. The plan is good. I pledge you my hands . . . my life, if need be."

"And I!" the young villager cried, stepping to Chávez's side.

The others followed, each vowing his support. Several asked to be included in the rescue party that would go to the Montaña Sangre.

Ruby waved them to silence, thanked them. "Such will be dangerous," he said. "And all of you cannot go. Since I do not know you well, I shall leave it to Ramiro Aramo and Gaspar Rodriguez to choose. After the ambush we will sepa-

221

rate and meet at a designated place. Then we will go to the fort. For now, ready yourselves for tonight. We gather here one hour after dark."

The attack was delayed until ten o'clock. It was learned that the sentries were reduced by half after that time, the soldiers alternatively sleeping and standing watch.

"It will be easier," Ruby explained to the thirteen men who clustered about him and Aramo in Gaspar Rodriguez's hut. "Is all else arranged?"

"Everything," Rodriguez said. "Even now the families are ready to flee. They only await the signal." The old Cuban paused, gazed wistfully at the men who were to participate in the fight. "I wish the years weighed not so heavily upon my shoulders. I would enjoy greatly using a machete on a Spaniard."

"You will be doing your part, old one," Aramo said. "To lead the women and children to safety is of great importance. There are always those who fight in a different manner."

"It is so," Rodriguez murmured. "I shall not protest. The children are of more importance to the future than we old ones. I am only thankful that a valorous man such as this *inglés* was sent to deliver us from the Spaniards."

"This is not a time of miracles," Cain Ruby said abruptly. "You are not yet delivered."

The Cuban moved his gnarled hands in an impatient gesture, dismissing the possibility of failure. "It is as good as done, *señor*. Of that we are all certain."

Cain shrugged, turned to Aramo. "We ready to move out?"

"All are ready."

"Go then to the far end of the village. Go singly. We

must risk nothing at this moment. Gather at the farthest hut."

"That will be my house," the young villager spoke up. "Me . . . Porfirio Díaz."

They faded off into the night, dark shapes slipping from shadow to shadow. Cain waited until the last was gone, then turned to Rodriguez. "The lady . . . Annette . . . she will be with you?"

"Yes. I shall care for her . . . my life be forfeit should I fail! Afterward, we will go to the village of Villareal. Your woman will be there."

His woman—Ruby grinned wryly at the phrase, wondering how Annette would react to such an assumption on the part of the old Cuban. Not favorably, he decided. But he was relieved that she would be clear of danger. It had been a matter of concern. He shook hands with Rodriguez, stepped out into the open. With Aramo beside him, he made his way to the hut of Porfirio Díaz. The men were all there, waiting.

"There is no need to talk again of the plan," Cain Ruby said, keeping his voice low. "You know what must be done. Go quietly and, when you strike, strike hard."

"Remember also to stay only three meters apart," Aramo added. "Move in pace with the man next you. Only thus can we act as one."

There was a murmur of assent and understanding. Ruby gave them a final appraisal. He nodded. "It is time," he said, and stepped through the doorway.

They circled the hut and crossed to the edge of the jungle. The ring of Spaniards lay a hundred yards from that point. For the first half of the distance Ruby kept the men hunched low. At the midway mark he lifted his hand, signaled a halt. He looked to both sides. The Cubans were flung out in an evenly spaced, straight line.

He lowered his arm, and as one the men of San Cristóbal moved forward through the tall grass.

XVIII

In the pale starlight Cain Ruby could scarcely make out Aramo. The man was only a shadow, inching slowly through the night. The Cuban to his right was a similar blur. Cain paused, listened. All was still. He moved on.

He hoped the report they had received was correct. If so, it meant the sentries would be spaced twenty feet or so apart, thus making the attack much easier. Including Aramo and himself, he had only fifteen men—all, except for the young Cuban, of unknown quality. But the determination to fight and be free was in their minds and that, Cain Ruby was beginning to realize, was a powerful weapon.

A man coughed. Ruby halted. He was near the sentry. Cain glanced to his left. Ramiro had not stopped. Cain crouched lower in the brush, resumed his crawling. The sudden, brittle clash of metal brought him up short again. Somewhere down the line contact had been made. He raised himself to his knees, looked ahead. A squat, thick-bodied soldier stood ten steps away. The Spaniard had also heard the metallic sound and now stared fixedly into the darkness. Cain Ruby rose noiselessly, closed with the man. The soldier wheeled, flung up his musket. Ruby's blade flashed in the half light, and the guard shuddered, crumpled.

Cain stepped over the man's body. He took up his weapon, ripped the pouch of bullets and flask of powder from the straps, and spun to see how Aramo fared. The Cuban was moving toward him, his job finished. The man to their right had found his chore a simple one, also.

Farther along on both wings of the line Ruby could see the men of San Cristóbal trotting toward the center. It had been absurdly easy. The Spaniards, expecting nothing, had been taken completely by surprise.

"Go . . . away from the village," Ruby told them as they came up. The men were smiling, flushed with success.

A musket blasted through the night. It was off to their left. One of the Cubans had run into trouble. Cain pivoted to Aramo. "He will need help . . . come."

"No . . . he comes now," Díaz broke in.

The Cuban was wounded. He was holding his arm, but he grinned, his teeth showing white in the starlight. "That Spaniard will never again pull a trigger," he said.

"You have an injury," Ramiro Aramo said, pushing forward.

"It is nothing. A scratch. But I have aroused the soldiers. They come this way."

Ruby stared into the darkness beyond the men. It was an unfortunate incident and would result in pursuit much sooner than he had planned. He could hear the Spaniards shouting questions. Another musket echoed through the night. It could not involve a member of their party—all were accounted for. But there was no time to wonder about it. He turned to Aramo. "Lead them to the place of concealment. Hurry."

"And you?" Ramiro said, hesitating.

"I shall wait to be seen by the soldiers. Then I will follow."

The Cuban wheeled, barked his instructions. The men moved on. Ruby held his position, intently watching the shadows. He could hear the Spaniards approaching, stumbling through the brush, calling out the names of the sentries.

Two men burst into the open. They saw Cain Ruby at the edge of the clearing, sent up a yell. He took aim, fired at the nearest. The Spaniard went to his knees, clutching at his breast. Ruby pivoted, raced to catch up with Aramo and the others.

More cries lifted as additional soldiers entered the clearing, began to pursue him. Muskets cracked spitefully in the sultry darkness. Cain heard the whine of balls, saw them dig into the earth ahead and beside him. He had delayed almost too long. Dodging back and forth, he risked a glance over his shoulder. The entire company was on his heels now. He looked ahead. He could not see Aramo and his men but knew, by that moment, they were in ambush. They needed only his arrival to open up on the charging Spaniards.

Ramiro Aramo rose abruptly from a clump of bushes. The Cuban shouted, and Ruby swerved, plunged into the dense cover beside him. Aramo shook his head. "You tempt luck, *amigo,*" he said, then cupping his hands to his lips, shouted: "Fire!"

The combined blast of muskets was a deafening explosion. A half dozen Spaniards pitched forward. The oncoming line wavered, stalled. Officers began to shout, curse. The Cubans reloaded, sent a second volley of death into the recoiling soldiers.

Ruby, standing next to Aramo, emptied his pistol, reloaded, fired again in a steady, methodical fashion. The village should be deserted by that moment, he thought. They could not have missed the sounds of gunfire.

"The Spaniards flee!" Díaz shouted joyously. "Like rats, they scurry away."

"Continue to shoot!" Ruby yelled hurriedly. "The charge has not yet broken!"

The Cubans unleashed another round. More soldiers went down into the grass. Immediately the Spaniards halted, flinching before an enemy they could not see. There was a moment of confusion, and then all turned and raced for the shelter of the trees. It was a complete rout. The soldiers had failed to score a single injury except for the one man who had been slightly wounded in his encounter with a sentry. Well over a dozen Spaniards lay dead or dying.

"Disperse!" Ruby shouted above the cheering and scattered gunshots. "We cannot stop them should they make a second charge!"

"But we have defeated them!" a voice protested from the smoke-filled shadows.

"For the moment only," Cain replied. "They will come again in larger force. It is best we take our small victory and go."

"Heed the *inglés!*" Porfirio Díaz shouted, stepping into the open. "It is plain he knows of what he speaks. To strike and run, and strike again, is a good way of fighting."

"Come . . . I will lead to Villareal," Aramo said, moving out in front of Ruby. "There will be other Spaniards in plenty."

They hurried off into the pale darkness, maintaining a slow trot that covered the ground steadily. An hour later, when they pulled down to a walk, Aramo dropped back to Cain Ruby's side.

"It is great hope you have brought to my people this night," he said. "There have been other encounters but none so successful as this."

"You make much of a small thing," Ruby said, but inwardly a core of pride glowed. They had administered a good lesson to the Spaniards. He shrugged. "What was done serves my purpose as well."

Aramo smiled. "You forget that I know you beneath the skin. I think you fear to be honored, Cain Ruby . . . that for such you portray dislike. But in this you will have no voice. By the time of sunset tomorrow your name will have spread throughout the island."

"They waste their strength. I have interest in only one thing . . . the Montaña Sangre. When it is destroyed, I am finished with Cuba."

"This you have said, but you can no more hold back the feeling my people shall have for you now than you can stop the wind. It will come to pass no matter how much you ignore it."

"Perhaps. I cannot prevent their thoughts, but it must be remembered that I am here only to do a job, and nothing more. When it is done, I shall return to New Orleans with the girl."

"That, also, is understood . . . and the hearts of all Cubans will be sad when you go, for this night you have truly won their love and respect."

Cain Ruby was silent for several moments. Then: "They would be fools to think of me as their new savior. We near Villareal?"

"Very near. It is just beyond the hill."

"Good. When we are there, select the six men who are to help. I would speak with them."

They reached the village almost alone, the others having forged on ahead, anxious to report the news. There was light in the church, and they turned their steps toward that structure, becoming aware of a gradual increase in sound as they drew close. Aramo opened the door, and they entered. A half a hundred persons surged forward as a cheer went up.

"*El Valeroso* is here!"

Taken aback by the unexpected welcome, Cain Ruby halted. The crowd moved in around him, shouting, weeping, touching him, babbling hysterically. Trapped, overcome by chagrin, he looked about helplessly. Over to one side he saw Annette. She was smiling.

"We have lit the fuse!" It was the young Porfirio Díaz. He was waving his arms above his head. "Soon will come an explosion that will blast the Spaniards from our land!"

"We have begun a victory," another voice cried. "And with one such as *El Valeroso* to lead us, we cannot fail."

Cain attempted to catch Ramiro Aramo's eye. The Cubans were taking too much for granted; his position must be explained to them.

"There is more!" Díaz shouted, shouldering to the front of the confusion. "It is good news for you, *inglés!* A messenger is here from Bahai Hondo. General Lopez has arrived!"

Cain Ruby stared at the Cuban in disbelief. Lopez was not due for several days. He reached forward, grasped Díaz by the arm.

"Of this you are certain?"

"It is true. The *Pampero* lies off the coast. The army will come ashore with sunrise."

The *Pampero*—that was the name of Lopez's ship. There could be no doubt. There should be three vessels, however, the second under the command of Governor Quitman, a third captained by Ambrosio Gonzales. Lopez was to rendezvous with them at Key West, on the Florida Chain. He had only a handful of men himself, and, while he was impulsive and prone to poor judgment, he would never be so foolhardy as to attempt an invasion alone. Or would he?

Above the tumult Ruby shouted his question at Díaz.

"There is only the *Pampero?*"

Díaz wheeled, pressed the courier for the answer. He came back to Cain. "There is only the *Pampero*. He tells that a sergeant who came ashore to see about horses reported that the general was so eager to engage the Spaniards he did not wait for the others."

Cain drew himself up sharply, a mixture of anger and exasperation forcing a groan from his lips. Lopez was even a bigger fool than he had been led to believe.

XIX

They lay in the brush and waited for midnight. The gates of the Montaña Sangre were directly opposite, perhaps a hundred yards distant. No repairs had been made as yet, but there were now two guards, one at either hinge post. A steadily fed watch fire kept the surrounding area well lighted.

Cain Ruby glanced at the men of San Cristóbal who accompanied him. They crouched in the dark shadows, awaiting his orders to move. Aramo was to his left. Farther along was Porfirio Díaz. Next to the voluble young Cuban lay Pedro Aragon, Rodriguez's friend who knew the interior of the fort well. Behind him were Carlos García and Esteban Salazar, the village strong man. A little apart from them were Ricardo Leclerc, who was half French, and a tall, thin black man named Manuel Vaca. It was an excellent crew; Aramo had made good choices.

Ruby shifted to one elbow and thought how pleasant it would be when it was all over. Then he could hurry to Villareal, get Annette DuRique, and together they would strike out for the coast—and leave Narciso Lopez to his own blundering devices. The *Felicity* would be waiting, and in a short time it would be New Orleans, his own ship under him again—and the start of a new fortune.

Annette had surprised him. Before departing for the Montaña Sangre he had halted her as she crossed the plaza and made her aware of his plans. He had told her in no uncertain terms that he would brook no opposition on her part. She had listened quietly, then leaned forward and kissed him lightly on the cheek.

It had startled him. "You are as emotional as these Cubans," he had said to cover his confusion.

"For luck," she had murmured and moved on.

I'll need it, he thought now. *A raid on the fort when the Spaniards aren't expecting it is risky enough. With them all cocked and primed and waiting . . . thanks to Saxon Carver . . . I've got a touchy job on my hands. It would have been better to wait a couple of days, let things cool off a bit, but Lopez's jumping the gun as he did knocked that idea into the brine. I'll just have to chance it, and hope to God it all comes out right.*

Before leaving Villareal, he had done what he could to stay Lopez. Dispatching a messenger to the general, he had suggested the landing be delayed until Quitman and Gonzalez arrived with their men. There were no island armies, Ruby had warned—only small, poorly equipped groups who could offer no effective support even if they could be contacted and assembled.

Wait. Hold up. That had been the substance of his advice, but he had little hope that Lopez would listen and heed. He could not tell the general the major reason why he should delay—that the destroying of the Montaña Sangre and the Spanish army quartered within it would do much to pave the road of victory for him. He dared not take such a chance. The Spaniards had many spies abroad, and that there would be none among Lopez's men was inconceivable.

"Soldiers. . . ." Aramo's voice was a quiet murmur in the darkness.

Cain threw his glance to the shattered gates. Horsemen broke into the fan of firelight. An officer followed by a score of men.

"Maspera," Díaz said, his voice going taut.

The Spanish captain was wearing a different uniform, one of white breeches, knee-length leather boots, and a brilliant blue, heavily decorated coat. He had exchanged his plumed helmet for one adorned only with a large, gold emblem of some sort. The officer rode through the gate, ignoring the saluting sentries, and turned south, his men, clad in the black and yellow of Spain, strung out behind him.

"The *asesinos* ride tonight," Salazar said. "Would that a bolt of fire from the heavens strike them dead!"

The sound of the horses faded. Ruby glanced at the Cubans. They had become restless, vaguely angered at the appearance of Maspera, even a little fearful, perhaps. He looked toward the slumbering fort, dark and silent, its grim walls etched starkly against the sky. It had been by sheer accident they had not run head-on into Maspera and his cavalrymen.

"Now it is time," he said to Aramo. "Tell the others."

He heard the men stirring, making final preparations as his order was repeated. For some it could be their last moments of life; it could even be the end for him, he realized. He possessed no special invulnerability to Spanish bullets or sabers. And this time it would be different; it would not just be a matter of getting through the gates and gaining the sentry hut. Before anything was done, Peréz-Rosario and all other Cuban prisoners, if there were any, must be freed and taken to a point beyond danger. And the prison, according to Pedro Aragon, lay far inside the compound.

Ruby felt fingers touch his arm. He came about. It was Manuel Vaca, the man selected to make the initial move.

"*Adiós, señor,*" Vaca said. "I go now."

Cain gripped his extended hand. "Go with God. We meet inside the walls."

"God willing," the Cuban replied, and slipped off into the jungle. He would circle, approach the fort's entrance from the east.

"We go, also."

Leclerc and Esteban Salazar. They had been chosen at the last moment because they most resembled the two guards at the gates in stature. Their task was to follow a like procedure but to come in from the west. They would move upon the sentries, diverted by Vaca, and overpower them from the rear.

Cain Ruby and the remaining Cubans waited, eyes on the guards who leaned wearily against the corner pilasters of the wall. On the catwalk behind them the sentries trod their prescribed beats.

"*Ai-ai-eeee-oooooo!*"

The guards came erect. Raising their muskets, they moved forward a step, stared at the man weaving unsteadily toward them.

"*Ai-ai-ai-mamacita!*"

Vaca staggered to one side, almost fell. His portrayal was convincing, one that could have been born only of long experience. The taller of the two guards lowered his weapon.

"A drunkard," he said to his companion.

The other Spaniard laughed. Cain Ruby swung his eyes to the catwalk. The sentries had paused to watch. After a few moments they wheeled about, resumed their marching.

Vaca drew up before the guards. He was singing some meandering ditty concerning a dark-haired girl in a far away port. The soldiers listened in stony silence. Vaca took a short step backward, caught himself, reeled forward. He lost balance, went to one knee. The tall guard reached down, seized his arm, and jerked him to his feet roughly.

"What are you doing here . . . drunk?" he demanded. "Where is your hut?"

Cain's glance again went to the top of the wall. The sentries were making their approach. They came to the gate opening, halted. Once more they watched the amusing antics of the intoxicated wanderer, listened to the harsh, impatient questions of the guards. Finally, they pivoted, picked up their monotonous routine.

Two figures disengaged themselves from the shadows beneath the wall. There was the quick glitter of metal as firelight touched the flat side of a knife blade. The guards crumpled silently into the arms of Leclerc and Salazar.

Vaca, still singing in his off-key voice, staggered to the gates. Cain Ruby rode out the long moments, eyes on the darkness into which the Cubans had dragged the two soldiers. Abruptly the guards were again at their posts. The sentries on the catwalk appeared, paused, reversed, and were gone once more.

"Go," Cain Ruby said.

Aramo and the others rose with him. In a compact group they crossed the open ground, reached the entrance. Leclerc and Salazar, dressed in portions of the guard's uniforms, met them with broad smiles. Vaca, apparently overcome by liquor and silent, sprawled against one of the uprights.

"It is done, and simple it was," Salazar said. "A Spaniard dies like anyone else."

Cain Ruby nodded, drew the others under the platform. The thud of the sentries' heels was distant. They were yet at the far end of their beat. He singled out Pedro Aragon.

"Lead us to the prison. We must move quickly."

Keeping close to the wall, they started. Salazar and Leclerc remained at the gate, Spanish guards to all appearances.

Aragon took them deeply into the silent fort. The buildings were dark, and there seemed to be no patrolling soldiers, save those on the catwalk. One of the dogs was barking, but the sound was stationery. Either the animal was chained to a post or was inside the kennels.

They passed a long, windowless building, broke into the open. A large plaza lay to their left. In the center a fire had dwindled to glowing coals. Beyond it a dozen posts reared blackly into the night.

"The whipping place," Aragon muttered, and paused.

"Someone is there," Aramo added. "See . . . he is tied to the center one."

"Poor devil. He hangs like one already visited by death."

"Better if he is. . . ."

Cain Ruby glanced at the sagging figure. He prodded Aragon's shoulder impatiently. "The prison . . . there is no time for talk."

"It is the building before us."

Ruby studied the rock structure immediately ahead. After a brief time, he motioned to the others to remain and, taking Aramo, cut in behind the building. Dropping to their knees, they crawled to the front which faced the plaza. Ruby drew up sharply. The door stood open. He heard the quick intake of Aramo's breath.

"It is empty! They have taken *El Profeta* elsewhere."

Cain Ruby came about slowly, his eyes reaching toward

the posts in the center of the square. "Come," he said in a grim voice, and led the way back to where the Cubans were waiting.

"What is wrong?" Díaz asked anxiously. "Can you not find him?"

Cain pushed through the cluster of men. Behind him he heard Aramo whisper: "The cell is empty. The man who hangs on the whipping post . . . perhaps he . . . ?"

Ruby moved to a point opposite the stakes, fifty yards or so distant. Overhead he could hear the measured tread of the sentries.

"It will be difficult to reach him," Aramo said quietly.

Porfirio Díaz murmured: "Only if there is a sentry to see."

He was gone immediately, a vague shadow beneath the catwalk. He reached one of the ladders, leading upward from ground level.

Aramo turned to the man beside him. "Another should also go."

Aragon wheeled, disappeared. Cain waited. There had been no interruption in the sentry's pacing. He could still hear the solid rap of boot heels on the wooden planks. "When all is clear, we cross," he said. "Have your knives in readiness to cut him down quickly."

"You think it is Peréz-Rosario?" Vaca asked in a faltering tone.

Cain Ruby shrugged. "It is not a matter of who. We cannot leave any man here."

"That is so."

But in his own mind Cain Ruby was certain of the victim's identity. The old Cuban leader had been brought to the fort. He would have been in the prison cell unless the Spaniards had already put him to torture.

There was a muted thump on the catwalk. A long silence followed, and then Pedro Aragon emerged from the darkness. "All is well, *señor*. Porfirio is now a sentry who walks a beat."

Ruby said: "Follow. Move with care."

They broke from the shadows and crossed the open ground at a soundless run. They reached the posts, large, square timbers with iron rings fastened high to all four sides, halted at the one near the center. The man hanging from it was little more than a shapeless mass of clotted blood and shredded clothing. Spanish whips had done a fearful job.

Cain Ruby took a hurried look at the slack, skull-like face. He had been right. "Peréz-Rosario," he muttered. "Release him . . . quickly."

The Cubans leaped to their task, caught the aged man in their arms, and lowered him to the ground.

"He still lives," Aragon said, wonder in his voice. "Miracle of miracles . . . he lives."

"No more . . . no more . . . *por Dios* . . . no more," Peréz-Rosario moaned.

"It is all right, *El Profeta*," Aragon said soothingly. "You are safe."

The old Cuban stirred weakly. "Safe? Safe?" he echoed blankly.

"We are friends. The *inglés* is with us."

"Friends . . . ?" Peréz-Rosario murmured, and lapsed into unconsciousness.

Cain Ruby, his face a mask concealing the anger that flowed through him, wheeled to the Cubans. "Carry him carefully. Make haste." They gathered the man into their arms hurriedly, handling him as gently as possible. Once he cried out, and then fell silent. "Return the way you came. Do not stop."

Ramiro Aramo looked closely at Cain Ruby. "What is it you will do?"

"The job I have not finished."

"In this I will help."

"No. It is for you to lead the others into the jungle where they will be safe. From this moment it is for me alone to act."

XX

He did not wait to see them leave. Bending low, he ran from the blood-stained line of stakes to the rear of a building on the far side of the plaza. The sentry hut with its entrance to the powder magazine would lie beyond that. There could be other entrances, possibly nearer, but he could not spare time for searching. He circled the low-roofed structure, a barracks it appeared to be, saw the sentry station a hundred feet farther on. He swerved in his direct course to take advantage of the shadows alongside another building and raced its length. He paused there, sucking deep for breath. His nerves were taut, and a grim anger still throbbed within him. At each turn he saw the sunken, tortured face of Peréz-Rosario, the battered, emaciated body, nor could he erase the sight of those stark, cruel posts and what they signified. His mind was as some tremendous force locked to a single purpose; he knew he would never again enjoy a moment's peace unless the Montaña Sangre was leveled.

The hut was just ahead. He waited for his lungs to normalize, then dropped to hands and knees. He was recalling the arrangement inside the structure: two windows, the door, a table, chair, and a bench. At that moment he heard something behind him. He sank back against the building, shifting about until his right hand, gripping Pablo Quintana's rapier, was free.

"*¿Señor?*"

Ramiro Aramo's questioning whisper reached him. His muscles went lax, and the hard promise of danger ebbed from his tense shape. "Here," he murmured.

The Cuban crawled to his side. "This thing you do . . . you will not do alone," he said reproachfully.

Cain Ruby stirred impatiently. He preferred to be on his own. "It would have been better had you remained with the others. They will need a leader."

"Díaz is clever. He takes charge."

Cain made no reply. He glanced about the hushed compound, began to crawl slowly for the rear of the hut, Aramo at his heels. Reaching the corner, Ruby looked back, motioned for the Cuban to circle to the right, while he went left. They separated, each working his way to the front.

Ruby halted abreast of the window. He heard the unmistakable growling of a dog. Crouched below the opening, he froze. The animal sensed his presence.

"What troubles you, *bruta?*" a voice asked.

A chair scraped across the floor. The clack of a dog's nails on the planks followed.

"It is nothing," a second voice said. "The bitch is in heat. She is nervous."

The chair screeched again. Cain heard the rattle of chain. He rode out another interminable minute, moved on. Gaining the end of the hut, he again paused. From the opposite corner Ramiro Aramo made a slight motion with his hand, revealed his presence. Together they converged on the open doorway, stopped.

Cain Ruby considered. It was not prudent to raise himself, look into the room, and see exactly the number of guards on duty—two, plus the dog, he thought—but he could not be certain without exposing himself. They would have to charge in blindly, take their chances. Surprise once more must be their ally.

He caught Aramo's eye. He pointed to himself, to the doorway, then to the young Cuban, and again to the entrance. He would enter first; Aramo was to follow. Ramiro nodded. Cain drew himself upright, flattened himself against the wall.

Inside the dimly lit room the dog whined anxiously. One of the guards muttered an oath. Cain Ruby bunched his muscles, the rapier in his right hand, knife in the left. The pistol was out of the question. They could afford no gunshots and must prevent the Spaniards from firing their muskets. Cain glanced at Aramo, nodded. Placing his shoulders alongside the door frame, he swiftly pivoted into the room.

Two guards. A dog. Ruby lunged at the nearest man, drove his blade deep before the soldier could move. He felt something brush his shoulder. It was Aramo, crowding in close. The dog sprang. Cain saw the Cuban's arm come up to protect his throat, saw the brute fasten its teeth in Ramiro's forearm, and drag him down. He stabbed at the bristling, squirming body a half a dozen times, heard the yelp of pain, and watched the dog wilt. He wheeled to the second guard. Aramo was before him, using his blade despite the attacking dog.

"*¡Por favor!*" the soldier cried, sinking against the wall in terror. Aramo's pitiless knife drove deeply into the man's chest, came out in a bright gush of blood.

"You are badly injured," Ruby said, glancing at the Cuban's set face.

"It is nothing," Aramo replied. "The animal got no

virgin when she bit me." He ripped away the tattered sleeve, wound it around his mangled arm.

Ruby turned quickly to the door that led below to the magazine. A chain now secured it. It was stapled into the wall at one end, a heavy padlock fastening the other end. The Spaniards had taken precautions.

"One will have the key," Aramo said. "I will look. . . ."

"There is no time," Ruby answered, and snatched up one of the muskets.

Using the barrel as a lever, he placed it under the chain, wrenched the staple from its mooring, and jerked open the door. Not hesitating, he started down the passageway. It was dark. He wished he had thought to bring one of the lamps. A moment later light flooded out before him. Aramo had remembered.

They hurried into the underground chamber. It was larger than Cain Ruby had pictured it, and well stocked. There were boxes of clothing, crates of supplies, saddles, harness, weapons, dried food—and row after row of gunpowder in wooden casks.

"Scatter these," he said, running toward the barrels. "Get them to all corners."

He tipped a cask to its side, placed his foot against it, sent it rolling into a far wall. The head burst open upon impact. Powder spilled out in a glistening heap. They moved swiftly, distributing the barrels. Those that did not break open, they did not bother with. Fire would take care of them. The primary need was to place explosive throughout the underground area. When it went up, the entire fort would go with it.

Ramiro, working near the passageway, suddenly hesitated. He listened, said: "*Señor*, there is fighting. I hear gunshots."

Aragon and the others. They had run into trouble. Cain Ruby rushed to complete his chore. He scooped up a double handful of powder to be used as a fuse train, began to trail it toward the passage. "Go above," he said to Aramo. "See if all is yet clear around this hut."

The Cuban disappeared into the corridor. Ruby followed, trickling the explosive in an unbroken string behind him. He could hear the shooting now; it came not as a sustained racket but in quick, short bursts. Evidently it was a running battle, as though Porfirio Díaz and the others were fighting their way to the gates.

"All is clear."

Aramo's words reached him, when he was almost to the end of the passageway. He continued, laying the powder string with care, making sure there was no unevenness and, above all, no gaps. To have the fuse sputter out would mean failure again—and this time he must succeed.

He came to the doorway, backed into the hut slowly, and dumped the balance of the powder into a pile. The firing near the gates had increased. He glanced at Aramo, drew an oilskin packet of lucifers from his pocket. "The powder will burn quickly," he said. "Perhaps, because of your injury, it would be wise to leave now."

Aramo smiled. He bent down, rolled one of the dead guards aside, and picked up his musket and ammunition pouch. "I shall wait."

Cain Ruby struck the match, dropped it onto the pyramid of powder. There was a quick puff of black smoke, and then a strong, sparkling flame began to race greedily toward the passageway. Ruby spun, snatched up the other musket, and, pushing Aramo ahead of him, stepped through the doorway into the open.

They sprinted for the inner fence, ducked into its

shadow. The shooting had ceased, and men were shouting from the catwalk. Cain and Aramo reached the opening in the fence, halted. No one was in sight. They bolted across the narrow alleyway, gained the shelter of the platform. The main gate was visible now. Three soldiers stood in its center, their faces toward the jungle.

Ruby did not hesitate. The powder fuse would be eating its way steadily into the magazine. He burst from the darkness at a hard run, Aramo a stride behind. At the sound of their pounding feet, the soldiers whirled.

"Here are more!" one shouted.

An answering hail came from somewhere along the catwalk. Cain paid no heed. The three Spaniards at the gate were the immediate problem. They had dropped to their knees, were leveling their weapons. Ruby swung the musket he had retrieved in the hut to his shoulder, fired point-blank at the nearest man. The guard yelled, went over backwards. In the same breath Ramiro also fired. The second of the trio spun, crumpled.

The third guard squeezed off his shot. The brilliant orange flash was so near that Cain Ruby flinched, momentarily blinded, but he plunged on. He saw the crouching figure of the Spaniard before him, frantically trying to reload. Raising his own empty musket, he swung it at the soldier's head. His arms tingled with shock as the blow connected. He dropped the useless weapon and with the guard's yell ringing in his ears rushed on toward the jungle.

Aramo lagged behind. The Cuban's injured arm was hampering him. Cain slackened his pace, allowed the man to catch up, and gave him support. Inside the fort soldiers were again shouting, their voices mixing with the furious barking of the dogs.

They reached the first growth, plunged into it. "We

cannot stop!" Cain gasped. "The explosion will. . . ."

"Over here!"

It was one of the Cubans, just which Ruby could not tell. They were much too near. He swerved in course, charged recklessly through the brush toward the sound of the voice, virtually dragging Ramiro Aramo with him.

"Retreat!" he cried. "Go farther. You are too close!"

He saw three men rise from the brush, bend to pick up a fourth. They began to move deeper into the tangle of vines and undergrowth. Ruby and Aramo caught up with them, and all hurried on. Ruby cast a look at Aragon.

"The others?"

"Dead," the Cuban said between gasps. "There was trouble at the gate. We fought."

We fought. The simplicity of the man's words, the pure understatement of fact registered forcefully upon Cain Ruby. His jaw hardened. "Who?"

"Díaz. And Manuel Vaca. And Esteban Salazar."

Young Porfirio Díaz who had been so anxious to battle the Spaniards, Vaca, the thin one, Salazar who seldom spoke. All brave men who . . . Ruby's thoughts died in his mind. The universe had paused, and from somewhere deep in the bowels of the earth there was a sullen rumbling.

"Down!" Cain Ruby yelled, and threw himself forward into the brush.

XXI

Ruby heard Peréz-Rosario groan as the Cubans laid him on the ground. Aramo said something, and then all things natural and human washed away in a flare of blinding light as a gigantic pillar of flame shot up into the night sky. The jungle became a lurid yellow and red land of awesome brilliance. It began to leap, to writhe and sway as a mighty wind bearing an ear-splitting roar swept through it. The earth shuddered. A powerful, almost irresistible force tore at Cain Ruby, plucked at him, strove to gather him in its arms and hurl him into the eerie glow.

A loud crackling arose as nearby trees snapped, were thrown to the earth by the man-made hurricane. The fire grew brighter, expanded in volume as it surged higher into the heavens. The roaring increased to a shrieking crescendo. Birds whirled helplessly off into the night, and no other sounds could be heard above the tumult, only the seething, crackling flames, the booming of thousands of pounds of gunpowder locked in its underground vault like some gigantic bomb.

As chain reaction set in, the flames spread farther. Rolling to his back, Cain Ruby could see the last of the Montaña Sangre. The walls had been ripped apart, lay crumbled. Some sections had fallen inward, others outward. A jagged rim had taken shape to form a volcano-like crater in which débris spewed upward continually, dropped back into the boiling maw as explosion followed explosion.

Ruby and the Cubans were silent, appalled by the fury. Gradually the wind lessened, became a stiff, hot breeze, but the jungle about them remained a strange, vivid netherworld of which, it seemed, they were no part.

There was no cheering among the Cubans. Cain Ruby glanced about him. Their faces, bronze in the glare, were stilled. As he, they shared the victory but were also struck dumb by the holocaust that had been unleashed.

"The Montaña Sangre is no more. . . ."

At the unexpected sound of Peréz-Rosario's voice, the

men turned to him. He had pulled himself to one elbow and was listening to the raging fires.

"It is finished, *El Profeta*," Aramo answered. "The day of freedom is at hand."

"Perhaps," the old man murmured, sinking back. "Would that I might be here to share with you that holy victory."

"You shall."

"No. My hour has come. I go no further in this life. It is upon your shoulders, and those with you, the weight of leadership now falls . . . be of strong will. Help our people. Protect them . . . guard them. They are as children . . . as the stalks of cane in the fields . . . bending with each new influence. Let not yourselves forget this."

"We will not forget."

"Beware the tyrant who would rise to oppress them. Many will appear. Destroy each as you have the Montaña Sangre. Heed only those your heart tells you are sincere, that are not blinded by the lust for power."

"It shall be as you wish, *El Profeta*."

"Is the *inglés* among you?"

"He is here."

"I would speak with him."

Cain Ruby moved to the dying man's side. "I am here, old one," he said, looking down into the Cuban's blanched face.

"It is good that you are safe. You have done much for my people. You return now to your country?"

"Such is my intention."

"There is more to be accomplished here. Only the first step has been taken. I think of you as a great leader. I could rest well, knowing you remain among us."

"The fight is not mine."

"It is every man's fight. We are lost . . . the world is lost if men who recognize the evil of oppression and tyranny turn their backs to it . . . and walk away."

Cain Ruby was silent. Peréz-Rosario seemed to sink lower into the warm soil.

"Margarita?"

Aramo bent over the blind prophet. He hesitated briefly, then said: "She is not here. But do not trouble yourself. She is in good hands."

Peréz-Rosario stirred faintly. "The moment comes," he muttered. "Go with God."

"Thou, too," Aramo said, and crossed himself.

For a time there was only the sound of the flames, and then Aragon said: "It is a great loss."

"True," Leclerc added in a sighing voice, "but it is good he knew of the Montaña Sangre before dying. Peace thus came to him."

"Also because of a lie," Ramiro Aramo said. "But I could not tell him otherwise."

"God will forgive a lie such as that," Pedro Aragon assured him quietly.

Cain Ruby looked toward the fort. Fires still raged, darting long, pointed tongues into the sky. It was true. The Montaña Sangre had been leveled—but the price paid had been high. Gavin Girard . . . Díaz . . . Salazar . . . Manuel Vaca . . . Pablo Quintana . . . Margarita. And now Peréz-Rosario. Those he had known personally. There were others, possibly thousands, who had perished because of it. Their deaths had been a factor in the destruction, for in dying they had given ultimate rise to the need for its obliteration. But he had not known them; they were only fragments of thought, bits of statistical information related to him by the living. Girard had been his friend, as had Peréz-

Rosario—Pablo—and the men of San Cristóbal. But his job was finished. He had earned his fee, and General Narciso Lopez could now move forth with his army of invasion and with average good fortune be successful. There would be an ample number of Spaniards for him to fight—groups such as Maspera's, the infantry patrols that skulked through the jungle, the small contingents that ravaged the villages. But there could be none of serious consequence. The proud army of General Enna was no more. The backbone of the Spanish force on the island was broken.

Another score had been settled—one of personal nature. Saxon Carver would have been with Enna, and no man caught inside the walls at the time of the explosions could have escaped. Thus Gavin Girard was avenged. Cain Ruby's only regret was that he could not have accomplished it, physically, with his own hands.

The glow of the fires began to diminish. Somewhere deep in the ruined fort a sharp crackling had arisen as some particular store of items burned with great fury. But the gunpowder had done its work; the devastation was nearly complete, and all that remained were the multitude of self-consuming fires among the scorched rocks.

"It is best we go," Ruby said, turning to the others. "All soldiers still alive on the island will come this way."

"We are almost ready, *señor*," Pedro Aragon replied.

Cain looked more closely. The men were scooping out a grave for Peréz-Rosario.

"When you are finished," he said. He glanced at Aramo. "How is it with the arm?"

"A matter of no consequence," the Cuban said. "A small price to pay for so great a victory . . . the bite of a dog."

"I am relieved that it cost you no more than that," Ruby said. "Others were not so fortunate."

"You are thinking of *El Profeta*'s words, perhaps?"

"I have thought of them."

Ramiro Aramo leaned forward, his sober face lighting with hope. "They have stirred your heart?"

Cain Ruby shook his head. "They hold no interest for me. I am sorry, but that is the way it must be."

Aramo lowered his face, hiding his disappointment.

"We are ready, *El Valeroso*," Aragon announced quietly.

Cain rose to his feet. He reached down to assist Aramo, but the Cuban pulled away, avoided him. Ruby frowned, shrugged, and moved off after the others. Pedro Aragon led, striking directly into the jungle and following an almost invisible trail through the brush, still aglow from the dying fires.

They traveled quietly, and twice they heard patrols of soldiers off to the side, hurrying toward the weird glare that hung above the desolated fort. Each time Ruby and the Cubans halted in the shadows and allowed them to pass.

"Wolves with no den in which to gather," Aragon observed once.

"But still with long fangs," Aramo replied.

"It is nothing . . . not with General Lopez and his army among us, determined to drive them into the sea!"

"Lopez!" Aramo exclaimed impatiently. "I think you expect too much of Lopez!"

Cain swung to the young Cuban. "What troubles you? These last minutes have found you strange."

Ramiro smiled apologetically. "Forgive me. My rudeness is unpardonable. It is only that I am aware of what lies ahead . . . that you go from us. With no one to lead, I fear all will collapse."

"You underestimate yourself. You have no need for me," Cain Ruby said. "Besides, it was understood from the beginning that I came only to do this one job. It was never in my mind to stay . . . and this you knew."

Aramo started a reply then, thinking better of it, shook his head, and trudged on through the night.

Just as the first streaks of dawn broke the eastern horizon, they reached Villareal. A cheer went up when news of the Montaña Sangre's destruction was told, followed by cries of anguish as word of the deaths was passed.

Cain Ruby, tired and in need of sleep, brushed aside those who would congratulate him and sought out Annette. He found her near the church. She was with several small children, and, smiling, she turned from them as he approached.

Before she could speak, he said, in English: "I'm getting a couple hours' rest . . . and then we'll move on. Be ready."

The smile faded from her lips at his abrupt manner. She studied his haggard features for a moment, looked away. "You're tired. We'll talk about it later."

He shook his head. "Nothing to talk about. We're leaving . . . as planned."

"I had hoped that you. . . ."

"That I'd changed my mind? That maybe I'd throw in with the Cubans?"

She raised her eyes, stared at him, shrugged. "I suppose it was a foolish hope."

"It was," he said flatly. "Nothing's changed. I've done my job, and now I'm going back to New Orleans . . . and you're going with me."

"And if I still refuse to go?"

"You'll go . . . if I have to tie your hands and put a tether around your neck."

She continued to study him. Finally, she nodded. "Yes, I believe you would do that."

"You can depend on it. Don't get any ideas about running off and hiding in the jungle, while I'm taking a nap, either. I'll just hunt you down. And I'll have help doing it. These people won't oppose me . . . they're my friends now."

"Better friends than you realize . . . or appreciate," Annette said. She pointed at the church. "There's a room in the back where you can sleep. I'll be ready when you awake."

He watched her turn away, rejoin the children. He felt the need to call her back, to say something that would soften the harshness of what he had said. But he could find no words, and he was too weary to search deeply for them. Wheeling slowly, he moved toward the church.

XXII

Oppressive heat awoke Cain Ruby. He sat up on the cot, glanced around groggily. He was soaked with sweat, his mouth was dry, and he was hungry. Abruptly aware, he sprang to his feet, wondering how long he had slept. He could not see the sun, and, therefore, he had no idea of the hour; midday, at least, he supposed, or it could be later. He stepped to the door, opened it, and walked the short length of the sanctuary. Immediately the low murmur of voices reached him. He halted in the entrance to the church and looked out upon the two dozen or more men collected there, talking quietly among themselves. At his appearance a shout went up, and then Ramiro Aramo, his arm neatly bandaged, detached himself from the crowd and came forward quickly. The others surged in behind him.

"There is bad news," the Cuban said, his face solemn.

Ruby frowned. "What is this? Does not Lopez make his landing?"

"Much worse. He is on the march to Havana."

"Then what . . . ?"

"The Montaña Sangre . . . it was deserted. Enna and the army had marched to meet Lopez. We destroyed the fort . . . yes . . . but inside were but a few guards."

Cain Ruby stared at the Cuban in stunned silence. Now he understood why the fort had lain so quiet in the night, why there had not been more soldiers in evidence. A bitter thought filled his mind as frustration rolled through him: all for nothing—Girard, the men of San Cristóbal, his own efforts—all for nothing. But not entirely so. The Montaña Sangre was gone, even if the muscle of the Spanish crown still lived.

"Of this you are certain?"

Ramiro nodded. "Two *pacíficos* were there, when the Spaniards marched. It was not long after the noon hour yesterday. Enna had been told of Lopez's arrival. He moved his legions into ambush."

"Has Lopez been warned?"

"We think not. There has been no time."

Ruby swore impatiently. "Why did you not awaken me and tell me of this?"

Aramo waved vaguely toward the plaza. "Anna would not permit it. She said you were in need of rest."

Cain felt a jolt of surprise. Annette thinking of him—considering his welfare. He shook his head in wonder, brought himself back to the moment. "Word must be sent to Lopez. He must be told to wait for Quitman and Gonzales, perhaps even to call off the invasion. With such few men he has no chance against Enna."

"Already he marches."

"He can halt, turn back."

"Narciso Lopez is known to you, *señor*," Aramo said quickly. "Do you believe he would turn back?"

Again Cain Ruby swore. "It is not likely. But he must be warned."

"Speak, *El Valeroso!*" a voice in the crowd shouted. "Tell us what must be done. We look to you!"

Cain raised his hands for silence. "Not to me. With the girl I leave soon for the coast . . . and my home on the mainland. This much I can do. I will carry the word to Lopez, warn him of ambush. All else must be done by you."

There was a minute of heavy silence, thick with disappointment at his blunt words. Ramiro Aramo broke it. "How shall we proceed?"

"Peréz-Rosario began the recruiting of men. Send new couriers to the villages, urge those who can fight to hurry and join Lopez if they would see the Spaniards driven from the island."

"It shall be," Aramo said. He wheeled and faced the churchyard. "You heard. Go quickly and spread the alarm. Tell every man you meet to take his weapon and hasten to the side of General Lopez."

"Where can he be found?" Pedro Aragon asked.

"He follows the road from Bahai Hondo to Havana. He will be somewhere along its length."

No one stirred. Aramo frowned, swept the men with his glance. "Go . . . there is no time to be lost."

An aged, bearded Cuban in the front of the crowd took a faltering step forward, his eyes on Ruby. He fingered his battered hat nervously. *"Señor Inglés,"* he said haltingly, "is it true what you have spoken . . . that you leave us?"

"Yes, old one, it is true."

"But you cannot! After San Cristóbal . . . the Montaña

Sangre . . . such glorious victories!"

"What I came to do is finished. There is no more. . . ."

"There is yet much you can do. We look to you, my valiant leader. The devil himself we would not fear to fight, if you led the way."

"Forget it," Cain Ruby said abruptly, slashing through the flowery Spanish. "Look to Ramiro Aramo, and to General Lopez. They are brave men."

"We do not question the courage of either, but you. . . ."

"There is no time for speaking," Cain broke in, changing the subject. "You must assist Lopez. I will warn him of Enna, also of your coming. But it should be done in haste."

Aramo extended his hand. "I go, too, *señor*. I am also needed in this. Perhaps we shall never meet again. It is best we say farewell now."

Cain Ruby took the Cuban's fingers into his own. "I have been honored by your friendship. Good luck."

"To you the same."

Cain moved forward, passing between the assembled men, shaking hands. There were tears in the eyes of Pedro Aragon, when he reached him. He grinned at the Cuban.

"Save those for the Spaniards you will slay," he said. "Farewell."

"*Adiós, Valeroso mío. Buena suerte.*"

Ruby crossed the plaza to where Annette DuRique waited. Wordless, she handed him a gourd of wine and a plate fashioned from a broad leaf containing several small biscuits, strips of dried meat, and some fruit.

"From the women of the village," she said. "It was the only way they could show their appreciation."

Cain Ruby looked back over his shoulder. The men had disappeared; only the wives and children remained. They appeared forlorn, deserted.

"Are you sure this is what you want to do?"

At Annette's question he came back around. "Sure?" he echoed. "Of course. Everybody keeps forgetting that I came here to do a job . . . and nothing more."

"And that job is finished. The real job, I mean."

"Far as I'm concerned. And the sooner we can get off this island, the better I'll like it. It's turning into a powder keg. Are you ready to go?"

"I am," she said coolly.

They moved off into the jungle, Cain finishing his meal as they walked. They traveled at a good pace, and Annette, surprisingly strong, matched his stride. When the afternoon waned, Ruby found himself marveling at her strength.

"Here we all change," she replied, when he commented on it.

Again he recalled the portrait in the New Orleans mansion. This was a different Annette. The delicate girl of fragile loveliness no longer existed; in her place was a woman—one of character, of strange, deeply moving beauty. Antoine DuRique would never recognize his daughter.

Near sundown they halted. Cain built no fire, since there was nothing to cook—and he would not have risked it, anyway, since there was certain to be soldiers in the area. Annette found berries and fruit near the stream where they rested, and a light repast was made of those.

At midnight they resumed the march, taking directions from the stars and moving always on a direct line for the coast. Sunrise found them worn from their consistent efforts, and again they stopped. Clouds had built up during the early morning hours, and the promise of a storm hung over them. They had yet to cross the river that had given the original party trouble on the inland journey, and the awareness of that set up a nagging worry within Cain Ruby.

They rested only briefly. Ruby now pressed the pace, the thought of facing the raging torrent weighing heavily on his mind as the threat overhead continued to mount. But finally they reached the stream and crossed. Cain heaved a sigh of relief.

The grueling miles had taken the best of Annette, however. He noticed she was no longer keeping up, that her steps dragged, and he realized they would soon be forced to halt for an extended period of sleep and rest.

"Can you go a while longer?" he asked. "Not much time to spare if we're to head-off Lopez."

She nodded wearily. There had been little conversation between them since leaving Villareal.

"We far from the coast?"

"Not far."

His own state of near exhaustion and her short replies turned him irritable. "It's for your Cubans we're doing this," he said. "I'm asking questions because I need to know a few things. Shouldn't we be coming onto that road Lopez is following?"

"I would think so."

"We'll stop, when we reach it."

Abruptly her manner changed. She turned to him. "It seems very important that I return to New Orleans with you. Is it only because of the money my father has promised you?"

Ruby looked at her in surprise. Denial leaped to his lips—and then he caught himself. He was about to say that it involved more than the commission, that somehow her welfare had come to mean much to him, but he brushed it aside. There was no place in his life for a woman—not yet, anyway. Perhaps later, when things were going well.

"That's it," he said. "That's what it's all about. The reason I'm here."

"Are you sure . . . or are you just avoiding the truth? Peréz-Rosario once said that no man can be entirely alone in life. That in some way he will be affected by others, mentally or spiritually. He believed that the good in one man could rub off on another. He even prayed that you. . . ."

"That I'd catch his freedom fever, too? That I'd become a *revolucionario* and stick around to fight? Not me . . . man's a fool to mix in other people's problems."

"And money is the only thing that counts?"

"It is. With it you can sit on the top . . . get anything you take a fancy to . . . I can even name a couple of kingdoms. . . ."

Cain Ruby's words broke off suddenly. Somewhere ahead in the brush a horse stamped. He caught Annette's arm, cautioned her to silence. Moving slowly, they made their way forward, halted at the edge of a small clearing. An oath slipped from Cain's tight lips. It was Maspera and his men.

XXIII

Legs spread, the Spanish captain stood a little apart from his men, smoking a thin, black cigar. The soldiers were sprawled about, taking their ease. Evidently they had been in the saddle for most of the night.

Cain Ruby's fingers strayed to the pistol in his belt. He felt Annette tremble beside him. Reaching down, he took her hand in his, pressed it reassuringly. Had he been alone, he would have drawn the revolver, put a bullet in the Spaniard's head, and taken his chances on escape. But her presence made that impossible. He could afford no risks.

Holding to her, he withdrew quietly to a safe distance, and continued on. Their pressing fatigue had disappeared in the face of danger, and for a full hour they traveled at good speed, and then once again they felt the need for rest.

Cain chose a spot in the deep brush well away from the trail. Annette sank down into the grass, her back to a rotting stump, while he simply stretched out. The rain had never materialized, but the stifling humidity held, and it was far from comfortable in the small pocket.

"We must be getting close," he said. "Maspera will be hanging around Enna."

"It can't be much farther. Do you have any idea where General Lopez is?"

"None. On the road to Havana . . . that's all I know. I'm not familiar with this part of the island."

"But if Enna's near, that means he hasn't yet come this far. He will be below us."

"Be my guess."

She was silent for several moments. Then: "You would have killed him . . . Maspera . . . if I hadn't been along, wouldn't you?"

"As quick as I would kill a Louisiana cottonmouth."

"Why?"

He raised his head, staring at her. "Why? Because he's what he is."

"His death shouldn't mean anything to you. You'll get paid whether he's dead or not."

Ruby lay back. She was right, of course, but he wasn't looking at it from that standpoint. Maspera had earned death, just as had Saxon Carver. "He deserves to die," he said, unable to think of another reason.

Annette smiled faintly. Cain Ruby, for all his tough worldliness, was having a difficult time understanding himself. Peréz-Rosario had been right.

A short hour later they moved on. They were making slow progress, Cain knew, but they could do no better. By that next morning, however, even allowing for a night's rest, they should be in position to intercept Lopez.

Around dark they reached the grass-covered banks of a small stream and halted. He found a hollow beneath a stand of musky-smelling flowers, and too exhausted even to look for food both crawled into it and were asleep almost instantly.

Cain awakened with a start. It was nearly dawn, for the jungle was already alight. He looked down at Annette. He was glad she still slept; she had needed the rest—and it afforded him an opportunity to try and sort out the jumble of emotions that had been battering within him. He had prided himself on being an uncomplicated man; if he were hungry, he ate, thirsty, he drank. Business was business, money was money—and women were women. He was experienced with all, and each had its proper place in the scheme of his life. But this woman—this Annette was somehow upsetting the balance.

He studied her in the meager light. She stirred, muttered faintly. Unaccountably a feeling of humility possessed him. That disturbed him. Never before had he been so acutely aware of another person. And, he realized with no small wonder, that for the first time in his life he was concerned with someone other than himself, something beyond the pale of his own interests. What was happening to him? What was breaking down that hard, impervious armor with which he had always clothed himself? The plight of the Cubans? The cruelty of the Spaniards? The deaths of Gavin Girard,

Peréz-Rosario, and the others? Or was it this girl, lying so closely beside him?

You're a fool, Cain Ruby, he thought. *You're letting this girl get to you . . . and it's all for nothing. You're from different worlds, and she has nothing but disdain for you. And you made it so. You've told her . . . you've made her believe that money is all that counts where you're concerned. She's tried to make you see it otherwise, but you won't listen. So forget it. Forget her. And forget all the other little things that keep bothering you . . . like what you saw in Cabezón, and that old man in Villareal, and the tears that were in the eyes of Pedro Aragon. Forget Girard and Peréz-Rosario and poor little Margarita. Forget them all . . . if you can.*

At loose ends, dissatisfied with himself, he got to his feet and stared out into the jungle. *I've got to get a hold on myself,* he thought. *Nothing's going to spoil my plans. Nothing . . . or nobody. I'm acting like a sentimental, soft-headed fool. I'm going to find Lopez, warn him, and then get the hell out. I'll do that much, but there it ends.*

He turned abruptly, leaned over, and shook Annette gently. She awoke immediately and sat up.

"Maspera?" she asked in a frightened whisper.

She had been dreaming about the Spaniard, he realized, and a sudden urge to take her in his arms, comfort her, possessed him. He stared at her intently for several moments, and then he shrugged.

"No," he said. "It's time we were going."

She nodded woodenly and followed him out of the hollow.

XXIV

They moved on through the early morning with only the drowsy chirping of birds breaking the silence. Cain Ruby's mind remained fixed on one solitary purpose: find Lopez and warn him, and then rendezvous with the *Felicity*. Once back in New Orleans he could turn Annette over to her father, collect his commissions—and that would be the end to all of it.

Toward dawn, with the first gray streaks scarring the east, they halted beside a stream. Wordless, he squatted at its edge, bathed his face in the cool water. Annette followed his example. Only when they had finished, did he speak. "We'll need food."

"There are villages along the coast," she said. "Should be reaching one soon."

He shook his head. "Probably soldiers quartered in all of them . . . waiting for Lopez. Plantation would be a better bet."

Annette said: "There are a few. I don't know exactly where."

They pushed on. He was trying to estimate their distance from the Gulf, but it was strange country to him, and he had no idea of the land. He asked the question of her.

"Four or five miles. I don't think it will be any farther than that."

The jungle now was bright. The sun had climbed above the horizon, and the world around them had taken on a clear, distinct look. Ruby glanced at the sky. It was clean, devoid of the clouds that had gathered the previous day. A thought came to him. If they were no more than five miles from the coast line, they had to be near the Bahai Hondo road upon which Narciso Lopez and his army of invasion were marching. Calculating from the time of the landing they—the sudden, completely unexpected blast of a score of muskets brought them up short. They were at the edge of a broad field. Cain seized Annette's hand, drew her into the shelter of brush. More gunshots welled up. A small-bore cannon boomed.

"What is it?" she asked breathlessly.

"Lopez . . . we're too late. He's caught in Enna's trap."

She stared at him. "What can we do?"

"Find Lopez . . . let him know what he's up against. We'll have to circle. Spaniards are right ahead of us."

Keeping low, they dropped back and skirted the field. They could hear the shouts of men now, and the firing had become a steady racket to which the cannon added its voice intermittently. They crossed through a palm forest in which smoke was beginning to hang and came in sight of several structures. The fighting was taking place in and around a village.

"What settlement is this? You know?"

"Las Pozas," Annette replied. "I recognize the church."

They reached the west end of the town without encountering any Spanish soldiers, found themselves behind the invaders. Halting at the rear of a small hut, Cain Ruby studied the area where the major engagement was in progress. His view was hampered by other structures and a jutting strip of jungle.

"Wait here," he said. "I'll find Lopez."

Annette shook her head.

He said no more, started for the center of the village with her at his heels. Several fires were burning along the dusty street, and they began to see the dead and wounded. The hard core of the battle, however, was at the opposite end of Las Pozas. They paused near one of Lopez's men. He stood behind the protective bulk of a shed, wrapping a bandage about his forearm. He was an American and sweat streaked his face and stained his uniform.

"Where can I find the general?" Cain asked.

The volunteer glanced up. "On down the street," he said unsmilingly, and resumed his chore.

A lull had come in the fighting, but there was still the sporadic snap of muskets as sharpshooters plagued the unwary. Beyond the town plaza a slant-roof building caught Cain Ruby's attention. He saw Lopez standing nearby, resplendent in a blue and gold uniform. Aides clustered about him, and a squad of soldiers, apparently his personal guard, lounged against a wall.

Ruby glanced at Annette. The dead, the cries of the wounded, the general din and confusion of battle had brought a depth of horror to her eyes, but he could see no fear.

"Got to run for it," he said. "You'll be safe here."

Again she refused. "I'll go with you."

He was in no mood to argue. "All right. Keep low, and dodge back and forth. Don't give those sharpshooters a target."

He broke into the open, sprinted toward Lopez with Annette slightly behind him. Muskets crackled from the far side of the field, but the balls went wide. They gained the safety of the metal-capped building and halted before Lopez. He stared at them, a frown darkening his face.

Cain Ruby did not stand on ceremony. "General, this is a trap. You've got to pull out."

The officer drew himself erect. "You presume to give orders to me . . . ?"

"I presume nothing. I tried to reach you in time to warn you."

"Are you from the rebel army?"

"There is no rebel army. That's why you've got to fall back."

Lopez shrugged. "That cannot be true. I was told Joaquín de Aguerro with several hundred men would join me. His scout was sent to conduct me to this village."

"De Aguerro is probably dead by now . . . along with his men. There is no rebel force, believe that. A few men may come, but that will be all. Whoever told you different is wrong."

"But I do not understand! It was reported to me that the Montaña Sangre had been destroyed and with it the garrison."

"The fort was deserted at the time. Enna had already marched to lay an ambush for you. This I know because I was one of those who was there."

Lopez looked more closely at Ruby. "You are, then, one of the men from New Orleans?"

"I am . . . Cain Ruby. My partner was killed."

Narciso Lopez fingered his pointed beard thoughtfully. A fierce hand-to-hand contest between a dozen or so volunteers and Spaniards was taking place in the extreme left corner of the field. Two men, drawing a small cannon by short ropes, were moving up to a position opposite the general's command post. Behind them four additional soldiers, in lieu of horses, were dragging a wagon loaded with ammunition for the weapon. The fight in the field ended suddenly. Evidently it was a victory for the volunteers as wild cheering broke out nearby.

"This is difficult to believe," Lopez said finally. "We face no large force here, and we defeat it. Even with no reinforcements, we should have little trouble reaching Havana. Of such I have been assured."

"Who is this scout of whom you speak?" Ruby demanded, holding to his patience.

"A man who joined me soon after the landing. He has credentials from de Aguerro. I have no reason to doubt his words. Is it possible you overestimate the strength of General Enna's forces?"

"You have not met his army yet. This is only a small part sent to delay you. I do not know where the rest is, but it will be of large size."

Lopez's lean, somewhat handsome face was thoughtful. "This engagement has cost me only a hundred men. I had thought to stand firm in this position until the rebel army. . . ."

"God's uncle!" Cain Ruby yelled angrily. "Can you not understand . . . there is no rebel army! You are alone. Enna is moving in to wipe you out. Who tells you different is a liar!"

Cain's raised voice brought several aides to the officer's side. He motioned to one. "Bring the rebel scout, Baca, to me."

Baca? The name struck no familiar chord in Ruby's mind. He glanced questioningly at Annette. She shook her head.

The aide returned in company with a thin, poorly clad Cuban. Oddly, his hair, mustache, and beard were neatly trimmed. A short scar traced one cheek, ended near the lobe of his ear.

Cain swept the man with a close look. "I doubt he is of the revolutionists."

Baca drew himself up stiffly. "I am a Free Cuban, *señor*. This cannot be disputed."

"I dispute it," Ruby said. "Why else would you tell lies to General Lopez?"

Baca shrugged, lifted his hands in a gesture of incomprehension. "These things I do not understand, my General," he said blandly. "I have never before met this gentleman."

Cain Ruby turned to Annette. "This lady has long been with Peréz-Rosario, the leader of the Free Cubans. Ask her if this Baca is one of them."

Annette shook her head. "He has never been to our camp."

"I admit such," Baca said. "There are many rebel armies. I do not happen to belong to that of Peréz-Rosario. I know of him. That much I can say."

"He is with the Spaniards," Cain insisted. "It will be wise for you to believe that. He is a part of the trap." Pausing, Ruby looked toward the field. "Are these all the men you have?"

"I brought with me three hundred. I detailed the remaining one hundred and fifty, under the command of Colonel Crittenden, to stay with the ship."

"Rejoin them. You will soon need all the guns you have. Delay there until Quitman and Gonzales arrive. That is my advice to you."

"But if the insurgents . . . ?"

Ruby shrugged in disgust. There was no convincing Lopez. He glanced at Baca. The scout watched the officer closely, his face sly.

The taste of the small victory was on Narciso Lopez's lips, sweet and encouraging. He was finding it difficult to accept Cain Ruby's warning, to believe it all a carefully planned scheme of Enna's to ensnare him. Baca's words were more to his liking. But his force had been trimmed to dangerous proportions in the engagement, and, if it were true no revolutionist reinforcements were *en route,* that Enna was moving swiftly through the jungle to strike—then prudence would be in order.

Lopez pivoted. He barked a command to the bugler, standing a short distance away. The notes of the retreat call peeled out high and clear above the shooting. A yell went up, and men began to drop back from the brush, working their way toward the village.

Cain Ruby smiled at Annette, heaved a sigh of relief. Beyond her, he saw a thin line of helmeted Spaniards appear in the wake of the volunteers. They halted, dropped to one knee, leveled their muskets. The officer accompanying them made a downward motion with his saber. There was a ripple of gunshots, and three or four of Lopez's men staggered and fell.

An enraged shout lifted, and the retreating volunteers halted. There was a concerted rush toward the kneeling Spaniards. They swept down upon the soldiers, using muskets as clubs, hacking with swords, stabbing with knives. There was a confusion of bitter combat, and then the volunteers resumed their retreat. No Spaniard stood upright to further dispute the withdrawal.

A number of officers had gathered around Lopez and were listening to a repeat of Ruby's report. They separated shortly, began to rally and regroup their commands. Cain Ruby, with Annette, turned and headed into the village. He had done all he could. He had warned Lopez, succeeded, finally, in convincing him of the danger that lay ahead for his small force. The volunteers could now return to the *Pampero*, rejoin Crittenden, and avoid the fate Enna had prepared.

They continued along the street. The army of Narciso Lopez was all around them now, victorious but in desperate straits. Lopez, himself, was near the front. The sun shone brightly on his handsome uniform as he strode briskly through the scattered ranks. To his left was Baca, speaking earnestly. At the sight of the scout, Cain's anger stirred, but he allowed it to cool. Perhaps he had not fully convinced Lopez the man was a Spanish spy, but he had managed to discredit him and induce the officer to ignore his suggestions. And that was all that counted.

Las Pozas with its brief victory fell behind, and they again entered the jungle. Officers were moving in and out among the stragglers, urging them to keep up, not lag and become victims of the sharpshooters. The day wore on. Noon. Cain persuaded one of the volunteers to share his rations with Annette, procured a small amount of food for himself from another.

Near the middle of the afternoon they reached a small valley through which a stream flowed. Lopez signaled for a halt. As the soldiers began to sprawl about, seeking rest and relief from the bludgeoning heat, Lopez summoned Ruby.

"I have been further considering the information you gave me," he said, stiff and formal. "I now wonder if you are not wrong."

Cain threw an angry look at the smirking Baca. "There is no mistake, General. Depend on it."

"Baca assures me there is a rebel force, that it soon will arrive. Possibly de Aguerro is dead. He admits to such rumors. But de Aguerro is not the only revolutionary on the island."

"Baca lies to you," Cain Ruby said wearily. "He hopes to keep you in the trap until Enna is ready to strike."

"I have decided to dispatch a courier to Crittenden," Lopez continued, as though he had not heard Ruby's words. "I shall order him to leave only a token force to guard the *Pampero* and with all haste march to join me here. Such will give me sufficient striking. . . ."

"You have yet to face the Spanish army," Ruby cut in.

"You engaged only a handful and the cost to you was a hundred men. How will you fare against thousands?"

"But with Crittenden . . . and the rebels that will surely come . . . ?"

Cain Ruby threw up his hands in despair, shook his head. "General, if you will not see, my words are of no use."

There was commotion beyond a group of officers gathered around a water cask. A horse and rider burst from the brush, raced across the open ground. Lopez's personal guard sprang to attention. The officer raised his arm quickly.

"Hold! It is Sanchez . . . a sergeant of Crittenden's."

The horseman thundered through the gaping volunteers and came to a halt before Lopez. Leaping from the saddle, he threw a hasty salute. "General . . . the Spaniards come! They move upon you. A great army!"

"The Spanish army?" Lopez said in a shocked voice.

The sharp crack of a hundred or more muskets drowned Sanchez's answer.

XXV

"Enna!" Cain Ruby yelled, and drew Annette down behind a shattered stump. "It's the attack!"

Narciso Lopez remained frozen. He looked about in a dazed, distressed manner. Two of his own officers, who had been standing close by, lay writhing in the dust. A dozen more soldiers were crumpled shapes on the slope and along the stream. The remainder scrambled for cover. The men assigned to the cannon were struggling to wheel it about, point it toward the still unseen enemy. Someone yelled for the ammunition wagon.

A second blast of gunfire ripped across the valley. One of the cannoneers fell. An infantryman leaped to take his post. The volunteers were beginning to recover from their initial surprise, and a return fire broke out. Cain Ruby drew himself to his knees, peered over the stump. He must find a safe position for Annette; better still, he should get her completely away from what surely would develop into a massacre. Once Enna hurled his entire force into the battle, he would overrun Lopez easily.

A slim figure darted from the shadow of a nearby tree. It was Baca. Crouched low, the scout fled for the jungle a hundred yards distant.

"General!" Ruby yelled. "The spy . . . he escapes!"

The warning seemed to snap Lopez from his lethargy. He wheeled, saw Baca, barked a crisp command. The men serving as his personal guard snapped muskets to their shoulders. Gunfire crashed. Baca halted in stride, pitched to the ground.

Lopez had recovered himself. Crouched low, he faced Cain Ruby. "I would ask a favor of you, *señor*. I cannot spare a single man, and I wish to get word to Crittenden. Go to him, say to him he is to come and bring all possible soldiers. . . ."

"It is of no use," Sanchez yelled above the crackling muskets. "I have tried to tell you. All is lost there. The colonel is dead. So also are the men you left with him. The Spaniards struck soon after you marched."

Again a stunned expression covered Narciso Lopez's features. "Are you certain of this?"

"Was I not there? Did I not escape only because I was in the village when the Spaniards came?"

Lopez was immobile.

Cain Ruby stared at him. "General!" he shouted.

Narciso Lopez roused slightly.

"Give the order to disperse! Your men must hide in the jungle. You cannot fight Enna with a hundred and fifty men!"

"It is so," Sanchez declared. "There are hordes of the Spanish. Thousands, I would say. They have many cavalry and much artillery as well as foot soldiers."

Lopez looked around. The volunteers had the cannon in position and now were firing regularly. After the first few rounds the muskets in Enna's forward line fell silent. From that the officer took renewed courage.

"We make a stand here," he said. "We are well entrenched . . . and the Spaniards have no taste for cannon balls."

"It will be suicide," Ruby said.

Lopez shook his head. "This slope can be held. And with darkness we can better ourselves."

Abruptly he leaped to his feet, hurried to where several of his officers had gathered behind the remnants of a crumbling wall. Enna's soldiers had resumed firing, the intensity of it picking up gradually. They were partially visible, crouched and lying just within the jungle at the western end of the valley. There was little cover available to Lopez's men. Some were prone in the open, relying solely upon the uneven contour of the ground for protection. Others had withdrawn behind the scattered bushes and few trees that had been overlooked when the area was cleared.

"Lopez is a fool!" Cain Ruby said. "They haven't got a chance."

"If he won't listen, you can't blame yourself," Annette replied.

He seemed not to hear. "That infantry fire is just to keep them pinned down until the Spaniards can surround the valley and bring up their artillery."

Lopez, daring enemy musket fire, moved away from the wall. He drew his saber, shouted at his men to give no quarter. A faint cheer sounded.

"He's either a brave man or an idiot," Ruby muttered. "I don't know which. But I know this . . . we're not waiting around to be slaughtered." He twisted about, studied the terrain that separated them from the jungle at its nearest point. "If we can make it to the brush," he said, "we'll be all right."

He looked at Annette. She smiled, and, taking her hand, he moved away from the stump and into a shallow ravine. They were out of sight of Lopez immediately. The depression led them almost to the wall of dense foliage, and then ended. A long ten yards of open ground lay before them. Cain Ruby glanced toward the Spanish line. They would be fully exposed to the soldiers' muskets, once they left the ravine.

Back on the slope and in the hollow the crackling of rifles increased, punctuated by the dull boom of the volunteers' solitary cannon. Enna would soon roll his artillery into position. Then would come a brief pounding by the Spanish field guns, after which the cavalry and infantry would move in to mop up survivors, if any.

Thinking of cavalry brought Cain's attention back to the jungle ahead. If his hunch were right, Enna's horse soldiers would be filtering through the forest at that very moment. Even if Annette and he survived the dash across the barren ground and gained the brush, there was no guarantee of safety. They could run straight into the arms of the Spaniards. Disturbed by that possibility, he studied the shadows beyond the edge of the jungle. He could detect no movement.

He crawled around Annette, placed himself between her and the Spanish guns. "When I say the word . . . run. Dodge back and forth, like we did at Las Pozas. No matter what happens . . . don't stop."

She moved her head slightly. He did not mention the possibility of cavalrymen awaiting them in the jungle. One thing at a time. He listened, held back until the shooting increased, indicating a concentration upon the slope. When it came, he released her hand.

"Now!"

They spurted from the ravine, raced across the clearing. Cain Ruby heard the whir of musket balls, saw the eruptions of dust in front and beyond them. They had been seen, but the aim of the Spaniards was poor. Breathless, they reached the brush, plunged into it.

"Can't stop," Cain said immediately. "Place will be crawling with soldiers. We must have been seen by every man in Enna's army."

They hurried on, swinging wide of the valley where the fighting raged. The shadows were lengthening, and for that Cain Ruby was grateful. Soon it would be easier to travel without fear of being noticed by cavalrymen and stray patrols.

Lopez was lost. There was not much doubt of that. The invasion had failed again, and the general would be fortunate if he escaped with his life this time. But the attempt had been doomed from the beginning—from the actual moment when Lopez had elected to move without Quitman and Ambrosio Gonzales. Even the destroying of the Montaña Sangre had been of no benefit to him.

Ruby wondered how many men would be lost in the engagement and fell to calculating. There had been a hundred and fifty soldiers with Crittenden; Lopez claimed to have under his command at Las Pozas three hundred or so. The total would be near five hundred, in all. It was a disaster that likely would discourage any more assaults upon the island for years to come. Possibly forever. The two expeditions led by Narciso Lopez had failed miserably. And there had been attempts by others before him—all financed by American capital. Now, when the news of this most recent fiasco reached the mainland, those who might have been interested in aiding the Cubans would most certainly change their thinking. *And well they should,* Cain thought. The entire venture had been poorly planned and organized. The ludicrous sight of two men drawing a cannon, another group pulling a wagon loaded with ammunition reflected precisely the mismanagement of the effort.

Looking back, Cain realized there was not a single horse in Lopez's army except the one Sanchez had obtained in the village and ridden to bring the alarm. Lopez should have arranged for several, even brought them on the *Pampero,* if there were doubts as to availability on the island. But it was typical of Narciso Lopez to depend on chance and rely on rumor. What would happen now to Cuba? Would the patriots, faced with Peréz-Rosario's death and Lopez's defeat, give up? Would they abandon their dreams of freedom? He turned to Annette for the answer.

"They won't give up," she said. "Not until they've won."

Cain Ruby shook his head. "Way it all ended, seems pretty hopeless."

"Peréz-Rosario and men like him have taught them that to fight for freedom is never hopeless."

"There's not likely to be any more help coming from the mainland."

"It won't matter. They'll go right on, doing what they can."

Through the brush ahead Ruby saw motion. He halted instantly, his hand going out to the girl in a cautioning gesture. "Soldiers," he murmured.

A moment later he saw he was wrong. It was Saxon Carver.

XXVI

Carver stood beside a clump of waxbush. He was staring off into the direction of the fighting. Nearby his horse waited.

Anger and hate rose within Cain Ruby. His hand moved to the pistol in his belt. *I'll get to square things for Girard, after all,* he thought. *And I'm going to enjoy it. I don't enjoy killing a man . . . but I'll enjoy killing this bastard. He's got it coming, if ever a man did. Better not use the pistol. The shot will be heard . . . and I've got to think of Annette. The knife. That's it. Wish now I hadn't given Pablo's rapier to Aramo.*

He felt Annette's fingers on his wrist. "What are you . . . ?"

"Kill him," he murmured before she could complete her question.

Shocked, she drew back.

He glanced at her. "You think I could leave here with him still alive? Not after what he did to Girard. And there's more. If he hadn't crossed me, Lopez and your Cuban friends would be doing all right. There'd be no Enna or Spanish army. And even Peréz-Rosario would be alive."

"I know, but. . . ."

He shook his head, again looked at Carver. Hatred burned more fiercely within him. "Was hoping for this," he said. "Keep down low," he added, and started forward.

Crawling, he worked his way through the tall grass and brush toward Saxon Carver. He could not see the man, but he had fixed his position in his mind and knew that by keeping the crown of the waxbush before him he could move in close.

He reached a vine-covered log, halted to recover his breath. When his lungs were again normal, he raised his head. Carver was less than a dozen paces away. Cain Ruby drew his knife, placed it between his teeth. His plan was simple: get as near as possible, leap to his feet, and throw himself onto the man.

His thoughts came to a stop. The solid thud of galloping horses came to him. He flattened himself behind the log, twisted about, endeavored to locate the sound. A flash of yellow among the shadows of the forest caught his eye. Cavalrymen.

"Here!"

Saxon Carver's shout echoed through the hush. More color appeared through the trees, and a dozen or more riders broke into view. Ruby swore grimly. Maspera and his *asesinos*. He was going to be cheated of his revenge. He thought then of Annette, glanced to where she lay hidden. She was safe. The soldiers would pass below her.

Maspera and his men rode up and halted before Carver. The officer removed his helmet, brushed at the sweat on his forehead. "Where are they?"

Carver shook his head. "In the woods. They have not appeared."

Maspera replaced his helmet with an angry jerk. "You have let them escape! They are not in the woods. In our passing we would have seen them."

"They can be no other place," Carver protested. "When I saw them leave, I sent the messenger to you quickly. Since then I have watched carefully."

Maspera shrugged. "You are blind. They have again made a fool of you."

"The hell they have!" Saxon Carver said, reverting to English. "If you're so god-damned smart . . . find them yourself!"

The Spaniard leaned forward, stared at Carver. "What is it you say?"

Saxon Carver turned to his horse. "I said it is best we all search," he replied in Spanish. "They will pass this way. The boat they seek is nearby."

Cain watched him mount, pull alongside the officer.

"I follow your orders, *comandante,*" he said dryly.

Maspera stirred impatiently, wheeled to his men. "Return to the woods. Keep a distance of ten meters between you. Search well. If the man and the woman are not found there, we will continue in the direction of the water. Advance!"

Immediately the horsemen cut around and began to infiltrate the forest. Maspera and Carver waited until the long line had taken shape, and then swung in behind. Delaying until all had disappeared into the shadows, Cain drew himself from the log and, keeping low, ran to where Annette waited.

"Got to get away from here," he said in a quick, clipped way. "They'll be coming back."

Her features were strained, and weariness lay deep in her eyes. "Where . . . where can we go?"

"The boat," he said, taking her hand. "Carver told Maspera about it . . . but it's our only chance. If we can find it, get off shore. . . ."

He did not finish, simply pulled her upright and hurried off into the brush. He did not alter the pace for several minutes, and then, feeling Annette falter beside him, he slowed to a walk.

"Is it far to the boat?" she asked in a dragging voice.

"Not far."

It was a mile, at least—and the odds for making it were small. They could not hope to outrun Maspera and his cavalry once they were seen. He glanced at the sun. It would be better to wait for darkness, then try to reach the boat, he decided. Accordingly, he began to veer left, away from the coast, and move deeper into the jungle.

Annette dragged at him. He turned his face to her. She was fighting to keep up, moving only because she was supported by his hand. He halted, drew her to him, and allowed her to rest against his body while he listened for the Spaniards. He could hear nothing.

"Aren't we going to the boat?" she asked, gradually recovering her breath.

He shook his head. "We'll stall until night."

"But if it isn't far . . . ?"

"Don't want to get caught in the open. Better to wait."

She trembled. He put his arms about her, held her tight. "We'll make it."

He heard the *asesinos* then—the thud of hoofs, a shouted, unintelligible command. Maspera had searched the woods, found nothing. He had swung about, was now concentrating on the area between the trees and the sea.

"We must go," he said.

She nodded wearily, pulled back from him.

"No need to hurry . . . just move quiet. Maybe they'll pass us by."

He had small hopes for that. Maspera would have his men flung out in a wide line, as he had done in the forest. They would sweep through the jungle with thoroughness.

There would be no escape.

The sounds of the oncoming horses grew louder, then slacked off as they reached the heavier brush. Cain Ruby tried to gauge the distance that separated them, judged it to be little more than a hundred yards. Maspera was proceeding confidently. He knew his victims were in a pocket, that he had only to drive them before him until, inevitably, they were forced into the open.

They moved on silently. The racket created by the cavalrymen neither increased nor lessened, indicating that the Spaniards pressed slowly, relentlessly. A bird fluttered from under Ruby's feet, beating its wings frantically as it sought escape. Annette uttered a frightened cry, flung herself upon Cain. Immediately a voice sang out: "Ho . . . Martínez! What goes there?"

The voice was so near, Cain Ruby stiffened. Maspera's men had worked in much quicker than he had thought possible.

"There is nothing."

The reply was equally close. Cain quickened the pace, looked ahead. The brush appeared to be thinning. Then, beyond, he saw a field and recognized the locality. He stopped, knelt, drew Annette down beside him.

"We're just below the boat," he said in a whisper. "I remember passing through here."

A small sound of relief slipped from Annette's lips. "Can we get to it . . . the boat, I mean?"

"Not together. Sure to be seen."

"Then how . . . ?"

"Just do what I tell you, and we'll come out of this all right."

She nodded. "Whatever you say . . . but first I want you to know this. I love you, Cain. I think I always have . . . from

279

that first day . . . and back in Villareal, I was going with you. I'll go anywhere . . . as long as it's with you. If we have to die, I want to die with you."

He drew her close, stilled her words with his lips. "We aren't going to die," he said quietly.

There was a crashing off to their right, a loud curse. Ruby felt Annette jerk in his arms, saw the quick lift of fear in her eyes. "Time's running short," he said. "I want you to hide. I'll go on, show myself in the field. That will draw them to me, give you a chance to run for the boat."

She looked at him in alarm. "What will happen to you?"

"Don't worry. Soon as you're gone, I'll duck back in the jungle."

The noise was increasing—the crackling of brush, the dull thud of hoofs. It came now from several points. He kissed her again.

"Don't be afraid. When you get to the boat, pull away from shore. It'll soon be dark, and you won't be noticed."

"But how will I know where to meet you?"

"I'll signal. The *Felicity* will be there after sundown. Row out to her."

"I'll make the captain wait."

"You leave it up to him . . . he's got the Spanish gunboats to worry about," Cain said. "Good bye," he added softly, and broke away from her.

He kept low, listened to the sounds of Maspera's men as they closed in. They were still behind Annette, now ten, possibly fifteen yards. It was important that he reach the field and show himself before they drew abreast of her. Success depended upon their seeing him, abandoning their minute search and racing on by her to get to him.

He raised himself, looked ahead. The clearing was less than a dozen paces. He drew his revolver, checked the cylinder. It was fully loaded. He came to the side of the brush, paused, his thoughts winging back to Annette. She would make it to safety. They would never guess she was not with him until it was too late. For himself he had no illusions. From here on in it was: *Katy bar the door.* . . . He grinned, wondering what it was that had brought one of Gavin Girard's favorite expressions to mind.

He took a deep breath, braced himself, and darted into the field. Instantly a yell went up. Soldiers farther down the line had been nearer the clearing than those in the center. He saw two riders come into view, wheel sharply, and start toward him. Lowering his head, he began to run for the brush on the opposite side.

More shouts lifted, coming from his right and also from the rear. Good. That meant those who were approaching Annette had not seen her, were taking the bait. A musket cracked spitefully, its report echoing through the jungle. The ball dug into the ground beyond him, sent up a geyser of dust. He heard Maspera's hard-edged voice coming from somewhere to his left.

The two soldiers who had first broken into the open were bearing down upon him at a fast gallop. He slowed to a walk, brought up his weapon. Taking careful aim, he pressed the trigger. The nearest of the pair folded forward, pitched to the ground. The other yelled, wheeled abruptly to the side. Ruby's second bullet knocked him from the saddle.

More guns began to crack. A ball tore into Cain Ruby's shoulder, spun him half around. He caught himself, fought to keep from falling. A rider thundered down upon him from the right. Ignoring pain, he brought up the revolver again, fired. The cavalryman wilted. Another appeared, seemingly out of nowhere. Cain got off a shot hastily, missed, but it turned the soldier, and he curved away.

Ruby heard shouts behind him—from the far side of the field. More soldiers. *God damn the luck . . . I've run into another patrol,* he thought. *But I guess it makes no difference. Ought to be happy. Annette's safe. And I sure as hell fixed that fort good for them . . . for the Cubans. There's no more Montaña Sangre. Got that much done.*

Two riders swung into his vision. They were side by side and coming on fast. Elsewhere in the field there was confusion obliterated by a pall of dust. He squinted at the approaching men, felt a tingle along his spine. One was Maspera, the other Saxon Carver. They were moving in to make the kill personally.

A tight grin crossed Ruby's face. He was being granted one bit of good luck before it was all over—a last chance to even the score with Saxon Carver. There would be time for one shot before they rode him down, and that bullet would be for Carver.

Why Carver? Cain Ruby thought about that. Why not Maspera? Carver was nothing. He would die, and his death would accomplish nothing more than the satisfying of vengeance. Kill Maspera. Rid Cuba of its worst enemy, its most evil blight. *It's your choice, Cain Ruby,* he thought. *One or the other, you can't have both. Forget Saxon Carver. Do one more thing for the Cubans. . . .*

His fingers tightened about the grip of the pistol. Ignoring the yells, the swirling dust, the crackling of muskets, he concentrated on this one last task. A musket ball seared across his leg. He winced but stood firm, his weapon raised and ready. The features of the two men were definite now. Maspera's lips were pulled back to show his white teeth. Saxon Carver wore a fixed smile.

Suddenly they were on him. Cain Ruby tensed, pressed

off his shot. Maspera straightened, flung up his arms. Ruby fired blindly, hurriedly at Carver, knew he had missed even as he lunged aside to avoid the horses. He was too slow. Maspera's horse struck him a glancing blow, knocked him to the ground. Fighting pain, he struggled to regain his feet. Through the dust he saw Carver wheeling. Bracing himself, he drew his knife.

"¡El Valeroso!"

The shout jarred his spinning brain. He steadied himself, suddenly aware of the furious fighting under way all around him. Men—ragged, poorly equipped men—were swarming about Maspera's asesinos, dragging them from their horses, hacking, beating, stabbing them mercilessly to bloody death. He looked again for Carver. His horse, saddle empty, was shying away.

"¡Valeroso!"

Again the yell went up. The Cubans! The soldiers he had thought to be Spaniards were Cubans. He saw a half a dozen of them trotting toward him. They drew near. He began to recognize some of them . . . Aragon . . . Carlos García . . . several he had seen at the church . . . Ramiro Aramo.

The young Cuban halted at his side. "¡Señor! It is good to see you. But you are injured!"

"A scratch," Cain Ruby said. He accepted a fold of cloth Aragon thrust at him, held it to the throbbing wound in his shoulder. He did not bother with the stinging furrow on his leg. "How does it happen you are here?"

"We were nearby," Aramo replied. "We heard gunshots. We thought it to be the Spaniards, attacking some of our people. I did not think it probable we would find you."

"Annette and I were trying to reach the dinghy. She is there by now."

"No, she comes," someone said.

283

Cain turned. Annette, her face anxious, was running toward him. The Cubans parted to let her through. She uttered a cry of relief, when she saw him, threw herself into his arms, weeping softly.

"Not one Spaniard escaped!" a man cried, rushing up. "All are dead. I, personally, slew the bad *inglés*," he added proudly.

Ruby looked beyond the crowd. Saxon Carver lay face down in the dust. Four blood-stained marks on his back showed where the tines of a cane fork had pierced his body.

"But it was the *señor* who struck down that devil, Maspera," Aragon said. "Was there ever such bravery? He stood until the horse was almost upon him! Truly he is the valiant one. We have won a very great victory. We have horses and weapons. Now it is possible to fight better."

Ruby, holding Annette closely, glanced around at the Cubans. One carried a spear—an ancient shaft with an improvised metal tip. Several had arm-length cudgels. He saw axes, sharpened spades, machetes, several forks, an iron stake. A familiar phrase crossed his mind: *the blazing guns of freedom speak loudly.* . . . But here were the real weapons of freedom—the simple, ordinary implements of everyday life buttressed by the strongest weapon of all—the will of men to fight, to die if need be, for their liberty. He felt a thickness rise in his throat. After a moment he asked: "Where do you go?"

"To join with General Lopez."

Cain Ruby shook his head. "It is too late. Lopez was trapped. I think none of the invasion army lives."

A groan ran through the Cubans. Aramo, his eyes reaching above the jungle to the darkening sky, was silent. Finally, he shrugged. "I dared hope the hour had come. With the Montaña Sangre no more, with Lopez marching to

Havana, with our own small victories . . . I felt the torch burned brightly. But we have again failed. I despair."

"No time to quit," Cain Ruby said, his words flat against Aramo's flowery Spanish. "Enna has beaten Lopez, but the Spanish armor has been dented."

"That is so."

"We cannot retire to hide. We must hammer at them, worry them, drive them mad."

Ramiro Aramo came around swiftly, eagerly. "We, *señor?*"

Cain Ruby nodded. "We . . . all of us. We will recruit every man on the island. We will pick the Spaniards clean, and, when another Lopez comes, we shall be ready."

Pedro Aragon pushed through the crowd. There were tears in his eyes again. "*El Valeroso* . . . he leads us!"

A cheer welled up. Cain looked at Annette. She was smiling. He knew there was no need for explanations.

About the Author

Ray Hogan was an author who inspired a loyal following over the years since he published his first Western novel, EX-MARSHAL, in 1956. Hogan was born in Willow Springs, Missouri, where his father was town marshal. At five the Hogan family moved to Albuquerque where Ray Hogan lived in the foothills of the Sandia and Manzano mountains. His father was on the Albuquerque police force and, in later years, owned the Overland Hotel. It was while listening to his father and other old-timers tell tales from the past that Ray was inspired to recast these tales in fiction. From the beginning he did exhaustive research into the history and the people of the Old West and the walls of his study were lined with various firearms, spurs, pictures, books, and memorabilia, about all of which he could talk in dramatic detail. "I've attempted to capture the courage and bravery of those men and women that lived out West and the dangers and problems they had to overcome," Hogan once remarked. If his lawmen protagonists seem sometimes larger than life, it is because they are men of integrity, heroes who through grit of character and common sense are able to overcome the obstacles they encounter despite often overwhelming odds. This same grit of character can also be found in Hogan's heroines, and in THE VENGEANCE OF FORTUNA WEST (1983) Hogan wrote a gripping and totally believable account of a woman who takes up the badge and tracks the men who killed her lawman husband by ambush. No less intriguing in her way is Nellie Dupray, convicted of rustling in THE GLORY TRAIL (1978). One of his most popular books, dealing with an earlier period in the West with Kit Carson as its protagonist, is SOLDIER IN BUCKSKIN (Five Star Westerns, 1996). Above all, what is most impressive about Hogan's Western novels is the consistent quality with which each is crafted, the compelling depth of his characters, and his ability to juxtapose the complexities of human conflict into narratives always as intensely interesting as they are emotionally involving. STONEBREAKER'S RIDGE will be his next **Five Star Western.**